PRAISE FOR *A STRI*

A Strike to the Heart is a compelling story. From the very first page, I was immersed into the thrilling action and remained gripped with intrigue until the satisfying ending. The romance escalated right along with the winding plot, creating a layered mystery that is sure to delight readers. A solid debut for author Danielle Grandinetti.

~ **Rachel Scott McDaniel**
Award-winning author of *The Mobster's Daughter*

A Strike to the Heart is an entertaining story that grabs you on the first page with its intriguing plot, as Grandinetti expertly balances action with the tender stirrings of a romance that will woo your senses until the very end.

~ **Natalie Walters**
Award-winning author of *Lights Out* and the Harbored Secrets Series

Danielle Grandinetti's novel *A Strike to the Heart* starts with a bang, literally, and doesn't slow down from there as her characters fight for their lives against unknown enemies. Lily and Miles aren't only facing physical dangers, but their hearts are also at risk as they join forces in their fight to survive. If you like stories full of action with plenty of romance mixed in, then *A Strike to the Heart* is a book you will want to read.

~ **Ann H. Gabhart**
Best-selling author of *Along a Storied Trail*

I loved this depression-era story. Danielle Grandinetti gives the readers an up-close-and-personal look at life in Wisconsin during the dairy strikes. And oh, Miles Wright is a swoon-worthy ex-Marine, and Lily is as independent as they come for a woman in the 1930s. A perfect combination for a page-turner historical romance. A well-researched, well-written, and intriguing look at a bygone era. I look forward to more from this debut author.

~ Cindy Ervin Huff
Award-winning writer, author of *Angelina's Resolve*

I've finally taken a breath after reading Danielle Grandinetti's novel, *A Strike to the Heart*. A story of running from an unknown enemy. A story of Lily not knowing who to trust. A story of escapes and fires and hiding. But unrest births a beautiful friendship, which blossoms into a sweet, tentative at first, then committed love between Miles and Lily. While the story is fast-paced, Grandinetti paints a vivid setting that is so tangible that it's hard to believe that this happened decades ago.

~ Sherri Stewart
Copy editor, author of *A Song for Her Enemies*

A Strike to the Heart is a gripping tale from beginning to end! Set against the turbulent backdrop of the Great Depression, this story of suspense, intrigue, and romance will keep you wondering and turning the pages until you arrive at the more-than-satisfying end. Kudos to author Danielle Grandinetti for a job well done.

~ Ann Tatlock
Novelist, editor, and children's book author

Faith and fear, trust and terror, love and longing . . . it's all here in this riveting suspense. *A Strike to the Heart* keeps readers on the edge of their seats as two headstrong people fight evil—and sometimes each other.

~ Susan G Mathis
Award-winning author of *Devyn's Dilemma* and
the Thousand Islands Gilded Age Series

A STRIKE TO THE HEART

DANIELLE GRANDINETTI

FICTION

An Imprint of Iron Stream Media
Birmingham, Alabama

A Strike to the Heart

Iron Stream Fiction
An imprint of Iron Stream Media
100 Missionary Ridge
Birmingham, AL 35242
IronStreamMedia.com

Library of Congress Control Number: 2021950797

ISBN: 978-1-64526-352-4 (paperback)
ISBN: 978-1-64526-353-1 (ebook)

1 2 3 4 5—25 24 23 22

MANUFACTURED IN THE UNITED STATES OF AMERICA

To my boys,

the sweet souls God has entrusted to us.

May we help you become your best selves so that you
grow into the men God created you to be.

Acknowledgments

Writing a book is a group effort, so I'd like to say a big thank you to …

My husband and sons for your smiles and hugs that keep me going. And for the time you give me to write.

My writing friends who have encouraged my progress, read pages, and offered suggestions. Friends like Ann, Jen, Alicia, Janyre, Kaci, Beth, Crystal, and many others.

My family by blood and heart. My parents, my sister and her family, my in-laws, my brother-in-law and his family, and my best friend, Ivy, and her family. You are my biggest cheerleading section.

My extended family and countless friends who have encouraged me along the way.

My editor, Denise Weimer, and proofreaders, Steve Mathisen and Lucie Winborne, for helping this story shine. And the Iron Stream Media team for your work on cover, design, and marketing to get my book into readers' hands.

You, my readers, for joining me on this journey.

And the One who first loved me and called me friend.

*This is my commandment, that ye love one another,
as I have loved you.*

John 15:12

CHAPTER 1

Friday, October 13, 1933
Northern Wisconsin

Miles Wright pressed his eye to the A5 telescopic sight attached to his Springfield long-range rifle. Instead of being hunkered down in the trenches of Europe or in the humidity of Central America, as he would be if he'd stayed in the Marines, he flattened himself against the rough branch of a monstrous pine one hundred yards from the ruins of a stone house lost amid the forests of northern Wisconsin.

He breathed deeply, the smell of decaying leaves filling his nose even as the action calmed his heart. Dusk had come, but he could still spot the shadows of his four fellow retired soldiers darting from tree to tree toward the stone structure where Lily Moore's kidnappers likely stashed her. His team was tasked with a simple rescue and had yet to meet any resistance. Miles's job was to keep it that way.

Tommy Darens, the lone British ex-soldier and their company leader, halted, and the others stood motionless. What had Tommy heard? Miles used his scope to scan the remnants of what could have been a happy home decades ago. Before the Depression. Before the war.

In the small clearing rose a four-foot-tall, hollow square of tightly layered stone—the roof now part of the forest floor that covered the interior with a bed of grass, rock, and saplings. A chimney, still intact, anchored the rear foundation wall.

Nothing moved. No breath of wind to stir the trees overhead. No scamper of chipmunks on the leaves below. No lifting of the rock sitting in Miles's stomach. Something was wrong.

Darens and the other three men crouched as they quick-marched closer to the house. They had followed a rumor that a woman matching Miss Moore's description was seen in this part of the forest three days ago. Was she still here?

Miles swept his scope over the deepening shadows. His companions reached the structure as darkness settled like a veil. Moonlight from the three-quarter moon struggled to filter through the heavy canopy. It was too quiet. Too still. As if the nocturnal animals saw what Miles could not.

Like a phantom of the night, Darens raised an arm, halting the men just outside the break in the stone foundation, the place where the front door must have been.

Miles gripped his Springfield. Searching. Searching. Memories of a similar feeling nagged him. The time he nearly got flanked as a green sharpshooter somewhere in the French countryside. Only a misfired shot and quick action saved his life that day. Where was the feeling coming from today?

He searched the area again, darkness deepening by the minute, making it harder and harder to see. Dampness pressed through his dark vest, the buttons digging into his breastbone and his sweat causing the cotton shirt underneath to stick. He never wore a jacket when sniping and always rolled up his shirtsleeves. It didn't help today, even with the October chill in the air.

He breathed out, slowing his heart. Darnes gave the silent command to move forward, to enter the stone ruins. Miles wanted to yell at them to stop, to wait until he figured out the puzzle. As a sharpshooter, he usually had more time for reconnaissance. What was he missing?

The four men rushed into the space. Miles's heart pounded against his chest.

One heartbeat.

Two heartbeats.

Three—

The ruins exploded in a blinding column of fire and smoke. Miles covered his head, nearly losing his grip on his rifle as debris flew. Visions assaulted him like a silent picture—men dying beside him as shell after shell ripped through their ranks. And then the picture stilled on two faces. Faces he should have been able to save.

He shook his disoriented senses into submission and looked through his scope, forcing his eyes to see the present, not the past. No movement. Not from his friends. Not from the unseen enemy. Bile pushed up his throat.

Suppressing the panic that was never more than a gunshot away, Miles shouldered his Springfield, snagged his suit jacket, hat, and pack from the branch where he'd stashed them, and scrambled down the tree trunk. Had anyone else heard the explosion? Would they send policemen? The fire brigade? The area had seen its share of forest fires lately. He stuffed his arms into his jacket and planted his hat on his head as he closed the distance between his tree and the old stone structure.

He still saw no movement as he neared the remnants of the house. Leaving his Springfield hanging from his back beside his pack, he snatched his Colt from where he kept it holstered under his left arm. Fire smoldered in the stone rubble, devouring the dry grass and lighting Miles's path. He picked his way through the blackened brambles and singed saplings.

His gaze snagged on a wire attached to one side of the doorway, snapped where his friends had entered. He followed it to the source of the explosion—the remnants of a booby trap.

He shook his head. Why hadn't he anticipated a trap?

That's when he saw Darens and the other three men. His gut roiled at the sight of them. He'd left the army because he couldn't stomach the violence any longer, but it haunted him even here. It took only a moment to confirm they hadn't survived the blast. Kneeling beside his team leader's body, he fought the urge to demand answers of the Almighty, but in truth, only Miles himself was to blame. He closed his eyes. Decay invaded his nose. Ash singed his skin. His lips tasted of salt—from tears or sweat, he didn't know.

Then, through the stillness, sticks crunched over the soft hissing of the smoldering fires. He had moments before he'd be discovered. If by coppers, they could think him a suspect. If by whoever set off the explosion … policemen would be the least of his worries.

Just as he turned to make his escape, his ear caught a cry. Someone had survived the blast? Could Miss Moore be here and still alive? He followed the sound to the center of the house but saw no one. The footsteps and voices outside the structure grew louder.

"Help me, please!"

The call came from below ground. He stepped back, brushed aside burned brambles, and uncovered a metal plate embedded in the dirt floor. The three-by-three-foot square wasn't anchored, so he crouched off-center and aimed his Colt at the opening in readiness for what he might encounter. Then, using his free hand, he flipped the hot cover away.

A hole gaped in the dirt. Miles leaned over the edge, gun muzzle first. A woman with the most gorgeous, albeit terrified, green eyes looked up at him. Oval face smudged. Brown hair hanging in a tangled mess about her shoulders. He couldn't recall ever seeing a woman so disheveled and yet still so beautiful. He'd found Lily Moore.

Never had Lily known such fear as she had over the last three days. Until a moment ago. The explosion shook the dirt walls of her dungeon, pooling it around her feet. She thought for sure the small hole would cave, burying her alive, so she shouted and shouted for help. Then the cover was pulled away, and she found herself staring at the shiny muzzle of a gun.

Her heart stuttered and she backed into a corner. Not far away, but enough that it gave her the courage to refuse to let her shaky legs buckle. Clenching her fists as if to keep a tight grip on that courage, she looked beyond the weapon to the person who planned to end her life. Perhaps she would find mercy there. Even if she had to beg for it.

"My name is Miles Wright," the man said, lowering the weapon to reveal his identity. The flickering flames and white moonlight gave him a shadowed appearance. He had a round face, covered in dark facial hair and grime and topped by a gray fedora. This was a man used to weapons, but would he use his on a defenseless woman?

The man's lips tipped into a smile as jaunty as his hat. "I'm here to take you home."

Home! Just hearing the word made her want to sink to the ground in relief.

Then her brain took over. How gullible could she be to believe a handsome smile? It didn't appear to reach his eyes, though he seemed sincere. With no idea how he'd found her or the motive behind his rescue, she could take no chances. He could be allied with her kidnappers, for all she knew. The only person to lift the lid to her tomb in the past few days had been a masked figure who tossed food scraps and a canteen of water down to her. This man showed his face, appearing to offer her a way home like a hero of old.

Father God, can I trust him?

"Are you hurt?" Mr. Wright broke into her rambling thoughts as he holstered his gun under his arm. This time, it was easy to see the concern in his eyes. He was worried about her?

She quickly shook her head. Her kidnapper hadn't done anything but toss her in the trunk of his car, then into this hole. No talking, no punches, no … She shivered at what could have happened.

"Don't be afraid. I'm here to help." He lay on his belly, his jacket bunched up over his shoulders as he reached into the hole with both hands. "Grab my wrists and I'll pull you out."

His deep voice settled her fear, and she reached up for him. Large, callused hands wrapped around her bare wrists. She clutched his forearms, feeling muscles ripple as he pulled her up. Somehow, he shifted to his knees while lifting until her ribs rested on the edge of the hole. But before she could fully register that his hands had moved, he gripped her under her arms, stood, and planted her on her feet.

Smoky air choked her, but it was air. The Good Lord's breath as it moved over the earth. It brushed her hair along her cheek. It filled her lungs. Even if the accompanying smoke made her cough and her eyes water. Or maybe those were tears. All she knew was that she wasn't in that hole any longer. She wouldn't be deserted. She wouldn't be buried alive.

Hands slipping to her waist, Miles Wright bent to look directly into her eyes. His were brown and warm and kind. "You okay to walk?"

She nodded, still unable to push her voice past the cascade of emotions rushing through her body. Relief. Fear. Wonder. And another emotion that instantly disappeared when he removed his hands from her waist.

"Good. We need to move quickly." The urgency in his voice warned of more danger, and she shoved her tumultuous thoughts and feelings to a place where she could worry about them later.

Mr. Wright propelled her ahead of him, toward what used to be a fireplace at the rear of the foundation. Behind them, indiscriminate noises turned into shouts.

"Don't stop." Mr. Wright pressed his hand against her back, urging her to move faster. Small fires licked at her clothes. Smoke clogged her lungs. A shot whistled by Lily's ear, and Mr. Wright shoved her to the ground. She cried out. He spun, unholstering his pistol in one smooth move, and fired.

"You're doing great, Miss Moore." He pulled her up by the upper arm. "We're going to get out of this."

If he said so.

"See that break in the trees?" he said. "Run for it. Now!"

His hand pushed her into a stumbling jog. Instantly missing his strength, she glanced over her shoulder. Mr. Wright crouched within the shadow of the chimney. One, two, three men, all with guns drawn, raced into the smoldering ruins.

Lily clapped a hand over her mouth. *Dear Father God, have mercy—*

"Miss Moore, go!"

Mr. Wright's direction forced her feet into action even as gunfire filled her ears. Within two strides, he caught up to her. Perhaps it was the flickers from the flames or the eerie light filtering through the trees, but the movement seemed to morph him into a giant bear. He towered over her with a deadly gaze. She shrank back. A simple swipe, and he could crush her life.

"Don't you go fainting on me." His paw clasped her hand, dwarfing it. But instead of intensifying her fear, as she expected, the connection spread comfort, and she found herself leaning into his tower of protection.

Not for long. A bullet chipped off a chunk of tree bark beside his shoulder. He aimed another shot behind them as he pulled her into motion.

"There are too many of them." He holstered his pistol with an air of decision. "I can't slow all of them down before they reach us. We need to get out of here."

Lily agreed wholeheartedly and tightened her grip on his hand. Even though she stumbled, he kept her upright, forcing her to keep up with him as they zigzagged up the tree-covered hill of whatever godforsaken place—no, even here, the Lord was with her.

She clung to that promise, heart beating in her ears. Lungs screaming for relief. Shoes slipping on dirt. Skirt catching on branches. Only three more steps to the top. To where they would be sheltered from death. If even for a few minutes.

Mr. Wright's inarticulate exclamation made Lily's attention swing to something bouncing along the ground behind them. The black device settled in a crevasse between two rotted logs. A grenade? She'd seen one before. Once. When her twin brother gave her a tour of the police station, his first day on the job. That one had been a dummy. This one would kill them.

With a yank, Mr. Wright snagged her around the waist and vaulted them over the crest of the hill. The last thing she felt before heat overpowered them was the hard surface of Mr. Wright's chest. At least she would not die alone.

CHAPTER 2

The grenade blast ripped Lily Moore from Miles's arms and sent him tumbling down the other side of the hill, careening off tree trunks and over fallen logs. Ears ringing, body screaming, Miles lay on his back cataloging each breath to assure himself that, yes, he was still alive.

What about Miss Moore?

Please God, he pleaded as he mentally worked himself into a place to battle the pain. He had to sit up. Get to his feet. Find her before the smoke cleared.

If she was still alive.

How could his mission go so horribly wrong?

He lay back against the hard ground, all manner of undergrowth digging into his ribs, his weakness taunting him. He needed to get them to safety before the enemy finished them off. The death of his friends was his fault, but they'd known the potential danger and volunteered anyway, and Miles would willingly pay the same price if it meant their sacrifice wasn't in vain—if an innocent would live despite his failure. He couldn't let Lily Moore become another victim.

Determination surged through him, dulling the pain, and he pushed to his elbows. As if she were a ministering angel sent to soothe his soul, Miss Moore appeared beside him. Worry clouded her filthy yet beautiful face. He shook his head to dislodge that thought. He couldn't think of her that way.

"You lay so still, I thought ..."

Her voice barely slipped past his ringing ears, so he watched her lips to be sure he caught her words. Blood dripped down her cheek. He followed it to a cut above her eyebrow. He raised a hand to touch the bruise forming around it.

"They're coming." The quiver in her chin revealed that she clung to the last shreds of her courage. Her tone hit a place in his heart he preferred to keep locked and buried but triggered the protective instinct that made him an excellent sharpshooter, providing the strength he needed to leap to his feet.

Miles's hearing sharpened. On the other side of the hill, loose stones clinked as they cascaded over one another. He and Miss Moore would indeed be discovered alive in moments. He snatched her hand and led her toward the untamed woods below.

Shouts behind them drove them through the trees, led only by the moon and stolen glances at his compass. They dodged brambles, thorns, and scampering nocturnal critters. Miles's every instinct strained to listen past the whispering wind and the soft crunch of their own feet for sounds of the shadows he could feel following them. Whoever wanted them dead now knew the grenade had not succeeded. As well trained as they were, they would catch up in no time … unless Miles came up with a plan.

He sorted through ideas as he kept Miss Moore within the darkest parts of the night-shrouded forest—a darkness that pressed on his soul. He hated leaving the bodies of his friends behind. Even though his boss refused to hire anyone with family, which meant his friends had no one to mourn them, it didn't mean he wouldn't grieve them. Deeply. After he got Miss Moore to safety.

Jaw clenched to keep his emotions at bay at least until he reached the car, he nearly crashed into Miss Moore when she caught her shoe on a vine.

"Sorry." She touched his arm while freeing her foot and skirt from the tangle. Her chest rose in a deep, unsteady rhythm.

Miles gave her a moment to catch her breath—even if they had no time to spare.

In the splinters of moonlight and with her hair falling about her shoulders, Miss Moore had an air of gracefulness despite the dirt caked to her sun-darkened skin. The green of her eyes reminded him of the lush grass that surrounded one of his home state's many lakes. At her shiver, he wrapped his dark coat around her shoulders. It dwarfed her narrow frame and made her appear incredibly vulnerable.

She tugged at the sleeves. "I should have said this earlier. Thank you for saving me."

"Just doing my job, ma'am." It's what he told all the victims he rescued, but today it felt hollow. Still, he could not burden her with the cost of her rescue.

She shook her head. "How did you find me? How did you know where to look? I don't even know where we are."

He stared at the yellow-green bruises peeking from under her cuffs, as visible in the moonlight as if someone shone a spotlight on them. Someone had bound her, dragged her into a forest, and left a bomb to kill any would-be rescuers. Who could feel such animosity toward such a captivating woman?

"Mr. Wright?"

He cleared his throat and cupped her elbow to get her moving again as he answered her question. "It began with a suggestion that you ran away. Something about being the last single woman in your family."

She stumbled over a clump of foliage. "That's what you heard?"

He tightened his grip to keep her upright. While he hated to see the hurt slicing her emerald eyes, he awaited her response with no little curiosity.

"It's not true. The running away, I mean." Her words and breathing grew faster as she spoke. "Yes, in the last year, both my elder brothers married neighbor girls. Now my baby sister, Amy, is married to Andy Booth. Wealthiest family in the county."

"Impressive," he said, not because he thought so, but because it seemed the expected word.

"But I didn't run away. Someone took me. And just because I'm not married can't be why …"—she took a shaky breath—"why I was kidnapped."

The confusion and betrayal in her voice ratcheted up his protective instinct, but the hairs on the back of his neck rose before he could voice his thoughts. He transferred his grip to her hand, pulling her faster through the brush, the branches that slapped his face providing the clarity he needed. He couldn't get distracted by her story, even if it made him strangely happy to hear confirmation that she was indeed unattached.

"My boss's company was hired to find you and deliver you safely to headquarters." He helped her over a fallen log. "That is my priority right now. We'll deal with the rest once people aren't trying to kill us."

"Headquarters?" She pulled her hand free, ducked under a low branch, and kept jogging. "No. I'm going home, Mr. Wright. I appreciate you rescuing me, but I need to see my dogs. I—I have to know they're okay. And, frankly, I want to get to the bottom of this mess."

"That's not the safest—"

"Returning to Eagle lets me face this head-on." Her tone became firmer as she regained control over her emotions. "I need to know if my brother-in-law's friends lured me to the restaurant where I was kidnapped. And if I was kidnapped for a reason or whether I was just a random victim. Then maybe I can find out who took me and why. What could anger someone enough to warrant this type of action? Trust me, I've had a few days to consider the options."

Miles halted her despite the danger following them. He needed her to hear him. He clamped both hands on her upper arms and bent so he could meet her gaze. "You can't investigate your own kidnapping." He resisted the urge to give her arms a gentle shake. "You'll just make yourself a target all over again."

The green of her eyes sparked like St. Elmo's fire. "I'll be a target until my kidnappers are caught, and I refuse to let other people decide my future."

A bullet splintered the bark of the tree just behind Miles's head.

He ducked, dragging Miss Moore with him as he zigzagged through the trees as fast as he could pull her. Never had a rescue victim been so infuriatingly stubborn. So insistent and determined and capable.

Which explained why she impressed him so much.

A thought for later. Right now, he had to keep her alive.

Lily sucked in as much air as she could gasp as her feet flew over the uneven ground. Her heart pounded in her ears, which were still sore from the grenade explosion. And she'd thought she was in good shape since she worked with her dogs every day. Apparently not.

Another bullet crashed into a tree as they dashed behind it. What had she done to deserve getting kidnapped—and now shot at?

Her brain raced wildly, and her feet tangled beneath her. She would have tumbled into a pile of dead leaves had Mr. Wright not caught her before her knees hit the ground.

"I can't—go—ow!" Pain shot through her ribs as they heaved with her effort to breathe. She bent double, hugging herself.

"Okay, okay. I'll buy us a few minutes." Mr. Wright pointed toward a small copse of bushes. "Crawl under there and do not make a sound."

She obeyed, slithering beneath the branches, thorns tearing her dress. She must already look a sight. Hat and gloves gone, hair no longer pinned up. Embarrassment heated her cheeks, but when she glanced behind her for Mr. Wright's expression, he had already disappeared.

Her protector. Her rescuer. Could she truly trust that God brought him to save her? That did seem to be his sole focus, and the man had risked his life, standing between her and danger multiple times. Yes, she could rely on him to get her to safety.

But would he follow through on his promise to see her home? Experience informed her that she wasn't a priority to most men unless she did as they demanded. Mr. Wright would likely be the same, which was all right. She could protect herself, and surely, the other Eagle policemen would help her brother keep her safe. Yet the thought felt hollow.

Huddled under the bush, the damp ground spread a chill through her body despite Mr. Wright's coat. She pulled the woolen fabric tighter around her shoulders. It smelled of smoke and pine, a comforting smell that did little to ease her worry. If Mr. Wright didn't come back soon, she'd be in trouble. And if he didn't come back at all?

He would. He had to. She couldn't rescue herself if she had no way of knowing which direction led to safety.

She strained to listen. Couldn't hear past the rushing in her ears and the erratic beat of her heart. Her teeth threatened to chatter. She couldn't make a sound, or the bad guys—whoever they were—would find her.

Noiselessly, she curled into a ball. One breath in. Nice and slow. One breath out. Not too fast. She pictured herself cuddled on her couch back home, her two dogs battling for room on her lap. A fire roaring in the fireplace. Stars dancing above her father's cornfields. Home. The best place on earth.

"Miss Moore." Mr. Wright's voice preceded his appearance as he peered under the branches. "I think I led them on enough of a circuitous route that if we move fast, we should be at the car in—"

"I'm not going to your headquarters, Mr. Wright." She crawled out from the bushes, destroying her dress even more, but she didn't care. Thinking about home had wrapped her in peace for the first time since she woke up in the trunk of a car three days ago. "I'm not asking you to come with me. I just want to go home. My neighbors in Eagle might not think much of me, but I have a way of life to protect."

Mr. Wright rubbed his beard. "You don't know who kidnapped you or why?"

Lily shook her head. "One moment, I was sitting at dinner, prepared to discuss business with two of Andy's friends. The next, I woke up in the trunk of a car."

He clutched her hand and urged her to follow, setting a rapid pace.

She kept silent, letting him think as he led them away from whoever followed them. Those people might have answers, too, but she doubted they'd ever let her or Mr. Wright live long enough to ask them any questions. She'd have to find answers on her own and a different way.

"My team discounted the runaway theory," Mr. Wright said quietly, as if they were discussing the situation over tea, not jogging through a dark forest ahead of unknown pursuers. "Your disappearance was not of your choosing, though no ransom was asked for as far as I know. That's why I want to inter …" He trailed off as if realizing he voiced his thoughts aloud.

Silence stretched around them, the woodland creatures quiet in the presence of human intruders. Normally, Lily would feel at home in a place such as this. Not now. Not today. Not when it could be her grave.

Mr. Wright cleared his throat. "Perhaps my questions would be better answered at the source of your kidnapping."

Lily froze. Did he mean what she thought he did? Would he really come with her to Eagle? Did she want him to?

CHAPTER 3

The green eyes that stared at him waited expectantly for him to clarify his statement. Miss Moore would dive headlong into the quest for answers as soon as she arrived home. Of that, he had no doubt. But a minefield of dangers awaited her when she followed that path.

He could not in good conscience let her return home without his protection. Craft had hired him because he was one of the best sharpshooters in the business. He might have failed his team, but second chances were meant for redemption. And there was no way he'd let his friends die in vain.

The snap of a twig propelled him into motion. He shoved away all thoughts except for the ones that would get them out of this forest unharmed. The car should be just over this rise. He would take an unlikely route from here so as not to lead these men back to Eagle.

But Miles's stomach dropped as they crested the hill. At least five armed men stood between them and safety. He whirled Miss Moore behind a tree, trapping her against him as he considered his next move—and ignored how it felt to have her so close.

Her breath came in shallow puffs. She turned her chin away from him as if embarrassed to be in such proximity to a stranger. She trembled against his vest, and his chest squeezed. He might be an ex-soldier, a sniper trained to kill, but he prayed daily that kindness would be the trait people would identify most when they interacted with him. He prayed doubly so in Miss Moore's case. She need not be afraid of him. He would find a way to protect her, to bring her home safely. Yet seeing her like this, duty no longer seemed a worthwhile motivation.

Perhaps his past made him susceptible to her vulnerability. Regardless, he'd allow all of it to fuel him to get her out of this alive.

He breathed soft-spoken directions against her ear. "We're going to circle around to the far side of the car. Quiet and slow. Just follow me."

She nodded and let him tuck her under his arm as he directed her to the left, keeping himself between her and the gunmen. He couldn't place them, but he had the distinct impression he knew them. Recognized how they worked together.

Miles breathed away the thoughts. He'd assess the question of their identity after he got Miss Moore to safety. Right now, he needed to focus on stealth. His sharpshooter experience guided him quietly through the brush, keeping the car in sight, each step painfully slow and silent. Finally, the gunmen were directly to his right. Seemingly oblivious to Miles's flanking, their attention remained ahead.

Miss Moore swallowed audibly, and Miles flexed his bicep, pressing her more tightly against his side in a silent cue not to speak. She looked from him to the gunmen and back again. He lifted a corner of his mouth, hoping it would portray a measure of comfort. She gave a nod. Breathed in slow, then out. Determination sparked her eyes like diamond dust.

Whom should he fear more ... the men who would kill them or the woman who tested the fortifications of his heart?

Who would have guessed that Lily's lessons in dog training would come in so handy? Or maybe it was her years of hunting. Whichever it may be, she called on those skills to keep her fear at bay and her panic under control while Mr. Wright led her around the men who wanted them dead.

After what seemed like an eternity, the car finally stood between them and the bad guys—a sturdy square of a car, shiny and brown, with headlights that looked like a pair of spectacles sitting low on its nose.

"Now what?" she mouthed, careful to keep any sound from slipping past her lips.

Mr. Wright raised his eyebrows to the edge of his hat and tugged her in the opposite direction from the car. She didn't understand but followed silently.

Through another set of trees, they came to the road where three cars had been pulled off to the side. Twenty strides brought them to the driver's side door of the lead car. Nothing indicated that the bad guys had seen them. Regardless, as Mr. Wright helped her into the car, he pressed her into a crouch, as low to the floorboard and out of sight as he could. Then he tossed his gear in the back seat, leaving the door open before dashing to the car behind him.

Lily sat up with a cry. Was he leaving her?

Pulling a knife from his belt, he sliced into all eight tires of the other cars. Lily pressed her hands into her knees. *Hurry. Hurry. Please, Father God. Please let us escape.*

A glance toward the woods and Mr. Wright darted back toward the car. He slid behind the steering wheel and cranked the engine, shutting his door. Shouts cut through the air. He shifted into gear and yanked the car into motion. Men emerged from the woods. Mr. Wright pressed Lily's head out of sight, then sharply turned the vehicle as a bullet pinged off the rear. Lily gripped the bench seat to keep from tumbling into Mr. Wright in the small space. Bouncing over the uneven ground, Mr. Wright shifted gears and urged even more speed out of the car. Intensity radiated off him, yet he seemed calm, as if he did this regularly.

Another gunshot. This one seemed to go wide, as it didn't hit the car. She raised her head. The men were clambering into the other vehicles, but they wouldn't get far with flat tires. The few minutes of extra time that action had taken would likely be the reason they got away with their lives.

Miles's heart pounded against his ribs as if it pleaded to be released from its cage. Electricity coursed through his body, the hum of it making him jittery and tense.

His sabotage of the other vehicles had bought them extra time. How much, he didn't know. That would all depend on whether he could effectively disappear for the night— a task, to be sure, since he didn't dare turn off the headlights on the dark, winding road, but he also didn't want to lead their enemies straight toward them.

Did they get off the road for the night so they could blend in with the other cars come daylight? Or did he bank on staying awake until—no. That was a foolish idea. He was on his second full night without sleep. Kidnapping cases required them to push to the end of themselves. Time was in short supply, so they worked without stopping. As a company, they could catch snatches of slumber while the others worked, but he no longer had a team. And as the sharpshooter, Miles had already sacrificed rest to hurriedly scout the terrain and find a place to perch to be able to protect his men.

All his planning usually benefited him. This time, he'd not only failed his team but left his body so exhausted, he couldn't drive much longer without risking his eyes closing of their own accord. Soon the energy would drain away, leaving him weak, exhausted, and struggling to keep emotion at bay.

Yes, they needed a place to stop for the night, a place where they wouldn't be tracked that was also safe enough for him to let down his guard for a few hours.

And he knew of just the place.

"Do you trust me?" He glanced over at the woman beside him.

She huddled against the far door, rubbing her arms through his coat, her brown hair catching the moonlight. She merely stared back at him.

He frowned. Restated his question as a statement. "You can trust me."

She shivered.

"I wish I could give you more than my coat."

This time, she stretched out a hand—barely had to lean forward in the small space—to touch his arm. Gratitude shimmered in her damp eyes. Then she reclined against the door and pillowed her head on her arm.

God help him. She looked so vulnerable resting there. Sure, he'd helped plenty of damsels in distress, but something about this one was different than all the others. Somehow, she touched a place in his heart he kept well buried. But that could also be his failure talking. Which meant, all he could hope was that he lived up to the trust she placed in him. Because the greatest sign that she trusted him was that she fell asleep with him at the wheel, willing to let him take her anywhere.

He followed a circuitous path toward a small, out-of-the-way farming community. It rested about halfway between where Miss Moore had been stashed and her home but not on the direct path between those two points. Hopefully, enough of a detour no one would suspect he'd turned off the road.

A wave of exhaustion swept over him, and he stared into the darkness, willing himself to stay awake. What worried him most was how slow his reaction time would be if danger—even an animal— jumped out in front of the car. His emotions felt so raw—his body in the heart of an electrical storm.

He'd reacted this strongly to trauma, in a physical sense, only twice before. Once during a particularly bloody battle during the Great War. And the other after witnessing his fellow soldiers massacre a village in the Dominican Republic not long after the war ended. It was the only time he had ever faltered in carrying out his duty, but the horror of what they had been commanded to do sickened him.

That was the beginning of the end for him as a soldier—his reason for not just getting out of the Marines, but also for letting Craft entice him away. Craft believed in protecting striking workers, in rescuing people taken as hostages by businessmen drunk on their own wealth. Miles agreed with that agenda and quickly became a part of Craft's Elite

Company. A company that had just been decimated.

To a man, each of the Elite Company members would have given his life to rescue an innocent civilian, but it didn't make their loss any easier. It did refuel Miles's desire for justice. Those men did not deserve to die. They had been ambushed while doing good. The least he could do to recompense his failure was to figure out the reason they died. To find that answer, he needed to know why Miss Moore had been taken and by whom. Because he was sure the answer to all of those questions was the same.

He'd barely made that promise to himself when an odd noise came from Miss Moore. It sounded like a cross between a moan and a whimper. In the darkened shadows, her face twisted in panic. A cry escaped her lips. Yet her eyelids didn't open.

Hang it all. He'd seen this before, too, in fellow soldiers back in France. Nobody talked about it because the worst cases were sent home to asylums, but everyone knew the nightmares plagued most of them. That Lily Moore should suffer the same cut deep into his heart. She didn't deserve this.

Should he wake her? Free her from the prison she was reliving? Not that waking moments were much better. He could attest to that. Which was why he needed a safe place to regroup. Collect his wits.

Then again, maybe his plan wasn't the best idea. She didn't need to be around his dark thoughts any longer than absolutely necessary. He should take her straight home, even if that meant risking being followed. He was surely strong enough to make it without sleeping. She needed to be around people who could love her, support her, help her heal from the horrible things she'd experienced the last few days. That definitely didn't describe him. But he could get her there.

Miles sighed. Yes, he'd get her home, just as she requested. Once he deemed it safe enough to do so.

CHAPTER 4

Saturday, October 14

Lily woke with a start, an uneasy fear crowding her mind. She blinked against the darkness, trying to wade through what was real and what had plagued her dreams. A car trunk. A hole in the ground. Explosions. Escape. Except the car they had commandeered was no longer moving. She glanced to her side to see Miles Wright watching her.

"I'm sorry to wake you."

She sat up, fully aware now. They were stopped in a grove of trees on the back edge of a farm. Corn covered a hill to their left. An empty field, whether deserted or left fallow, lay in the darkness beyond the trees in front of them. Everything else was hidden—even Mr. Wright, who watched her from the shadows covering the other side of the car.

She really ought to be scared of him. So big and powerful and definitely dangerous. Especially since they were alone in a car together. Parked. And she had no idea where they were. But fear was not the emotion she felt around him. He'd saved her life. Several times. He was her hero.

"Miss Moore?" Mr. Wright shifted, and Lily caught an awkwardness in his tone.

She raised an eyebrow. "Mr. Wright?"

"It would be safer to pause for the night." He hesitated. "Being the only motorcar on the road is too dangerous. We'd be singled out instantly."

Lily nodded but suspected there was more to his decision than he told her. She wanted him to know he didn't have to coddle her. Even if her sore body protested, she leaned forward to give him her full attention. "What is your plan?"

"We still have several hours of darkness left. If it is acceptable, I need those hours to close my eyes. But ..."

Ah. That's what he was getting to. "You can speak plainly, Mr. Wright. I'm not going to criticize you, and you won't disturb my sensibilities."

His beard moved ever so slightly as if he quirked a smile. "First, while you're so agreeable, let me try once more to convince you to return to my headquarters."

Lily shook her head.

He held up a hand before she could offer her protest. "I had to ask, but my plan revolves around returning you to your home, so no need to discuss it."

Relief washed away the last vestiges of the bad dreams.

"We are stopped on the outskirts of a small farming community we passed through while looking for you." He rubbed his beard. "I apologize for my weakness, Miss Moore."

"Weakness? You mean your need to sleep?"

"Aye. But I honestly do believe it will be safer to blend in with other motorcars come morning."

"Do you wish me to keep watch?"

"No. I couldn't rest easy unless we were in a safe place." He shifted again. "This grove is about as off the beaten trail as I could find. But I worry for your reputation, Miss Moore."

She should as well. "I suppose staying overnight together in a parked car won't help if my neighbors catch wind of it."

"No ma'am." He squared his shoulders. "So I will sleep on the grass right outside. You are perfectly safe with me, Miss Moore. I only request that we stop because I believe it is the best way to handle the situation."

Something in his tone made it sound as if there were more to the *situation* than he was telling her. Should she worry about it? Try to drag it from him?

Lily fingered the cuff of his coat, now as dirty and torn as her dress. She decided to go with honesty, even if she could hear her brother in her head, screaming for her to get out of the car and run. Or at least demand perfect transparency. She just didn't feel afraid. Not as she had while trapped in that hole, sure she was about to be buried alive.

She shuddered. Made eye contact with her rescuer. "The truth is, I trust you, Mr. Wright. You've saved my life multiple times. I'm confident in your ability to get me home. And if this is the best way, then this is what we shall do."

Even the shadows couldn't hide the blush that bloomed over the man's face.

Lily pushed away her sleeves, resolved to thank Mr. Wright through her support. "You might be rescuing me, but if I'm not mistaken, your life has been equally in danger as mine. Please tell me what I can do to help."

"Rest." He didn't hesitate. "Stay in the car. Trust me with your protection. I sleep with one eye and half an ear open, so I'll know if anyone gets close. And no argument about that arrangement, understood? I'm used to sleeping outside. A little cold won't faze me. As long as you promise to stay inside the car."

Lily's pulse quickened with the idea of being stuck in a car alone. Four sides. Like a box. It reminded her too much of the hole she just escaped. She gulped a breath of air, but the steel walls closed in on her. She struggled to claw through the panic, school her voice into a normal-sounding one.

"I'd like to walk for a few minutes first." Desperation muted her tone, leaving her unable to form a coherent explanation for why she had to get out of the car. Now. Lily didn't wait for Mr. Wright's permission but turned to push open the passenger door. It wouldn't budge. Her mind clouded, her vision darkened, and she jiggled the door handle with a frustrated cry.

"This way." Mr. Wright's voice broke through the panic as he slid out of his side of the car and offered his hand.

She scrambled over the seat, planning to tumble by Mr. Wright on her way to freedom. Instead, her skirt tangled on her legs, sending up a dust cloud of panic. She couldn't breathe. Images of dirt and creepy-crawlers hemmed her in.

With the same ease with which he'd lifted her from her dirt dungeon, Mr. Wright raised her from the car and set her on her feet. He kept a hold on her hands, his humongous paws covering her small, slender fingers. And, as if a lever had switched, a feeling of safety traveled up her arms and settled in her heart, banishing the fear. It was like a warm blanket, wrapping her in a cocoon of refuge. Her lungs released and her heart slowed.

Until he let go.

Then she backed against the car, trying to get a handle on the juggernaut of emotions racing through her tired body. Fear and safety and worry. But particularly, the desire to grab hold of Mr. Moore's hand and never release it. Ever.

Cold air sent shivers down her spine. Or maybe it was residual fear. It couldn't have anything to do with Mr. Wright.

"Here." He adjusted his jacket over her shoulders. "Let's wander up the road some."

"Shouldn't you rest?" She pulled the coat tighter against the cold wind or maybe to shield herself from his answer. She wanted him to join her, even if she knew he really needed the sleep. "You don't need to walk with me."

"Who said I don't need to take a stroll?" He offered his elbow with a smile that infused her with good feelings. "A little walk will help me sleep."

Lily didn't believe a word of it, but he sounded so confident and convincing, it wouldn't be right to contest him. Not that she had any desire to do so. She grasped his arm, clinging as if her life depended on it. Maybe it did. Even if her past record showed her to be a self-sufficient woman. Out here in the unknown, with danger just out of reach, she wanted to hang on to security a while longer.

"It's too bad there is so much cloud cover." He spoke as slowly as his steps led them along the road. "I do like sleeping under the stars."

The collar of Mr. Wright's jacket brushed her chin as she raised her head to see the sky. The garment enveloped her, filling her senses again with the smell of pine and burnt leaves—a very October smell. It conjured happy images of plentiful harvests and cozy nights with her family. A time of bounty, even when the country's economic outlook appeared so dismal.

Lily breathed deeply, cold air bringing her fully conscious of the world around her. Golden rows of feed corn rose up beside them, towering above Mr. Wright, who easily stood well over six feet tall. She loved losing herself amid cornstalks. Row upon row, blocking out everything but the sky above. This time of year, the stalks were heavy with their produce, and each day, another field would be turned into feed for the cows. Neighbors helping neighbors.

Especially now.

She tightened her hold on Mr. Wright's arm, drawing in the security that radiated from him. Ever since the Great War, Dad and her brothers had toiled for pennies, yet with the whole nation enduring difficult times, crops and milk were valued even less—which made the past year an even bigger deal for their father. Two of his sons had married into the farming families on either side of the family farm, creating the largest dairy farm in the county. And then, the marriage of one of his daughters had provided a link to the milk-distributing company to which they sold their milk. Not to mention, when Lily's twin brother, Joey, solidified his position within the police force, it offered extra security to the family.

Then there was Lily. She had no interest in farming—not after the years of heartache and struggle to earn enough to eat, to save enough to buy a tractor to harvest enough corn for more cows. On and on it went. Had her grandfather not willed her the land on which she lived, Lily wasn't sure she'd still be in Eagle. Not that she had anywhere else to go.

"We should turn around." Mr. Wright broke into her thoughts as he positioned himself as a pivot to reverse their direction. Like a dance with him leading her around a ballroom, the heavens above a vaulted ceiling.

For a suspended moment, her imagination took wing. Feelings of safety and freedom wrapped around her soul. This quietest part of the night was her favorite time. The nocturnal animals had lulled, and even the breeze had grown gentle, as if the world sat poised between night and day. Darkness and light. Evil and mercy.

Then dawn would come, and with it, light, teeming with life in all its brightness. A new day. New mercies. New chances for a better tomorrow. The hopelessness of night turned into a world of possibilities come morning.

Yet, it was this moment, this suspension between worlds, between days, where she could almost hear the small whisper of God. That was what she loved most of all.

"Miss Moore?" A chuckle brought the vivid scene crashing around her like breaking glass. They had stopped moving. Embarrassment warmed her, but instead of letting her pull away from him, Mr. Wright resettled her hand around his arm with a smile.

Up to this point, he'd seemed as lost in his thoughts as she had been in hers, but the idea of him as a dance partner made her aware of him again. His height, which made him tower a foot above her. His broad shoulders, which made him seem like the sturdiest of men. His muscled arms, which strained the seams of his cotton shirt. The rise and fall of the vest that covered his chest as he puffed out white steam. The way he stayed at her pace, even if his long legs could match three of her strides.

No. She put proper distance between this man and herself. She was simply enamored over the hero who'd saved her, that was all. She knew nothing about him and, of course, a man like Miles Wright would have a family or at least a girl he was sweet on waiting for him back home.

Questions dashed across his features, and his shoulders, no longer squared with success, rounded under an invisible weight. "I admit, I could use some shut-eye now."

"Of course." She tugged on his elbow to head back toward the motorcar at his side. Offering up a hesitant smile, she caught a glimpse of some secret sorrow that weighted his brow. This was the human side of him, not the hero who rescued her. The real Miles Wright. And much to her chagrin, her heart wanted to reach out to him in comfort.

"If it isn't too forward of me, Miss Moore," he said suddenly, as if parroting her own recent thoughts, "how is it someone like yourself has not decided to marry?"

CHAPTER 5

"What?" Lily froze, dread sinking her stomach even as heat spread up her face. She slipped her hand from his elbow. Had he been all too aware of her perusal?

Miles Wright turned with a saunter, stuffing his hands into the pockets of his trousers and looking so handsome, she risked putting her own cold hands against her cheeks to cool down her face.

"The original rumor was that you ran away because of your singleness," Mr. Wright continued as if he were unaware of her mutinous thoughts. Surely, they were stamped across her forehead! "Tell me, Miss Moore, for I cannot puzzle it out—why would they think such a thing?"

This she could answer. She'd defended her choices enough times, it came easily, even if it still stung. "Eagle is a traditional, old community. They have been hounding me regarding my lack of choice for a husband since I came of marrying age. But I am content with my life as it is. Something they can't seem to comprehend."

"They?"

All of Eagle. But her family too. Especially with her decision not to aid in the dairy business. Frankly, her views had made her an outcast in Eagle. The older ladies wagged their tongues over her, and the men avoided her, having given up on the potential for a match. Not that she minded the latter. She had no interest in any of them. They had teased her mercilessly and humiliated her, particularly over her opinions on women's suffrage. She'd been sixteen when women were granted the Constitutional right to vote—too young to vote herself, but not too young to be aware of the incredible victory her elders had won for her and all the women who would come after them.

Only one friend, their local vet, Katy Wells, had stood by her—perhaps because Katy was one of only a handful of female vets in the country, or maybe—and Lily suspected this was more likely—because Katy had come to America seeking freedom from a past of which she never spoke.

"Miss Moore?" Mr. Wright's voice was quiet. Curious.

"Sorry." She shook her thoughts into the present. "It's just that most of my neighbors don't like my choices and find ways to show their displeasure with me."

"I get the feeling," he said as he got them walking again, keeping his hands casually in his pockets, "that your singleness isn't the entire story. What are these choices that have landed you in hot water?"

"Oh, just—" Lily snapped her lips closed. Embarrassment spread like lava. Not because of what she was about to share but because she feared dampening Mr. Wright's opinion of her. Would he be like everyone else and judge her for her choices? Why should it matter? She refused to care what anyone, especially a man, thought of her, yet here she was doing just that.

And not just anyone, or any man, but a stranger, no less. One she wouldn't see again once he delivered her home. And didn't that just put her thoughts right back where they belonged? She was nothing more than a woman he was rescuing. A damsel in distress. A job to be done before returning home to his real life. So why did it matter what he thought of her?

She didn't know, but, merciful heavens, it did matter, and she was too tired to fight the feelings that battled inside.

Mr. Wright cocked his head. "They wouldn't happen to be choices that stemmed from the idea that women are strong and capable, would it? That you have learned to stand on your own regardless of the darts thrown at you by your community, maybe even your family? That your actions are born of a willingness to defy convention, to plow a new path, to—"

"I wouldn't go that far." Lily's fingers sought her sleeve hem but found the cuff of his coat instead. Her insides hitched at the familiarity. Frustrated with herself, her emotions, she let her irritation infiltrate her tone. "I don't just defy tradition for the sake of it. I really am quite careful. And I would never willingly put myself in a position to be kidnapped. I was attending a business dinner. One within sight of many people."

"I wasn't—"

"Being alone with you like this is a first for me. I don't make it a habit. Even if I do run my own business, live on my own, and am completely capable of taking care of myself. In fact, if you let me borrow your Colt, I'll keep watch while you sleep tonight."

A laugh slipped out before Mr. Wright covered his mouth with his paw. His face sobered, but humor still shone in his eyes. What startled Lily was the lack of condescension there. She knew full well what that type looked like because most of Eagle gave her that expression. Miles Wright had an entirely different response, one Lily had no idea how to interpret, even as she tried to tell herself that she shouldn't want to know.

"I have so much I want to say." Mr. Wright rubbed his chin, all traces of his response gone. They'd neared the motorcar again, and Lily was ready to hide before he showed himself no different than any of the other men in Eagle. Than her own father and brothers.

She reached for the handle of the passenger door. "Won't it be too cold for you to sleep outside? You do not need to suffer on my account."

"No." He rested a hand against the car. "You can trust that I'm keeping watch even if you are sleeping."

His words brought reality back with a slamming force. She backed against the motorcar. "You don't think trouble will come tonight yet, do you? You don't think they'll find us? You said it's too deserted of a place to be happened upon." Had he just been placating her?

"I don't expect trouble tonight." He offered a shadow of a smile, and then, as if a mask slipped from his face, she could see just how tired he was. The lines deeply etched in his skin, the smudges under his eyes. And yet, he'd walked with her, was making sure she felt secure before he dropped into an exhausted slumber.

She mercilessly tamped down her fluttering heart. *Horsefeathers and hogwash. You are not a blithering fool, Lily Moore, so stop it this instant!*

"After morning comes, it's a different story," Mr. Wright was saying. "But one we will address in the light of day. For now, get some rest."

A plan with which Lily could heartily agree.

Miles stretched out on the grass beside the road. Rocks pierced his back, cold nipped at his nose, and his muscles complained. He pulled the wool wrap over his body, the one he kept in his pack for overnight sharpshooting missions. It was black and warm and made him appear like a hole in the night.

It'd taken some insisting to convince his charge that he wouldn't freeze to death. During the Great War, he'd been outside in much worse conditions than tonight's chilly October weather. And even if it was on the edge of uncomfortable, he couldn't make Miss Moore uneasy by staying in the car with her. It wasn't right.

Usually, they had a team for a situation such as this. Then a woman wouldn't fear for her reputation. Not that she had anything to fear from *him*. He just refused to be the cause of gossip for any woman. He was the protector, the rescuer—not trouble.

But with the way his insides were spinning as if churned by a hurricane, trouble had definitely found him. His stomach rolled with nausea born of fatigue. His muscles screamed at the abuse they had taken in the last several hours. With no strength left, he let his eyelids close, allowing the waves of emotion to overtake him.

Grief choked him as the explosion replayed in his mind's eye. His brothers-in-arms. His family. Gone. A single moment changing life as they knew it. Plans destroyed. Hopes obliterated. Worst of all, he should have been able to prevent it. His job was to see danger before his friends reached it. He should have listened to his instincts and more thoroughly scouted the ruins before taking his position in the tree.

Somehow, knowing that no one—save him—would grieve Tom, Nick, George, and Bill made the pain that much worse. These men would live on only in his memory. That he'd had to leave them behind in the charred remains of that forgotten place galled him, but he would find their killers. It was the only way to honor them.

As fresh determination cleared the smoke in his mind, leaving him with a battered and bloodied heart that only time would heal, green eyes stole his thoughts. His aching heart pleaded for a healing touch. Would he find it if he veered off course and surrendered his plans for revenge and redemption in favor of comfort?

Before the answer came—and with it, peace—sleep claimed his troubled mind. It left him fitful. Dreams repeated the questions that bombarded him. Emotions smashed his heart like a giant fist. Then came the cold. It pressed in on him as despair threatened to drag him down into the deepest ocean.

Hope faded, and his mind told him to just give in. Sleep the sleep of the dead. Only there would he find the peaceful repose he yearned for. All he had to do was let himself drift. Relinquish the fight.

Just as he was ready to lift the white flag, a hand plunged into the water. It reached for him. Begged for him to hang on. To swim for the surface. But dampness soaked into his bones, aching yet numbing.

He was freezing! Heaven help him, he needed to fight the cold that wanted to take him, or he wouldn't live much longer.

A shiver raced through his body. His teeth clenched.

Fight!

He had too much yet to accomplish. He couldn't leave his mission undone. His brothers needed restitution, his charge needed a protector, and he needed redemption. No. God couldn't be finished with him yet. He could feel it. This wasn't his time. He needed to wake up.

"Miles, please." Lily Moore's voice penetrated the fog that kept him captive like a siren's call. "You must open your eyes."

Hands patted his face, shook his body. He pushed his exhaustion aside to dig deep into the reservoir of his inner strength. There he found just enough to force open his eyes. A frozen droplet splashed on his cheek. Another on his shoulder. His forehead.

"That's it, Mr. Wright. Wake up."

More frozen water landed on his face, as if the sky spat at him, deriding him for nearly giving up hope. He blinked rapidly. Dark clouds covered the moon, blotting out any hope of light, like the despair that had nearly cost him his life.

Then a beautiful face blocked his view. Emerald eyes, full of worry, fear. "Miles Wright, you wake up this instant!"

Yes ma'am! This was no siren but a general to be obeyed.

"I'm awake. I'm awake." It took effort, but he got the words out.

Relief caused her to sink beside him. "You scared me, Mr. Wright. People have died from cold, and you seemed awfully close."

Closer than he liked to think and much closer than he would tell her. Indeed, it felt as though winter had arrived this very night, and every part of him was wet with sleet and sweat. He shivered. She'd saved his life. He lifted his hand to her cheek. Whether his fingers were frozen or her cheek was, the cold spread up his arm. But heaven help him, in this moment, Lily Moore was the most gorgeous woman he'd ever met. If God changed his mind and called him home, he could let his body succumb and die a contented man.

CHAPTER 6

"No. No. No." Lily clasped Mr. Moore's large hand as it slipped from her cheek. His head lolled to one side. Eyes closed. "I forbid you to fall back to sleep. You hear?"

He didn't stir. A snowflake landed on his cheek.

She should have noticed the sudden temperature drop sooner with the way the clouds rolled in, threatening to lay a blanket of early snow over the half-harvested fields. She hadn't been sleeping as Mr. Moore had wanted her to. She couldn't close her eyes without being back in that hole. So she'd stayed awake, watching her rescuer fight inner demons as he attempted to sleep.

She would never admit to him that was what had alerted her to the danger. For what seemed like hours, he'd lain in agitated sleep. She'd taken too long arguing with herself over whether to wake him from his nightmares when finally she'd realized his black blanket had slid into a heap at his side, and he'd gone still, as if the cold had added rocks to his limbs. In essence, it had. It wasn't peace that calmed his thrashing, not if the expression on his face was any indication.

As she jumped out of the car, the cold had hit her like shards of ice. She was not dressed to be out in the wet snow, but she refused to let that stop her. Miles Wright had insisted on sleeping outside, in a snowstorm, just to protect her sensibilities. No one would see them here or start any gossip, but she would know, and he would know. For that reason, she'd respected his choice, even if she'd missed the safety of his presence. She certainly wasn't about to let a man like that die on her watch.

She tucked the wool blanket around his damp body. He needed warm, dry clothes, and fast, but since that wasn't a possibility, getting him out of the elements would be a start.

Standing and placing a foot on either side of him, she hooked her arms under his and pulled. He was heavy, but just because she was a woman didn't mean she didn't haul heavy things. She would never be able to lift him to her shoulder like a sack of feed, but she could drag him to the car.

With waddling steps, she moved him toward the back seat. He didn't even moan as she slid him over the pebbles that lined the road. At the car, she climbed inside and lifted Mr. Wright in after her. Once she got his shoulders onto the seat, the rest of him followed easily. Of course, he was too long to fit, so Lily scrambled back around to the other side in order to stuff his legs into the car. She fought back embarrassment at touching him in such a way.

Day would break soon, even if the clouds hid the waking sun. That meant, surely, she could find a diner opening soon where she could get a cup of strong, warm coffee. And maybe a doctor if Mr. Wright didn't reawaken by then.

She slipped into the driver's seat. This was a different model than the pickup truck she owned, but a quick survey showed the mechanics were the same. Clutch. Gear. Pedals. She managed to do it all in the right order without too many ear-bleeding noises and got the old horseless carriage rattling down the road.

In no time, she found her way into a small town nestled in the farmland. So this was Mikle Lake. They were one of the towns against the dairy strikes, according to her dad. The buildings showed the wear of the last several years of drought and hardship. No extra money to make the businesses pretty. In fact, half of the shops looked deserted. Just south of the center of town, the barber was opening up for a waiting customer. Next door, a pharmacist swept the dusting of snow from his walkway.

Across the street was Mel's Diner. Was it open?

Lily parked and took the keys from the ignition as a well-dressed yet threadbare gent left the building, patting his belly. He glanced at them, and Lily quickly avoided eye contact. No one would know her here, but she hadn't expected direct scrutiny from a stranger.

"Where are we?" Mr. Wright's groggy voice came from the back seat, and all the tension drained from Lily's body.

"Good morning." She looked over her seat. "I'm getting us coffee. Or I can if you have any money in your pack."

He sat upright. "You can't go inside alone."

"No. I am perfectly capable. You just don't want me to. But you're in no condition to leave that back seat."

"You realize, this is the gossip I was trying to avoid." He nodded his head toward the barber shop and pharmacist where the three men watched them with open curiosity.

"Maybe they know where the doctor is—because he should make sure you're healthy. I had a hard time waking you up last night, and you slept through me dragging you into the car."

At that statement, Mr. Wright blinked several times as if he realized the truth to her words. "I remember you waking me from—never mind—but nothing else." He stared at her. "I'm really heavy."

Lily shrugged. "Just because you saved my life doesn't mean I can't help you too. Now let me get the coffee before we have the whole town watching us."

"We'll go inside together."

"And that will get tongues wagging unless we're a married couple."

"It will, no matter what."

"Not if I ask for the doctor and say I found you on the side of the road."

"Hate to say it, but that would only be true if I found you."

Lily's good humor died. He was right. Mr. Wright may have been exhausted and half frozen, but Lily's clothing was torn, her hat and gloves missing, and a woman wouldn't have allowed a strange man into the back seat of her car. They really were in a pickle. And the longer they sat there, the worse it was going to get.

"Do you trust me?" Mr. Wright straightened his vest and dashed a hand through his hair before he settled his hat on his head.

Lily nodded.

"Then we're a married couple who ran into some ruffians. They left us worse for wear but alive. And no, we wouldn't recognize them and do not need to file a local police report."

"That's not too far from the truth."

"Exactly." He tried to hide the grimace as he pushed open the rear door, but Lily saw it plain as the daylight burning away the snow. Nevertheless, she waited for him to open her door and help her out.

She handed him the keys as he did. "Are you sure you can walk?"

"Once I get moving, I'll be fine." He flashed her a grin. "I'm hardier than I look."

A laugh leapt out. And though her body ached, for the first time since she'd been kidnapped, her heart actually felt light.

The middle-aged man looked up from the contract as the younger man entered his study, igniting his anger. "You know better than to come here."

The young man shuffled to a stop, wringing his hands. He wore an ill-fitting suit and a tie, askew. Did he not know how to dress appropriately? He paid the boy handsomely. Could the young man not find a new set of clothes so he would not bring embarrassment? And if that thought hadn't stoked his ire enough, the fact that the young man refused to follow directions turned his anger into an inferno.

The young man cleared his throat. "We have a problem."

The fire banked. Simmering. "Speak."

"She was rescued."

He laid down his pen, the tremble in his fingers the only outward sign of his controlled fury. "Explain."

The young man shuffled.

"Now!"

The young man fumbled for a letter. Held it out. "I paid a scout to deliver food to her. He got this to me this morning."

The missive told of four men, like shadows, entering the ruins where the young man had stashed Lily Moore. It didn't say who they were or how they knew she was there.

"He said they looked like soldiers," the young man said, a whine in his voice. "And there was an explosion."

"Tell me she's still alive. I need her alive." He would show this young man an explosion if Lily Moore was dead.

Finish the letter. He stored his anger for the time being and continued to read. The scout reported a single soldier, as well armed as the others, entering the ruins after the explosion. He found the hole where the young man had put Lily Moore and carried her to freedom.

A curse died on his lips as the letter told of a handful of armed men following the pair, shooting at them, and finally, tossing a grenade. Who were these people? He hadn't authorized lethal force.

"This doesn't tell me whether she's still alive." He slammed the paper on the desk, mind reeling over the implications.

The young man stuffed his hands into his pockets. "Then you'll like knowing I saw her in the passenger seat of a motorcar before I came over here. She was with a man."

"The same soldier?"

The young man shrugged, but the insinuation was clear.

He rubbed his professionally shaved chin. The plan could still be salvaged. "I have another job for you."

"You want to kidnap her again?"

"Don't be an idiot. We got away with it, thanks to your rumors. Kidnapping her again would make her brother's claims stronger, and the police couldn't brush away her disappearance again. No. We change tactics." His mind whirred with possibilities.

"What should I do?"

"We can't let her get comfortable. She—"

"You need someone to cause mischief." A light bloomed in the young man's eyes. "That's much easier than kidnapping."

"I want her alive."

"Easy."

"And I don't want it traced back to you. Or me."

"Don't worry."

But he did worry because trusting a kid went against everything in him. Yet this young man had accomplished everything asked of him thus far. The rescue wasn't his fault. Or was it?

"Anything else?" Cockiness overcoming his nerves, the young man sauntered to the door.

"Just keep her off-kilter and report to me what she does next." Information. That's what he needed for his plan, but it would also tell him about the young man's true loyalties. "And I want to know the name of the man who is with her."

"Mischief and a name. Consider it done." The young man gave a mock salute.

He tapped his pen on the contract as the young man slipped from the office. Mahogany, floor-to-ceiling shelves covered two of the four walls. Behind him was a wall of windows. Lush carpet comforted his feet, though he always wore dress shoes. And an electric ceiling fan slowly rotated above his head, keeping the air moving.

He leaned back in his desk chair. His original plan was to use Lily Moore as leverage before turning the screws to her. Now he might have to reverse that plan. He slammed the pen down. A few more hours, and he would have succeeded.

It couldn't matter. He wasn't about to let this new development derail what he'd worked years to accomplish. What the market crash had opened the way to achieve. Violence wasn't his *modus operandi*, but he'd use it if he must. This contract meant thousands. He'd get it signed one way or another.

CHAPTER 7

"Are you sure you want to do this?" Miles asked as he turned onto the country road that led to Miss Moore's house. Golden cornstalks rose high on either side, creating a tunnel effect that made him uneasy. "You just survived a horrible experience. Isn't there someone who can stay with you tonight?"

"I'll be fine." The way she'd been rubbing her cuffs since they reached the outer farms of Eagle said otherwise.

A mile farther, the road veered sharply to the right, and the corn on the left side gave way to browning grass and a smattering of fallen leaves. He turned onto the gravel drive that ended behind a small, white farmhouse. A gnarly oak left a bed of russet leaves in front of the house, and a host of yellow flowers swayed under the large picture window to the right of the door. Not a hundred yards to the left of the house sat a bright red barn. A pine stood sentry at its closest corner. Behind the house was a large garden, mostly bare except vining plants at the far end, and a couple small outbuildings, including a silo and metal windmill.

"Wow. This is all yours?" Miles set the brake and leaned over the steering wheel for a better perspective. He'd never met a never-married woman who owned her house, let alone property this expansive. "It's—"

Without warning, Miss Moore leapt out of the car and jogged to the door at the back of the house. Barking echoed from inside as he chased after her, getting to the door a step before she did.

"Slow down a minute." He pressed a hand on the screen to keep her from opening it. "Let me go first."

She raised her chin, a flash of fear and determination in her eyes, as she kept her hand on the knob.

He knew he presented an intimidating figure, especially towering over her as he was. He forced himself to turn down his intensity and soften his tone. "It's for your safety. Please let me make sure it's safe before you go inside."

"I see your point." Her shoulders relaxed. "But listen to my dogs, Mr. Wright. No one is in there, and, frankly, for your sake, I should go in first."

She had a point there. Palm resting on the butt of his Colt, he backed away and scanned the yard for danger. The corn isolated Miss Moore's house, making it nearly impossible to see anything but the clear blue sky above, the road winding past, and the woods at the back.

"Mama's home!" she called as she cracked open the door. "That's it, boys. Sit."

A yearning pang he thought long buried struck Miles like a sniper's bullet as he watched her kneel in front of her two dogs. She wrapped her arms around their necks, and their tails moved so fast, their hind ends wagged too. The larger one rested its chin on her shoulder, rubbing its head against her neck. The younger one bounced on rear legs as he reached up to furiously lick her cheek. They'd certainly missed her.

"Ready to meet the duo?" Miss Moore swiped at her eyes as she stood.

Miles simply nodded to hide the choke in his own voice. He loved his work, the ability to rescue people from awful situations, but he rarely witnessed the homecoming, and he never had anyone waiting for him at the end of a mission. The tradeoff always seemed worth it.

Miss Moore held up a hand, palm out, to the dogs, and two canine hind ends hit the wooden floor. They studied Miles as he entered the tiny mudroom, tails swishing slowly, muscles tense.

"This is my Pieter." She rested one hand on the black dog's head. Curly hair covered his lean body. Intelligent eyes shone through the hair that flopped from his forehead. He came up to Miss Moore's knee, which he pressed against as she spoke. Next, she scooped up a gangly, curly-haired puppy with the saddest eyes. "And this ball of energy is Smokey. He just joined our little pack."

"He's adorable. May I?" He held out a hand, fingers down, palm flat, to let the puppy smell him.

Smokey nuzzled Miles's hand, then squirmed his way into Miles's arms.

"You know dogs," Miss Moore said, then released Pieter. He circled Miles, sniffing his shoes, his pants, his free hand, tail moving nearly as fast as it had for Miss Moore.

"I had a couple growing up." Miles scratched Smokey's ears as he searched over her shoulder for any sign of trouble.

Miss Moore distracted him, moving from foot to foot, tension again coiling around her shoulders. Was she worried about staying alone? How couldn't she be, after all she'd experienced? Or was she nervous because she was alone with a strange man in her house? Gossip could cause damage, and he didn't want to cause her any more. She'd handled the questioning looks at the diner that morning with admirable grace. Here, people wouldn't be so accepting of any old story. The dogs might offer a sense of security but not propriety, and he refused to put her in an uncomfortable situation.

"I'll wait outside." He set the puppy on the floor, but before he could exit, Pieter plopped down on his shoes. "Or I suppose I can stand right here with the dogs. You'll be safe either way."

She glanced at the dogs, then back at him, a small smile lighting her eyes. "Come wait in the kitchen. I'll only be a few minutes, then we can take the dogs out. I hope they haven't been cooped up since ..." She ran light fingers over Pieter's curly head, then dashed away. Smokey trotted after her.

Miles peered through the mudroom doorway at the lower level of Lily's home. The kitchen was small. A wooden table stood in the center, surrounded in an L-shape by an electric refrigerator, woodstove, and cupboard. Pots hung from the ceiling around the stove. He slid his foot free of Pieter to step into the kitchen. Jiminy, an electric light hung above his head.

He slipped farther into the kitchen to peek through the archway that separated the kitchen from the other half of the house, Pieter at his heels. The picture window allowed the late-afternoon sun to bathe the sitting room in a soft glow. Miles didn't spot a radio, but books overflowed the short tables beside the single couch and the two armchairs. The walls were covered with a pleasing cream wallpaper with hazy roses, causing the fireplace to stand out with its reddish brick surround. Tension eased from Miles's shoulders, and he fought the urge to sink onto the couch and page through Miss Moore's books.

In a word, it felt like home.

"You are a couple of lucky boys." He gave Pieter a pat, and the dog turned soulful eyes back at him.

He lived in a stark boardinghouse near Craft Headquarters in New York City but was rarely there. Partly because he worked so much and mostly because he missed the country life of his youth. In fact, he hadn't been in a home, especially one as warm as this, since his parents died months before he signed up to go to war. Now, after losing his team, he found great comfort just standing in Miss Moore's kitchen.

"All set," she announced as she descended from the stairs that led to the story above, a closed door tucked underneath.

"All ready?" That was barely ten minutes.

She gave a little shrug as she came into view. And wow, what a view! She wore a simple, long-sleeved, floral blouse that showed off her waist, a bow under her chin, and her hair was swept back into a knot at the base of her neck. Her blue skirt followed her hips until it flared at her knees.

"Do you want to clean up?" Her voice filtered into his consciousness.

No amount of scrubbing would make him presentable enough to accompany her, even to take the dogs for a walk. "The dogs are waiting."

Her green eyes sparkled. "We have time if you stop standing there, gawking."

His heart gave a *ker-thump*. Plenty of women flirted with him, but none made him forget his surroundings quite like Lily Moore.

Lily breathed in a deep breath of outside air. Tinged with burning leaves, cow refuse, and damp earth, it surrounded her with a sense of safety. Even so, after the events of the last few days, perhaps she should have listened to Mr. Wright and called her twin brother to stay with her. But no. He would be overprotective. She needed to tell her family she was back, but first, she needed some semblance of normalcy. Anyway, right now, a stranger seemed to offer more comfort than the thought of her large family. Granted, he was an awfully good-looking stranger.

She couldn't believe the transformation Mr. Wright had undergone in the five minutes he'd taken to wash up after hauling fresh water in for her. The dirt-stained shirt and vest he'd worn during her rescue had been discarded. Now he wore a white shirt and dark vest under a dark suit coat that made his already dark hair even darker. He wore dress shoes, too, though perhaps not the best choice to walk in a cornfield.

Who carried a change of clothes with them on a rescue mission? Was that common? She'd never met anyone like Miles Wright before. But the simple change of clothes caused him to go from intense protector to confident friend. His muscles and broad shoulders perfectly filled out the suit, and yet he seemed the picture of ease. If only it was proper for him to stay with her tonight.

Heat rushed into her cheeks. Not in that way, of course! Any attraction she felt was entirely due to his heroic rescue or his dramatic change of clothing, nothing more. It couldn't be anything more because she knew nothing about him. She was simply a job, and once the task was concluded, he would return to his normal life. She, on the other hand, well, she doubted she'd ever be the same woman as before the kidnapping. Life just looked different now.

Pieter stuck close to her leg, while Smokey bounded toward the dog pen and then dashed back to them, distracting himself with the various smells in the grass. Seeing them gave her hope that she would feel completely safe again. No explosions, no deep dark holes, no freezing weather.

That morning, the man who left the diner just as they emerged from the car happened to be a doctor. One look at Lily, and he'd insisted on helping them. Mr. Wright had offered their curated story of being attacked, and the doctor hadn't questioned it. It turned out, Mr. Wright had several bruised ribs, which led the doctor to suggest his *wife* make him take it easy for a few days. If the doctor had noticed her embarrassment, he hadn't mentioned it, and she'd felt horrible for having dragged Mr. Wright into a car with such injuries, but the doctor said getting him out of the cold had been the right plan.

Thankfully, Lily had injuries no worse than a few bumps, bruises, and scrapes, which the doctor had easily cleaned and bandaged. She fingered the bandage on her temple. How had she made it out alive, let alone with so little damage? It made the past few days feel like a surreal nightmare.

"How do you feel about being back?" Mr. Wright asked, his voice blending with the crickets.

"You keep asking about my feelings." Lily stopped in the middle of the yard, emotions weighting her feet and making her words terser than she intended.

He touched her shoulder with a gentleness that belied his size. "You've been through something horrible. It's helpful to talk about it."

Her heart melted just a little bit more. He'd seen firsthand what she'd been through, so she didn't need to prove the truth of her story. It made Lily want to answer his questions—she just didn't know what to say. He stayed quiet and still, as if time had paused until she could turn her troubled thoughts into coherent words.

"I should probably talk to the police." It was the only thing she could think to say aloud. "But reporting my rescue would include telling them about how you saved me. It invites more questions." About them. About her reputation. About everything.

He sighed and dropped his arm. "This is why taking you to

headquarters was the better plan. It would keep you from having to answer malicious gossip. You would be safe, and I could find your kidnapper. Plus, my boss hates involving local police."

"I'm sorry, I—"

"Don't apologize." Mr. Wright shifted to face her. "Bringing you home instead of to headquarters was ultimately my decision. I know you wanted to come here to find answers, but you need to focus on healing from what happened first. Let me worry about everything else right now."

With compassion like that, how was she supposed to keep her heart from falling for—

"Do you hear that?" He spun toward the road, pushing her behind him.

"It's a car?" The words scraped her throat.

"Take the dogs into the barn. Now." He gave her a nudge. "Go."

Lily couldn't force her feet to move. She clutched the back of his shirt, memories of their flight the night before flashing before her eyes. And here, she thought she'd be safe.

CHAPTER 8

Miles failed to react fast enough. With Lily—no, Miss Moore—frozen behind him and the dogs racing to meet the arriving Ford Model A, his only option was to bluff this to a hopefully peaceful conclusion.

"Lily!" A man leapt out of the car without turning off the engine. Tall, muscular, obviously able to handle himself. And looking uncannily like the woman behind him. "Where in heaven's name have you been?"

Miles tensed. Best not to escalate the situation by showing himself armed, but he still kept himself between the stranger and Miss Moore until he could determine the level of danger.

"Joey?" Her voice came out more like a squeak.

"You need to tell me before you decide to disappear for a couple days. I've been worried …" The man skidded to a stop as if he suddenly registered Miles's presence. "Who are you?"

Eyes unsettlingly identical to Lily's brilliant green ones issued a silent challenge, and when Miles didn't back down, the man squared off. Miles eased a hand to his suit jacket, underneath which lay his Colt. The man made an identical move, revealing a police badge on his chest. His boss would kill him if he tangled with a local copper.

"It's all right." Lily slipped out from behind Miles, tugging at her sleeves. "Mr. Wright, this is my twin brother, Joey, and Joey, this is a friend of mine, Mr. Wright. He …"

"Is just visiting from out of town." Miles smoothed his jacket over his weapon. He didn't offer a hand since Joey didn't either.

Without taking his eyes from Miles, Joey swept his sister into the strongest of bear hugs, lifting her off the ground for good measure. Miles backed away, feeling like an intruder. Yet Joey's greeting set him on edge. Could the man not know his twin sister had been the victim of a kidnapping? The niggling worry that should have warned him of the explosion that killed his friends crept up his spine.

He needed to think this through before he missed something big. Because, for the second time in two days, something didn't feel right.

"You scared me to death." Joey pulled Lily close as Miles reentered her house after asking to use the telephone and promising to cover any long-distance charges. Smokey trotted after him.

"It wasn't my intention." Lily leaned into her twin brother. She felt Miles's—Mr. Wright's—absence, but maybe familiarity did have its comfort.

"I made sure your dogs were fed when I noticed you hadn't been home. Usually, you tell me when you need someone to watch them. Where were you?"

Then again … She frowned. Joey had switched to his policeman's voice, suspicion lacing his tone.

Lily pushed away. "I don't want to talk about it."

A crash snapped her attention to the house. Her heart jumped into her throat as she frantically sought the cause and braced for impact. Smokey. The pup had knocked a potted plant off the steps when Mr. Wright left him outside. Lily pressed a hand to her racing heart. It wasn't another grenade.

"You're as jumpy as a toad." Joey grabbed her elbow. "Tell me what's going on. Who is that Miles Wright guy? And what were you doing with him?"

"Not now, Joey," she hissed. Between being a policeman and her twin, he'd always been extraordinarily protective of her, and sometimes, it drove her mad. She felt too raw to deal with it right this moment. Had the strangest urge to find Miles. He would understand why she was so jumpy.

"Lil?"

"I'll tell you, just not right now. Please." Anyway, she needed to think first. Consider the implications of everything—from her reputation to her sanity—before she revealed anything that would steal her chance at getting the answers she desperately needed.

"I can't help you if you don't talk to me."

"I know that." Tears pricked her eyes. As soon as Joey learned what had really happened, she wouldn't get a say in anything that happened next. He'd seek to manage everything, keep her locked in a protective bubble. She looked around for Miles. How long of a phone call was it?

"You're as distracted as I was this morning," Joey was saying, frustration icing his tone. "It's been an irritating day. Not only was I worried about you, seemingly for no good reason, but the boys in the office kept arguing about milk and crop prices. Again. There's going to be another strike, and Dad's in the middle of it."

The dairy strikes. There'd been two earlier this year already. Lily's heart picked up speed. That's exactly what Andy's friends had been discussing right before she'd been kidnapped.

Visions of creepy, crawly bugs coming out of the moist dirt that held her captive sent shivers down her spine. She hated feeling like a victim, hated the claustrophobic fear that threatened to entomb her. She had to find the person who did this to her. Had to look him in the eye and find out why. It was the only way she'd be free.

"Buck up." Joey bumped her shoulder with his fist, transporting her back to the here and now. "Forget all that. How about I stay at your place for a night, and you can fill me in on where you've been the last few days?"

Did no one know she'd been kidnapped? Could her closest family member truly believe she'd just been out of town? She hated leaving her dogs, so why would she leave them behind on purpose, especially without providing specific care for them?

Lily blinked away the tears and grabbed hold of her resolve. She wasn't going to back down. Not this time. Not when she'd survived the scariest days of her life. She wanted answers, and she wasn't going to depend on anyone else to find them. She would do it herself.

"Thank you, Joey." She yanked her hands away from her sleeves. "Not tonight."

Miles held the phone's earpiece away from his ear as his boss let out the string of curses, his reaction to Miles's coded message on how the rescue mission had gone. It took a good minute for the man to finally calm down enough for Miles to speak again, wording his response carefully, knowing he was being overheard by at least one operator.

"I decided it was my gentlemanly duty to assist." Meaning, to escort her home. Miles leaned a hand against the kitchen wall beside the mounted phone box, ear cone in the other, and wished the room had a view of the yard so he could keep an eye on Lily.

"I agree." Craft's still-angry voice came clearly over the line. "But it was not your call."

"But my companions—"

"They're mine too."

"Of course, sir." Miles scanned the cornfields he could see through the picture window, past the oak. The corn seemed to stretch for miles all around Lily's house. If he could soak in the peace of her home, it might allow him to keep a level head with his boss.

"I won't hesitate to make your next delivery to a more grueling location. Is that understood?"

"Absolutely, sir." Miles squeezed his eyes closed. The threat was not an idle one.

"But …"

Miles waited out his boss. The man was right that Miles completed his assignment. He successfully rescued Lily, but Miles wanted answers and didn't feel right about leaving her alone with her unknown kidnapper on the loose.

Craft finally spoke, the anger simmering under his tight control. "You are my top deliveryman and a gentleman."

Miles pushed off the wall. His boss was caving. The patience of a sniper worked every time. Especially with a man as emotionally volatile as Craft.

"I'd fire you if you weren't so good at your job." Craft grumbled, a few extra swear words slipping out. "Finish this as quickly and quietly as possible, then get home."

"Thank you, sir." Miles signed off and bounded back outside.

"Mr. Wright?" Lily appeared as if from a cloud, crashing into Miles's chest as he closed the back door behind himself. She sucked in a quick breath as her eyes popped wide.

"Lily." Miles cleared his throat at her sudden close proximity. "Miss Moore." He snapped himself out of his reaction. Steadied her before she toppled and tried to step back, only to bump into the door. And he still must have gazed at her for too long because over her left shoulder, he spotted Joey moving closer. Not good. With his boss's warning to stay away from police notice ringing in his head, he didn't dare give Lily's brother reason to think Miles was anything other than a friend.

"Everything okay?" Worry darkened her green eyes.

"Absolutely." He gave her a wink, and pink spotted her cheeks. The same pink that was surely coloring the tips of his ears. Evidence of how she flustered him, despite his attempt at covering his reaction.

She glanced over her shoulder at her brother, and Miles felt the tremble that raced through her as she spoke. "Joey was telling me about his morning. About another dairy strike."

Another one? That would make three. The first two had grown increasingly more violent. A third could ignite the mounting anger like Big Bertha come to the farmland of Wisconsin.

He struggled to keep all reaction off his expression as Joey approached. In Miles's experience, union strikes often turned deadly. Had for a long time. And the resolution of the inevitable clash with law enforcement seemed to depend on who had the political sway to deploy the police. Which, in this case, could pit Joey against his family.

"You know it's too dangerous for you to get involved." Joey practically growled the statement at his sister, interrupting yet echoing Miles's own tumultuous thoughts. "People have already died over this and surely will again."

"I know that." Miss Moore folded her arms across her body. "I'm not planning to get involved with the strikes. That's Dad's business. But we are children of a dairy farmer, after all, and I'm not so dense as to not understand what's going on."

Miles covered the smile that peeked out. He couldn't help but admire the woman's spunk.

"I didn't call you dense." Joey rubbed the brown scruff on his chin. "But with Dad solidly supporting the Farm Holiday Association's encouragement to strike again, the so-called alliance between our family and the Booths gained by Amy and Andy's marriage could really blow up."

"Because Andy's dad owns the distribution and processing center." Miss Moore waved her hand for Joey to continue. "I know. Get to the important part."

"Mr. Booth is refusing to pay a higher price for the milk he buys, and you know Dad. He's already led the way with the other farmers in dumping milk. But this next strike is threatening to become the biggest one yet, and the most personal since our sister is now a Booth. Those are all the facts I know."

Or want to share. Miles could hear the unspoken caveat.

"Tell me something I can't figure out on my own." Miss Moore rolled her eyes. "What about Harry Williams and Alex Chiff? They're Andy's friends. Have they expressed opinions on the strike?"

The two men who were at O'Reilly's Restaurant with her when she was kidnapped? Miles clamped his mouth closed. He wanted to elbow her to keep her from asking more questions, even of her brother. Joey appeared of a similar mindset, which made Miles's antenna rise even more. Was it because he knew more than he was letting on? Or because he believed a woman shouldn't be involved? Or was he simply concerned for his sister?

Miles needed more information. Background. Especially on the immediate persons involved, but also on the larger picture. The strikes. And the only person he trusted to help was his old war buddy ... Giosue Vella.

The man was a genius. Always ready and willing to help a friend. Frankly, Gio was the only person Miles trusted with the most personal parts of his life. He had proven himself by standing beside Miles in the trenches, the first person who'd witnessed his grief after the death of his parents. Since those dark days, their friendship had deepened to that of brothers.

Once he knew he'd have Gio watching his back, perhaps Miles would finally breathe easier for the first time since the explosion murdered his team.

CHAPTER 9

"Tell me why you want to know about those two troublemakers." Joey darted a look at Miles over Lily's shoulder.

Lily descended the two steps that led up to her back door to rescue Smokey from digging in the dirt from the pot he'd knocked over. At least, that's what she told herself as she wrapped the pup in her arms. Miles followed her but kept his distance. A helpful thing, since running into him had flustered her more than she cared to admit.

Joey narrowed his glare at her. He could see right through her action, and she didn't like it. It didn't help that he was no happier with her right at this moment than she was with him. She despised it when he withheld information just because she was a woman. It was the only subject that threatened a significant rift between them, and this time, Lily wasn't interested in bridging the gap.

"I only ask because Harry and Alex seemed invested in preserving the farms without protesting." She tossed the information out as casually as she could—not that she could fool Joey, but a girl could hope. "You're sure you don't know anything more about it?"

A strange spark lit Joey's eyes. Lily suddenly got the distinct impression she had turned into his prey … a feeling she'd never had before. She shifted closer to Miles, and Miles responded in kind.

Joey didn't miss a thing. He spoke with deadly calm. "I asked around when I couldn't find you. You went to dinner with them. Why?"

"We were discussing dog training. Not that it matters. You've never worried about the people with whom I conduct business."

"That's because you've never *disappeared* before." Joey emphasized the word as he eyed Miles. As if Miles had something to do with the reason she left.

For a moment, she considered blurting out that Miles was the reason she came home. Alive. But she was too tired to explain Miles's presence, especially with the distrustful glint in Joey's eyes. "Why are you questioning me as though I'm one of your criminals?"

"I'm trying to protect you!" Joey flapped his arms in exasperation. "Women should stay out of danger and leave the question-asking to the authorities. I can take care of you. You don't need to run to the first muscle you see." He narrowed his eyes at Miles.

Clanging alarms sounded in her head. She had no intention of staying out of anything. Nor would she avoid a lead that could get her answers. She would never forget she'd been kidnapped. Nor would the days spent as a prisoner slip her mind. But, of course, Joey didn't know about that, and Miles's agency did not want the police involved.

Trapped by her own green eyes staring so intensely back at her, Lily's heart stung. Joey, her other half, might be two minutes older, but they looked as alike as two twins could. Well, they used to. Something had changed in him lately, and the five inches he had on her in height seemed like even more. It gave him an intimidating stance she never remembered noticing before. Joey's belittling attitude had pushed her away when she needed him more than once before. Now her brother made it clear he'd tell her nothing even if he could.

A warm hand settled on her shoulder, and Miles's quiet voice cut through her frustration and hurt. "Joey can do his job, and we'll get our own answers. Together."

Joey's jaw hardened as his gaze dashed between her and Miles. Lily leaned closer to Miles as Smokey squirmed against her tight hold and Pieter pressed against her legs. Miles kept his hand on her shoulder, his fingers gently kneading as if he could communicate through the simple touch. She couldn't deny that it spread calm to her heart, just as it had during their escape last night. She'd never met a man who had that much effect on her. Her experience was quite the opposite. Her lack of feminine curves that other women could so easily show off and her vocal support of women's suffrage had turned away many a masculine eye. Unless they thought they could get a piece of her dad's money or influence.

Lily focused on the issues at hand. She wanted to believe Miles that they would find the answers she needed. That the bad people would be brought to justice. But if her overprotective family had their way, she would be carefully tucked away from any hint of trouble—and any possibility of finding answers.

As if shouldering her concerns, Miles shifted to a casual stance behind her and spoke up. "I wasn't around for the first two strikes, so I wouldn't mind hearing more about them."

"What's it to you?" Joey's gaze darted away from Miles's hand on Lily's shoulder to pierce him like a bayonet. She'd hear more about Miles's presence as soon as her brother had her alone again, which meant she had to avoid Joey at all costs.

"Just trying to get to know more about the family of my friend." Miles oozed a charm that could make every female in Eagle fall for him in an instant and every man want to be his buddy. Sorrow snuck up on Lily. She was always the loser in that scenario. Dare she hope this time would be different?

Joey scowled and turned back to Lily. "I'm not the only one worried about you. You know Mom hates that you're alone in this drafty old farmhouse. Dad fears for your safety."

Lily shifted the dog's weight in her arms. "I can assure you, everything here at the farm has been peaceful, as always."

"Maybe for now, but you really are isolated out here." Joey continued with the argument she'd heard a hundred times but that felt even more threatening after the past few days. "Nobody liked it when Grandpa left you this parcel of land." He glanced at Miles with a disapproving look. "We all wonder why you don't want to get married like Amy or our brothers—or at least move to town to be closer to me."

Lily closed her eyes, ran her hands over Smokey's curly fur, and breathed deeply. She'd answered these questions a dozen times and didn't need to make things worse just because she was irritated with her brother. "You all know I love being here on my own. Tell Mom I'm fine."

Joey shook his head and took a step back toward his Model A. He muttered under his breath. "Hard-headed, irrational woman. No daughter of mine will live alone."

Her anger unfurling, she jabbed her finger at him. "Who are you to talk, Mr. Bachelor Policeman whom the women adore but who refuses to pick even one to court?"

Her arrow hit its mark, evidenced by the red that infused Joey's cheeks. But he flipped it on her with the speculative glance he gave Miles. Lily felt herself turning a similar shade of pink at the silent implication and censure in Joey's look.

She ducked her head, uncertain whether she was more ashamed by her outburst or Joey's silent condemnation. What must Miles think of her now?

"Do you have a place to stay, Mr. Wright?" Joey asked with a sweetness that belied the fact that he was turning his interrogation techniques onto a new target. One he'd no doubt enjoy putting behind bars. "I ran into Mrs. St. Thomas today. She said she has a couple open rooms."

Miles glanced at Lily. She could feel his questions. The only thing she knew was that she needed to end this conversation before any of them made a bigger mess of everything.

"You know what?" She set Smokey down and pushed her brother toward his still-running car. "Let's talk again tomorrow, Joey. I'm tired and do not want to continue this conversation right now."

Joey frowned. "I don't like leaving you here without a chaperone."

"I know, but I'll be fine."

Joey hesitated before planting a kiss on her cheek and getting in his car.

"Good night, brother dear."

Her shoulders sagged as Joey finally backed out of the driveway. Tired didn't begin to explain how she felt. If she could sink into the cool grass and sleep for hours, maybe then she would be merely tired. Her fight with Joey left her empty.

"How about we get you inside." Miles wrapped an arm over her shoulders. "I'll get a room at the boardinghouse, as Joey suggested. I would hate to be the cause of gossip for you. And you need to rest."

She glanced up at him. "Do I look that done in?"

"You look—" He stopped, then restarted. "If anyone deserves a quiet evening, it's you."

Not what he was going to say. She forced a chuckle. "Kind of you, but you must be as tired as I am. Mrs. St. Thomas really does have a lovely boardinghouse."

She left off how much she would prefer Miles to stay, propriety or not. She'd made a life for herself, and she could stand on her own two feet. She'd built a business, managed her own property. She could spend the night alone in her own house without any help from a man.

"All right, then." Miles nodded and pressed his lips into a smile. "I'll see you tomorrow."

As he stepped away, the reality of being alone, even with her dogs, made her heart race—something she would never admit to Joey. But her fear slipped out with this protective stranger. "Come in for a cup of hot chocolate before you go?"

"Lily." He caught her hands, her name a caress against her hair as he leaned closer. "There's no need to be anxious. Part of why I'm here is to make sure whoever got to you once won't do it again."

She chewed on her lip. "Part?"

He glanced toward the dust rising up in Joey's wake. "You've had a long enough day. Let's talk in the morning."

Her heart stuttered. "What aren't you telling me?"

CHAPTER 10

Joey found his dad finishing up his twice-daily chore of milking the cows. Thin and weathered, the older man gently pulled the Surge Milker off the cow's udder and emptied it in a five-gallon milk jug. A jug that in less than a week—if the strike went on as planned—would be dumped out on the side of the road in protest for the low milk prices, a waste Joey didn't understand.

Dad wiped his brow with a cloth and waited in silence for Joey to state his business.

Joey dispensed with niceties. "She came home."

An odd look flashed in Dad's eyes. "How is she?"

"Ornery. And she was with a man."

Dad's eyebrows rose. "Explain."

Not the response Joey expected. Honestly, he hoped his dad would demand his sons join him in dragging Lily to the safety of their parents' house.

Dad's brows raised higher at Joey's silence.

Fine. "Some stranger by the name of Miles Wright who she said was a friend from out of town. Big man. Could be someone's muscle."

Dad's expression turned curious but relaxed. Not at all what Joey expected.

Time to try goading. "He seemed possessive of her. Protective. Even from me."

A quirk of a grin flashed across Dad's face, only noticeable because it forced wrinkles out of its way. He leaned an elbow on the cow's rump, rubbed the stubble on his chin.

"Do you know this man?" Joey demanded. He and his dad rarely saw eye to eye, especially on matters of money—where Dad saw progress, Joey saw extravagance—but neither approved of Lily's independence. "Do you know where Lily has been or why she left without telling us? But you can't know because you were worried sick. I saw you. You were in worse shape than Mom was. Why this sudden cavalier attitude? What changed?"

Dad's answer was to turn the cow out to the yard and tie in the next cow. Several years back, just before milk prices began to fall, Dad orchestrated bringing electricity out from town to the farm—including the neighbors and Lily's place. It had been an unprecedented move, and his had been one of the first farms in the county to get electricity. Joey disagreed with his dad's reasoning that progressive farms elsewhere were making the move, which allowed them to expand because milking went so much faster with the Surge Milker. More milk meant more money for things like indoor plumbing and the latest John Deere tractor—a Model D—which allowed Dad to grow even more feed to support a larger herd. Or so the plan had been before the Depression.

Now Dad never mentioned his business plans—at least to Joey. But Joey had his suspicions, especially with Amy's marriage to Andy, whose father owned the closest dairy processing plant and was one of the wealthiest men in the community. It smelled of the type of arrangement meant to consolidate kingdoms rather than a marriage of love. No matter what Andy said.

Dad attached the Surge Milker to the next cow's udder, and it began its automated milking. Dad raised a graying eyebrow. "I'm not a suspect for you to intimidate, son. Your sister is quite capable of defending herself. If she felt in danger, she would have told you."

"Then why didn't she?"

"Obviously, she felt safe with this man."

"You don't find that strange?"

Dad sighed. "If I worried about Lily the way you and your mother do, I would have a full head of gray hair."

Joey mumbled a comment about the lack of brown strands left.

"She has a mind of her own." Dad leaned down to check the milker. "And a set of values that are not as old-fashioned as anyone in the town would like. Including you."

Joey zeroed in on a potential reason for his father's nonchalance. "Is she being courted?"

"If she was, do you think she would tell you?"

Joey squinted at his dad. "You didn't answer my question."

"And you didn't answer mine." Dad straightened and brushed his hands against his overalls. "This is a conversation you should have with your sister. And, unless you plan to help me organize the dairy strike, you should go see your mother."

He hated when his dad dismissed him. "You know I'll be one of the officers charged with keeping the peace. Again."

Dad's eyes flashed. Ah, there was the emotion Joey was waiting for. His old man rose into a younger version of himself. "You best remember who filled your belly as a boy, who supported your decision to become a police officer, who paid the first month's rent on your apartment in town. The cows did. With their milk. And now Booth dares to lower the price even more. All he cares about is protecting his wealth. If we don't get a decent payment, we'll lose the farm."

"So you're going to dump the milk? During a depression." *And further antagonize your daughter's new father-in-law?*

That quirk of a grin lit his dad's face, and this time it stayed. "We are losing money, anyway. Might as well keep him from getting any too."

"Are you set on staying here alone?" Miles scanned Lily's yard for the third time before answering her question about what he wasn't telling her. Call it stalling. Call it attentiveness. Call it the unease of coming night. In the minutes since Joey left, dusk had crept over the sky. An orange moon rose over the woods. Perfectly crescent, it cast an eerie shadow over the cornfields that stretched beyond her property.

"I have no reason to worry while I'm at home." Her breath puffed out in a white cloud, and she rubbed her arms through her sleeves. He couldn't tell if she was trying to convince him or herself. "Let me feed the dogs, then I'll make us hot chocolate, and you can tell me what is really going through your mind. Why don't you wait for me inside?"

Letting her wander in the dark alone? Not a chance. He kept pace with her, the dogs running ahead as if they knew her purpose. "Do you come out to the barn frequently?"

"Usually, I have a kennel full of dogs I'm training, but with the wedding last Saturday, I didn't schedule any clients for this week since they usually arrive on Saturdays and I wouldn't have been home. I was hesitant to not have any dogs for a whole week because the Depression requires taking as many clients as available, but now I'm glad I made the decision I did."

Not wanting to be sidetracked, no matter how much he wanted to ask her about her work, her clients, the life she built, Miles rephrased his question. "Do the dogs go out often at night?"

"Smokey is basically housebroken now." She led him into a large pen connected to the barn by a dog-sized door that lifted by a rope. It also shared a fence with another large, fenced area to the rear of the barn. Lily shut the gate behind them. "Once in a while, he still wakes me up in the middle of the night, but nothing like those first few weeks. Watch your step. I don't know if my brother cleaned up after the dogs while I was … gone."

She grabbed a trowel from a box secured to the wall and bent down to scoop up a steaming pile that Smokey just deposited. Was it because she was a farmer's daughter that she had no hesitation to clean up after her animals? It had been a long time since Miles met a woman who was unafraid to get her hands dirty. In fact, not since the Great War and the women who served as nurses, ambulance drivers, and doctors to the wounded soldiers.

A high-pitched *yip* sliced through the night—and Miles's memories—sending a shiver down his back. "You have a lot of coyotes here?"

She dumped the smelly mess in a covered can in the far corner and wiped her hands on a towel hanging from it. "With the dogs here, most wild animals stay away from the yard. But something must be close because Pieter is never this distracted."

Distracted must mean pacing the fence line, sniffing along the bottom, and failing to leave his own stinky deposit.

If Pieter was worried, Miles was done being diplomatic. "Wild animals aside, Miss Moore"—he crossed his arms, knowing his next words meant battle—"I have to agree with your brother. I don't like it. You being out here in the dark. Alone. It's not safe."

"Tough." She matched his posture, St. Elmo's fire appearing in her eyes once again. "I've had enough of the overprotective act from my brother tonight. I don't need it from you too. In case you haven't noticed, I've made myself a home here. This is my sanctuary. My safe place. I will not let anyone take that from me. Ever. So you can stop telling me how the darkness scares you and tell me why you're more spooked than you were last night when you slept on the side of a cornfield."

"Evidence that I'm not scared of the dark." He waved his hands to make his point. "Can't you trust my instincts here? Or Pieter's, if you don't want to listen to me or your brother? There's something not right, something that has me on edge here that I didn't feel last night. Put it this way, this situation is exactly the type where I do my best work. You know what work that is? I'm a sniper, Lily. A sharpshooter. I could put myself in a tree behind your barn, and you'd never realize what killed you."

He watched fear drain the color from her face as she stepped away from him. A punch to the kidneys would hurt less. He softened his voice, trying to get a grip on the fear that was putting the irritation into his words. "Look. I'm not trying to make you afraid of me. Trust me, that's the last thing I want to do. I'm just saying that I know how a hunter thinks, how a hunter acts. If someone is after you, this is—"

"You are not the only hunter here, Mr. Wright. And I will not be considered a defenseless female." The anger lacing her words took him aback. It was cold, deadly. "I plan to find the person who kidnapped me, not hide while I let other people, especially two men, fight my battles. Nothing will make me cower. Is that clear? I will not let them win again."

Pieter whined, pressing his furry body against his mistress's skirt. Little Smokey sat and watched them with worried eyes. Miles felt like a heel.

"Come on, pups. Let's get you fed." She turned with head held high, then added with a slight glance over her shoulder, "Mr. Wright, I'll give you Mrs. St. Thomas's address once I'm finished here. We can talk again after church tomorrow."

Miles deflated. He'd done the exact thing he'd promised he wouldn't do—get emotionally involved. Now he'd caused a rift that put Miss Moore—forget it—Lily's life on the line. Because, if Miles was honest with himself, his protective instinct had soared to new heights when it came to this spitfire with emerald eyes. If he didn't bring it back down into normal range, or at least normal for him, that instinct could be the very thing that would get them both killed.

"You had one job to do. How did you let them escape? Alive!" The dapper gentleman hissed into the phone's receiver while glancing around the hotel lobby, alert for anyone close enough to eavesdrop. As it was, conducting business over the phone lines was ill-advised. Any number of people, including the operator, could be listening in. But he needed this update in order to plan his next steps.

"It was effective." The man's trademark cavalier attitude that made him bribable apparently also made him a liability.

"But you discounted the sharpshooter." He wanted to pound his fist against the wall on which the phone box hung, but that would draw undesired attention. Instead, he smoothed his suit coat with his free hand. "How did you forget about the sharpshooter?"

"We attempted a second attack and ambush to eliminate him, but he eluded both." The man had the grace to clear his throat before adding, "Then we lost them when he sliced the tires on our cars."

He took several breaths to control his voice. "Well, I found them … exactly where I didn't want them to be. So just follow directions for once and lay low until you hear from me. I'm calling in reinforcements who will take care of the situation once and for all."

"Sir, I can—"

"I gave you a chance. Now back off. I'll handle this myself."

"Yes sir."

He slammed the receiver into place. Money might buy loyalty, but it did not buy intelligence. It just meant he'd have to engage his trigger man. It wouldn't be cheap, especially for the tight timeline and the secret nature of the job, but he would get the job done. And done right. Like it should have been done the first time.

CHAPTER 11

Sunday, October 15

Lily rose with the sun, same as she had every day of her life. The life of a soul that lived off the land. Only this morning, pain radiated throughout her body unlike she'd ever experienced. Getting kidnapped and almost blown up—multiple times—then napping in a car took a greater toll than she'd anticipated. So did her restless attempt at sleep.

She stretched out as many of the knots as she could, then pulled on Levi's—which she'd lied about buying for her brother—and one of her grandfather's flannel shirts. Her mother would be scandalized, but October mornings were crisp and bracing in the fields, and Lily refused to wear a dress just because she was a female. It wasn't practical or warm. Anyway, the clothes reminded her of Grandfather, and she needed to hold his memory close this morning.

More than anything, she wished he were still here so she could hear his gravelly voice assuring her of God's wisdom, His grace, His comfort. The nightmares and noises, not to mention the fear that had laced Miles Wright's voice, kept her tossing and turning all night.

But it was a new day. A crisp October day. The type of day where the weather would remind her of God's promise to restore her soul and lead her in His path, just as Grandfather had reminded her so many times as she walked with him in fields full of abundance. Perhaps there was a mercy in Grandfather not being alive to see the financial depression that held everyone captive. She would not lose her land because Grandfather had owned it outright when he'd willed it to her, but she knew her father had taxed every last line of credit to update the farm with electricity, plumbing, and equipment. If milk prices didn't rise, what would it cost him?

Coming down the steps that led from the upstairs hallway, Lily listened for her dogs, anticipating their excitement. She'd not only sorely missed them but desperately worried and prayed for them while she'd been in that hole. With no way to care for them or get word to someone who could, she'd had visions of them clawing their way out of the house to find food and water. At least she hoped they would, rather than perish.

Her heartbeat raced at the memory, and her ears strained for sounds of them. When she heard nothing, she quickened her steps. She held her breath until she reached the wooden floor of her living room and saw her two furry friends sitting there, waiting for her. Just as they knew to do.

Her breath whooshed out. No need to worry. She was safe. She was home.

"Good morning, boys." She ran her hands over each one, assuring herself of their well-being.

Pieter, her eight-year-old American Water Spaniel, bred by the one and only Dr. Fred Pfeifer of New London. And Smokey, her six-month-old Water Spaniel, a gangly runt she'd rescued from a scoundrel who was trying to get rich off Dr. Pfeifer's work. The tiny puppy's joy had enlivened her life the past several months.

Now, Smokey ran in circles. Pieter stood at her side as she stirred up the woodstove and filled the kettle with the last of the water in the kitchen bucket. His soulful eyes watched her every move as if drinking in the sight of her. Tears pricked. How she'd missed them!

"Outside we go." She cleared away the emotion with a wave of her hand toward the rear door. The old farm coat she shrugged on smelled of wood and smoke and wet dog. The scent wrapped around her like a hug as she stuffed a knit hat on her head and her hands into mittens.

Smokey's scampering grew more frantic, and Lily didn't wait to lace up her work boots. She scooped the pup in her arms and led the way out to the dog run. She'd structured her dog barn like her father's cow barn, providing a doorway to release the kenneled dogs into the run. However, with just Smokey and Pieter, she used the exterior gate to enter the muddy area.

Once she set Smokey on the dirt and latched the gate behind them, she performed her morning ritual, rain or shine, warm or frigid. Today, bracing air tinged with the smell of leaves and cow dung filled her lungs as she drew in several deep breaths. Each one a prayer. With the horrible memories clinging to her, she couldn't help thanking God for His grace in allowing her to live another day.

Even kidnapped, she'd been fed. No hunger pains to assault her like so many fellow Americans felt each day. She'd seen farmers forced to leave their land, their homes, in search of another way to bring in money to support their families. Dad thought the strikes would make people pay attention. So far it hadn't worked.

Hopelessness nagged her and she forced it away. Birds called as they flew through the air. Dew sparkled on the grass like crystals in the morning sun. Yes, this was a morning full of hope. Not despair. To that she would cling.

While the dogs attended to their business, she turned to practical matters. First, she freed her fingers and put her mittens in her pockets, rubbing her hands together to warm them before bending over to tie her boots. The thought of shoes brought a smile as it reminded her of how ill-prepared Miles Wright had been to walk through the mud last night.

Last night.

Her smile wilted. She was ashamed at how she'd reacted to Mr. Wright. He was just trying to keep her safe. But she'd struggled to push aside how smothered she felt after Joey's visit. His overprotective brother routine, his reminder about Mom's desire to see Lily married, and his commenting about her isolated home had put her on edge. Not to mention Dad and his fight over milk prices. It seemed everyone had a plan for her life, but no one considered what Lily actually wanted.

That's why she wouldn't give up. This place, her home, it was her last stand. She couldn't give up the refuge she'd created. On her farm, she didn't have to answer to anyone's opinions or battle any rumors or manage anyone's expectations. Here, it was just her and the Lord.

Smokey ducked between her legs.

Her, the Lord, and the dogs. Just the way she wanted it.

"Did you do your business, little one?" She rubbed Smokey's curly haunches.

Smokey jumped around, wanting to play. Lily found only one pile steaming in the hard mud.

"Which one of you is dawdling?" She eyed Smokey. "Smokey, privy."

The puppy cocked his head. Lily maintained her stand. Smokey gave way and trotted to the corner to obey. Lily heaped him with praise and pulled a treat from her coat pocket. Then she grabbed her trowel from beside the can and stopped. She distinctly remembered replacing the cover last night. She always did, or it could attract the wrong type of critters, critters that could be harmful to the dogs.

She leaned closer and covered her nose against the atrocious smell, dampened only by the frosty temperatures. Nothing appeared out of the ordinary. Puzzled, she cleaned up after the dogs and made sure to securely replace the cover. Smokey raced ahead as they passed through the gate leading from the pen to the corral and then into the rear barn door. Pieter, as usual, stayed right beside his mistress as she let them inside for breakfast.

The smell of dog greeted Lily. The line of kennels to the right felt strangely empty. Her forced absence made her long for her work. She'd been training hunting dogs since she trained her first puppy—a gift from Grandfather—as a girl of thirteen. Not only did she discover she loved it, but others recognized she had a knack for it too.

Since then, she'd studied the work of Colonel Konrad Most and his book explaining the training of working dogs—even if he'd worked for the Germans during the war and she'd struggled to translate the language. She'd also learned from Dr. Pfeifer, who was vital in the development and promotion of the American Water Spaniel, specifically as a hunting dog that could thrive in Wisconsin's challenging conditions.

With her grandfather's support, people from all around the area began hiring her to train their hunting dogs. The fact that she was a woman still hindered her, more so now that Grandfather was gone, but overall, her business had grown. She could house up to seven clients' dogs at a time and had clients from all over eastern Wisconsin. Grandfather would be proud of all she'd accomplished in the years since his passing.

Pushing away the bittersweet feeling that thought caused, she set out two bowls and instructed the dogs to wait. Their kibble came in fifty-pound sacks that she kept stacked in the storage room of the barn. She preferred the dry food over the more common canned food because of the ease of packaging. Hefting feed sacks had been a similar chore until she left home, so it made sense to her.

She kept a covered pail filled with kibble near the door for easy access. A pail that was empty? It had definitely been full last night when she fed the dogs. Oh well, she must not have been thinking clearly after her argument with Miles. She lifted one of the large bags to her shoulder only to have it split open. Fifty pounds of kibble showered down her body, catching in her collar and piling at her feet. Unable to resist, Smokey poked his little black nose into the storage area.

"No, Smokey," Lily commanded. "Out!"

Instead, the pup dove into the food. Honestly, she couldn't fault him for disobeying. Try telling a child not to jump into a pond full of penny candy. But too much food too fast could damage a dog's stomach, so she quickly tossed the bag aside and freed her feet from the kibble.

"Smokey. Out." She lifted the dog and removed him from temptation, securely fastening the door to keep him out.

Then she turned back to consider the mess. She'd never had a bag break open like this before. She must've accidentally sliced one open, but she didn't remember making such an error. She smoothed out the bag, looking for the telltale slit. None. Instead, both ends appeared to have been opened, then reclosed with a loose thread that had snapped in several places.

No wonder it had broken open so easily. She definitely hadn't bought it like that. There would have been no way to get it home without spilling the entire bag. Someone had purposefully designed the closures to fail after she'd placed it in her storage area. But who and when and why?

An uneasy feeling rising in her chest, she quickly swept up the kibble and fed the dogs before hiking out to the windmill pump. She filled two buckets, then carried them to the low trough designed to serve as a water bowl for her dogs. Not surprisingly, it was empty.

She gripped the handle of the first bucket and poured. A bump on her ankle made her pause once she set down the empty bucket. Smokey stood at her feet with puppy eyes. She lifted him into her arms and let him lick her chin.

"Missed me, huh? Don't worry, I'm not mad at you for eating the kibble."

Smokey yipped and wiggled to get down.

"Okay, okay." She set him down and dumped the other pail into the trough. "I'm getting your—"

The wooden trough cracked open, spilling water over her boots and flooding that area of the pen. Cringing against the cold, Lily shooed Smokey out of the mud and studied the trough. The edges had been sawed away from the base and then placed back together with one tiny nail each. This was not how she left it. That she knew for sure.

A chill wheedled its way down her back. First the trash can, then the kibble, now the trough. Was this someone's version of a bad joke? A welcome-home prank gone horribly wrong?

Even as she asked herself the questions, she knew the answers. These were not harmless antics. They had to be done by someone who wished her ill, someone who could have sent her dogs, and potentially a client's dog, to the vet.

Did that mean Miles was right? Was her home no longer her safe harbor? Had she just put her dogs and her business in danger by simply returning to Eagle?

Horsefeathers and applesauce. Why had she gotten so angry at him last night? She really did need his help.

CHAPTER 12

Miles slipped into the far end of a pew halfway down on the left side of First Church. He knew that in a small town such as Eagle, it didn't matter whether a person was as devout as a monk or believed God didn't exist—everyone went to church.

He scanned the room for Lily Moore. The dark wood and stained-glass windows of the small church provided a balance of elegance and solemnity that he liked. It made him wish work didn't get in the way of attending his own church as often as it did. But for now, God had him in the rescue business.

And that meant listening to his instincts. They began to needle him more urgently that morning when he couldn't reach his boss. Now they were quickly turning into a cattle prod as, one by one, the Moore brothers—he could tell because they all looked alike—filed into the row ahead of him, including Joey, who gave Miles a long glance. Still no trace of Lily.

The pastor walked to the pulpit to give the welcome. Miles's sharpshooter training had taught him to spot anomalies, the absence of something as much as suspicious activity, and this morning's lack of communication with his boss, plus Lily's absence, screamed at him. Why hadn't he insisted on picking her up this morning? Why had he backed down on keeping her safe? He'd failed his team and they'd died. He couldn't let his actions cause her death too.

Just as he'd made up his mind to track her down, a hand pressed his shoulder, and Lily slipped into the row in front of him. She wore a green dress that moved with her as if she were a sapling swaying in a warm breeze. It welcomed him, beckoned him to experience home and peace—two things he hadn't had for a long time. He let out a deep sigh. All was right now that she was here. Alive.

"Where have you been?" A young woman who had to be Lily's sister leaned over Joey with a deep scowl. She clasped her hat with a gloved hand as she leaned forward, her profile more angular than Lily's, yet she had the same brown hair knotted at her neck.

"Not now, Amy." Joey pushed the woman back to her side of the pew.

Lily squared her shoulders, then invaded Joey's space, her beret nearly smacking him in the nose. "You're supposed to be on your honeymoon, Amy."

"Andy had a meeting, so we postponed." Amy crossed her arms with a pout. "Dad is going to ruin everything with this protest of his."

Miles leaned forward as much as he dared in order to eavesdrop. Lily scooted closer to her brother. Miles found himself studying how the varying shades of brown hair interlaced each other in the intricate knot pinned at the back of her head. It reminded him of a sailor's rope. Plus, the jaunty angle of her beret accented a whimsical side that drew him. Made him want to get to know her more. Which had him shaking himself into focusing on what really mattered.

Unfortunately, Joey stopped his sisters' conversation by prying them apart with a harsh word to be quiet.

Lily squared her shoulders with enough emotion that Miles made a mental note to get her to explain her conversation later. That is, after he got her to talk with him at all.

Last night, he'd put in a long-distance call to Gio. The man was the most outgoing person Miles knew. Gio cultivated friendships like the prized roses he grew outside his Chicago home, and if Miles needed anything, he always knew exactly the person to help him. In this case, Miles asked his friend for information on Lily's family, then told him to get to Eagle as quickly as he could.

Until then, Miles should turn his attention to the preacher, but instead, he spent the rest of the service considering how to convince Lily she needed his protection and praying he wouldn't let her down once she agreed to his help. Because he couldn't leave her to fend for herself. Yes, she intrigued him more than was good for his heart, but that wasn't the reason—all right, the *only* reason—he wanted—no, needed—to help her. If something happened to Lily Moore, he would blame himself for the rest of his life.

Before the pastor finished the *amen* of his benediction, Miles tapped Lily's shoulder. "Miss Moore, can we—"

"Come with me." Lily grabbed his wrist with a cotton-gloved hand and, much to his surprise, expertly wove them down the side aisle. If her absence hadn't gotten tongues wagging, this behavior certainly would. Not that he minded her determination to have him accompany her.

Within moments, they exited a rear door that led to the church cemetery. Miles blinked against the bright sun or at the abrupt change of scenery—he wasn't sure which. He gathered his wits as she brought them to a wooden bench in front of a stone statue depicting a shepherd with sheep at his feet located at the center of the cemetery, far away from prying ears. The quiet of the gravestones offered an oddly fitting choice for the conversation he needed to have with her, yet the memorials to the dead only heightened the guilt he desperately tried to keep at bay.

Lily's skirt fanned out beneath her coat as she perched on the edge of the bench, the fabric brushing against his knee as he sat beside her. She clutched her hands in her lap. Her head angled so that the beret cast a shadow over her eyes. It didn't hide the determination, yet trepidation, he saw there. He needed to smooth things out between them before she derailed him with whatever she needed to tell him.

"Look, Lil—Miss Moore." Miles played with the brim of his hat as it hung from his fingers between his knees. "About last night—"

Lily held up a hand. Her fingers trembled, and she clasped them again. "I overreacted. We need to work together, figure this out, before anyone gets hurt."

"I agree, but I expected more of an argument." Miles studied her. Tried to look past the obvious. She looked so different from the woman he'd rescued two nights ago, only wisps of hair escaping the knot instead of it all askew. Pink cheeks with a host of pinprick freckles instead of colorless features under streaks of grime. Confident elegance instead of—no, that's how she'd appeared in church. Now, she was folding in on herself as if fear was taking over.

"Something happened, didn't it?" Miles held himself from reaching out to her. "Something changed your mind about working with me."

The story of her morning tumbled out. "At first, it seemed like mischief. Spilling food or destroying the water trough wouldn't necessarily hurt me, but could someone be coming after my dogs? Pieter and Smokey would have tried to eat all fifty pounds of food, and that could have killed them. I hate that someone would try to intimidate me, but to come after my dogs?"

He wanted to reach out to her, tangibly ease her distress. Instead, he pushed the feeling away. Remained professional. "You think there is a tie between what happened this morning and you being kidnapped?"

"I have no idea, and that's why I wanted to talk to you." She played with a string on her glove, avoiding eye contact. "Why would they sabotage my barn *after* they kidnapped me? None of it makes sense."

"No, it doesn't." He rubbed his chin, missing the beard he'd shaved that morning for attending the church service. "What is clear is that someone wants something from you, and we have to figure out what that is."

Lily nodded.

"First, do we agree that you must let someone keep watch over you and that I'm in the best position to protect you?" He hated feeling like a manipulator, using her fear to get his way, but he went in strong, still expecting her to balk as she had last night. Mentally, he even prepared a counterargument.

Instead, she simply nodded. No fight. No sassy statement. Only quiet acquiescence.

Miles's stomach dropped. This wasn't the woman he'd rescued. Her dogs were her Achilles' heel. The weakest spot in her defenses. She might face off with death, but the thought of someone harming her dogs turned her to putty.

Lily barely lifted her chin. "Should we get Joey involved? He is a policeman."

"Not yet." Miles wouldn't break that agency rule now but softened his planned response and veiled his distrust of her brother. "I'm worried they didn't treat your disappearance like a kidnapping. And we still might tell him everything. Just not yet. Which brings us to step two. If you're okay with me protecting you, your family is going to need a reason for me being around."

"Isn't it too late to create a story?" Color bloomed on her cheeks. "Joey saw us together, and now here we are …"

"But he doesn't know who I am." He leaned closer. "If we want to smoke out the kidnapper, it's best no one know I'm one of the people who rescued you."

"One of?"

He froze. How could he be so off his game as to make such a slip? She didn't need to know about his team. Especially not when the thought of danger to her dogs affected her as much as it had. How could he fix this?

"Mr. Wright?" She turned those green eyes on him. "You can tell me the truth."

And there was his problem. He wanted to tell her. To unburden his heart. To let her share in his grief. He didn't see her as a client, a victim he'd rescued. They were partners in finding the persons responsible for causing all this heartache. But they weren't supposed to be.

"Please." She rested her gloved fingers on his arm, ending any resistance he had left.

"My boss's agency was hired to find you, rescue you," he said, working his jaw to keep the emotion at bay. "I am—was—part of a five-man company, an elite company within the Craft Agency. My job as the scout and sharpshooter means I make sure my team has a clear path and then the protection they need to accomplish the assignment. I knew something about the rescue didn't feel right, but I didn't warn them in time."

"The explosion." She gasped, tightening her fingers on his arm. "They died in the explosion, didn't they? Oh, Miles, I'm so sorry. How selfish I was to demand you get me home when you'd lost your brothers-in-arms. You should go back to your headquarters. There must be family to visit. Funerals to attend. I'll be fine here."

"Oh, no, you don't." He captured her shoulders in his hands. "I decided to come to Eagle because whoever kidnapped you also killed my brothers. I want to find them so they can't hurt you or anyone else ever again. I have the full power of my boss behind me. And if we work together, we both can find the answers we need, and I can keep you safe."

She again found the string on her glove. "Miles—uh, Mr. Wright …"

Her lapse warming his heart, he smiled down at her. "I think it's Miles now."

She nodded, more of a ducking of her head. "Miles. Are you sure you're the one who should be doing this?"

"You're saying I'm too close?" He dropped his hold on her. "That is exactly why I have to see this through. I need to see justice done. To understand what happened. What I missed. They were more than people I worked beside, Lily, they were my friends, and they deserve answers." He bowed his head. "It's the least I—"

Something whizzed by his ear, and he jerked Lily behind the fountain, covering her with his body, yanking his Colt from the holster under his arm as he tried to spot the shooter. Heaven help him. If he didn't get his head on right, he'd get them both killed.

CHAPTER 13

The fear Lily felt when the explosion rocked her dirt-walled cage in the forest roared back like a wave as Miles took her to the ground. She'd recognize an errant bullet anywhere. Normally, she'd call out, let the confused hunter know he was shooting the wrong direction, but Miles's reaction confirmed what she intuitively knew. The gunman meant to kill them. So, as terror liquefied her muscles, she let Miles tuck her under his arm.

His large body shielded her, and she shoved aside the guilt. She'd already cost his team their lives—how could she let him put himself in harm's way for her again? She was better than this. Stronger. Another shot glanced off the stone fountain, and she swallowed a whimper. *Father God, protect us. Please.*

"We need to keep moving." Miles spoke into her ear. "I don't want to lead him toward the church, so we're going to use the headstones for cover. Can you do that?"

She nodded as another shot pinged off the fountain. Miles shoved his hat on his head and clutched her hand, and they dashed toward the Schmidt family monument. Two *pops* followed them. Miles pressed her head to his chest as they leaned into the stonework. Lily couldn't tell whose heart pounded in her ears, hers or his.

"I don't have a clear shot and won't risk hitting an innocent bystander, so we have to keep our heads down until the police arrive." Miles risked a glance around the monolith. Jerked back, pressing her into the cold stone, as a bullet pinged by his head. He shoved his own weapon back into its holster under his jacket.

"Why shoot at us here when they could have gotten me at my barn this morning?" Lily asked between clenched teeth to keep them from chattering. Her body was already shaking, despite the strength Miles wrapped around her. She needed to dig deeper for the courage to think clearly, or she could be the reason Miles died.

"I wish I knew." He glanced behind them. Pointed with his chin. "On the count of three, we're headed to that oak. Got it?"

Lily nodded. Just as in the woods, his calm direction kept fear from freezing her mind and body. His gentle push to run unglued her feet, and she hiked her skirt, hunched low, and dashed for the oak. A bullet slammed into the dirt by her foot as she skidded into the shelter of the old tree.

"Police!" Joey's disembodied shout sounded far away. "Put down your weapon!"

Her heart jumped. Her brother was in danger because of her too. She tried to wiggle free, be sure he was safe, but Miles kept her cocooned.

"He knows his job," Miles said in her ear. "But when he comes to get you, he is going to want answers, and we need a believable story. Something we didn't give him last night."

"We need to come up with that now?" She took a beat to control her voice. And not because Miles's brown eyes were so close to hers. "With someone shooting at us?"

"There hasn't been a shot since your brother showed up, so the shooter likely hightailed it back to his hidey-hole. For now, at least. And until we get the all clear, we might as well decide how we're going to explain being huddled together under a tree."

His grin made Lily's stomach flip-flop, which made her cheeks warm. Oh dear, she couldn't go down that rabbit hole. People talked about her enough as it was. This incident was going to further annihilate her reputation, whereas, for Miles, this was simply a job. She really didn't want to be left with a broken heart and mangled relationships when he went back to his real life.

"What if you're training one of my dogs?" Miles asked.

"That doesn't answer why we're here." She swallowed. "Like this. Or why you were at my house yesterday … without your dog. We should have thought this through before returning to Eagle. Joey—"

"All my fault." He rubbed her upper arms. "I've been off ever since—"

"Since you lost your team. Miles, I'm …" She lost her train of thought as he moved one roughened hand up to cup her cheek. She could almost feel his grief, as if he drifted on an open sea, desperately searching for safe harbor—and finding it in her.

Her brain screamed at her to break the connection, but she couldn't pull away. His sorrow tugged at her heart, yes, but she also didn't want to leave him stranded there, alone in his grief.

He blinked, ending the moment as a shadow fell across them. Joey loomed, gun pointed directly at Miles.

"Having a pleasant chat, are we?"

Miles inched away from Lily as he adjusted his jacket over the gun holstered under his arm and raised his hands. "Did you catch the man?"

Joey's green eyes glinted. "What were you doing with my sister?"

Lily put a shoulder in between him and her brother, forcing Joey to change his aim. Leaves and dirt clung to her skirt, and the knot of hair at her neck looked like frayed rope. She'd also lost her beret at some point.

"That's enough, Joey." Lily's voice was sharp. "Miles is. … Mr. Wright and I … I wanted to show him the cemetery. Then that crazy person started shooting at us!"

"Uh-huh," Joey muttered but holstered his pistol, and Miles relaxed just a smidgen. "Any particular reason the guy was shooting at you, *Miles*?" Of course, he'd caught her slip.

"No sir," Miles lied. Sort of. Fact was, motive eluded him. Them. Why had Lily been kidnapped? Why was his crew ambushed? Why was Lily's barn sabotaged? Why couldn't he reach his boss? Why was someone shooting at them? And why was he letting himself get distracted by the captivating woman standing between him and her brother?

He should have seen the shooter coming long before a shot was fired. He could have identified him, tracked him, even captured him. Instead, he'd let the shooter chase them into hiding, risking Lily's reputation and their lives. Worse, he couldn't act on any feelings he had toward her if he wanted to keep his job, a job that was his very way of life. It wasn't fair to Lily to lead her along only to break her heart. He deserved Joey's anger. Felt it toward himself.

If he wanted to keep her safe, he needed to focus on the investigation, find information, and track down a lead. He could start by getting a look at one of the bullets the shooter had fired. It might tell him what type of rifle the man used. But right now, he had to figure out how he was going to keep his real purpose a secret while keeping near Lily without bringing the wrath of her brothers down on both of them.

Joey put a protective arm around Lily, boxing Miles out. Miles didn't like it, but he understood and backed off. If he had a sister, he'd act the same way if a strange man, especially with someone of Miles's bearing, suddenly showed up and people started shooting at her.

"Let's head to the church," Joey said. "Lily, Dr. Holland will—"

"I'm fine." She pushed out of Joey's protective hold but tucked her hand in his elbow.

Miles dropped back even farther. He made a mental note of the shooter's line of sight. Stiff wind, crisp air, and noonday sun. The shot came from the trees separating the cemetery from the road. Had the shooter simply emerged from the cover of the trees to creep closer or factored the breeze better, Miles had been distracted enough that the shooter shouldn't have missed. His gut twisted. That's why Craft had the rule—no attachments.

He wished Gio had arrived already. He needed someone who could keep him focused. Miles greatly admired the Italian for his close walk with God. Though Gio never missed a church service, his relationship with God went far deeper than only attending for attending's sake. It was as if Gio had access to a secret line of communication with the Almighty.

Miles pushed away the envy. God might not listen to his prayers the way he did Gio's, which only meant Miles needed the peace that always emanated from his friend even more.

Miles stashed his weapon in his car before he gave one of the policemen his version of events. Since staying away from local law enforcement was out of the question, better to not give them more reason to question him. All the while, he kept Lily in his sights. Trouble was, as soon as the deputy finished with him, Miles couldn't hang around her or the crime scene without arousing suspicion from the coppers and anger from her brother. Nor, with the way brother bear was hovering, could he get Lily alone to make future arrangements. It left Miles no choice but to return to his room and more carefully plan his next steps. Joey would keep a close watch on his sister for now. Miles would meet up with her at her house once she forced her brother to leave. No doubt, she would do that sooner rather than later.

Mrs. St. Thomas's boardinghouse was a moderately sized Victorian a couple blocks off Eagle's town center and only a few blocks from the church. He'd driven instead of walked, so he had the means of a quick escape. He didn't like that he had to keep using the car he'd stolen from the men chasing them, but until Gio arrived with options, he was stuck.

Now, like last night, he felt like an uncouth barbarian as he climbed to the wide porch and entered the front hall. Doilies and flowered wallpaper decorated the communal area. Teacups and fine china rested on shelves. Dainty figurines of all varieties perched on exquisitely carved furniture. Yet it did not feel grimy or cluttered. His hostess kept an immaculate house.

"Ah, there you are. Lily Moore's friend." Eliza St. Thomas was an older lady with silver hair and spectacles hanging from a chain around her neck. She shuffled out of the dining area, appearing frailer than she had even last night when she'd agreed to give him a room on the Moore twins' recommendation.

"Yes ma'am. You may call me Miles." He tried to take the intensity out of his expression with a smile.

"Miles." She gave him another once-over, and a twinge of fear mixed with her curiosity. "You were with Lily when ... you know ..."

The shooting. Of course. "Yes ma'am. Were you at the church when the ... incident began?"

She nodded, and Miles's protective instinct surged. He gently wrapped her nearly translucent hand around his bicep and led her back to the kitchen, settling her in a chair.

"I hear a cup of tea and something sweet can wipe away all troubles. You sit here and I'll bring it to you. Just tell me where to find everything."

"No, no, dear."

"I insist, Mrs. St. Thomas. I need a cup too."

She obviously didn't believe a word but let him go with nothing more than a few directions and a firm warning about breaking her teacups.

Miles set the kettle to boil on the stove, carefully chose two teacups from the sideboard in her dining room, and found her choice of tea. Then he added two cookies to the saucers.

"I'm impressed." Mrs. St. Thomas smiled at him when he carried the steeped tea in a pot to the table and poured her a cup. His team's leader, Darens—God rest his soul—had been particular about his tea, being a Tommie and all, so Miles wasn't unfamiliar with the brew. Not that he enjoyed it, no matter how hard the retired British soldier had tried to get his fellow Craft Agency mates to observe afternoon tea.

"Knowing how to brew it comes in handy every once in a while." Miles took a chair kitty-corner to her where he could see both exits.

Her eyes latched onto the way he carefully cradled the delicate china in his large, callused hands. Hands that had killed too many and now sought only to save. "Were you in the military?" she asked.

"Cut my teeth in France during the Great War." Fresh from a

Minnesota farm, a lad of just eighteen. The death and destruction he'd seen since made him feel much, much older than his thirty-some years.

"My late husband served." She hesitated. "Was Lily okay after …"

"Physically, yes." Emotionally …

In the last two days, she'd been nearly blown up three times and shot at more. He marveled at her deep inner strength to continue on in the face of such nightmarish cruelty, and her spirit drew him to her like a beacon calling him home. If he didn't figure out a way to resist, things could turn ugly again rather quickly. The problem was, he didn't just want to give in—he wanted to run right into the shelter Lily didn't even know she offered.

CHAPTER 14

Lily couldn't relax until she had her dogs in the corral behind her barn. She leaned against the north wall of the building and let the afternoon sun warm her as the tension seeped from her body, leaving her chilled, shaky, and weak. Instead of giving in to those feelings, she forced herself to focus on her dogs.

Pieter was a master at obeying her commands, but even experienced dogs needed to remain sharp. Today she planned to focus on him since she wasn't up for the harder work of training Smokey. She rummaged in her supply room for her jar of venison jerky. Tearing it into small pieces, she pocketed the handful and returned to the corral. She made both dogs sit and handed them each a piece.

She released Smokey to play and instructed Pieter to heel. He whipped his hindquarters around to plant himself at her side. She expected Pieter to stay beside her until given direction. Whether she moved or stood still, Pieter stayed beside her left leg, sitting when she stopped and lying down when she knelt.

With a smile, she tossed a jerky piece to where Smokey rolled in the fallen leaves. He might be playing, but he watched Pieter, learning as he did so. He'd get to be just as good a sporting dog as Pieter with training and practice. Something she knew just how to do. And that confidence allowed Lily's riot of emotions to gradually settle to a low simmer.

After an hour of drilling Pieter on hand signals, she jumped the corral fence to set tin cans on a beam she'd nailed to two posts pounded into the ground, forming an upside-down U. The hay bales behind it kept the shotgun pellets from continuing into the woods on the north side of her property. Grabbing her shotgun and leaving her dogs safely in the corral, she backed herself against the fence so the dogs would be near the gunshot sound as a way to accustom them to the noise.

She checked to make sure the area was clear, then she raised the gun to her shoulder. Sighted the middle can. Eased back the trigger. And sent the can tumbling to the ground. A strange feeling—fear, perhaps—swam in her belly at the noise. She refused to let the unease take root. Sighted the next can. Fired again.

Her father, like his father before him and most of the farmers in Eagle, were dairy farmers. Sure, they had a few other animals, and her mother maintained an extensive garden that dwarfed the one Grandfather had left Lily, but dairy cows were their bread and butter. So much so that not only had her brothers married Amy's best friends, they married into the farms on either side of their father's farm to extend the family property. It was a business move as much as a personal one. Just like Amy's marriage to Andy.

It didn't leave much of a hole for Joey and Lily to fill in the sense of marital responsibility, except maybe with grandchildren, but with Joey in law enforcement, his lack of help on the farm was understood. Their parents were proud of Joey's service and supported his choice to rent a room above the bakery across from the department. While they would like him to marry, they were happy with his decisions thus far.

Not so with Lily. She had done nothing to help the family name. She spurned attempts at matchmaking and chafed against more feminine pursuits. She preferred wearing men's jeans and her grandfather's flannel shirts with mud on her boots and leaves in her hair. Her dogs at her side.

According to her father, bird dogs weren't a helpful part of the dairy farming business and were thus unnecessary mouths to feed. Perhaps if she trained cattle dogs or herders or guard dogs, her training skills would be useful, but hunting dogs? Her father disapproved of the sport. Thought it wasteful. It had been her grandfather, her mother's father, who'd taught her how to shoot and, in death, left his parcel of land as her own, free and clear.

Whenever Lily held her shotgun, she could feel her grandfather's presence. A stalwart man of faith, he'd been proud of her choice to follow the path she believed God had for her. He'd championed a woman's right to vote since she'd been a girl. And his confidence in her had given her strength to continue despite the small-town tide that flowed against her ... and the peace that she had made the right decision. But she missed Grandfather, missed his wisdom, his insistence that God would always be with her.

Lily took aim at the seventh and final can when Pieter gave a bark and came to stand as close to her as the fence allowed. Smokey jumped against the opposite fence, the one facing the drive, barking as fiercely as a pup could. Lily lowered the weapon, noting her shaking hands. She was still more rattled from the shooting this morning than she cared to admit.

"Target practice?" Joey sauntered around the barn. Not the person she wanted to see.

"Got one more." She raised the rifle, more to ignore him than to finish. Her irritation roared back. He'd been insufferable after the cemetery shooting, and she'd gladly left him behind when the other deputy finished with her. Much to his intense disagreement. But he'd had to finish at the scene and couldn't see her home.

"Lil, we need to talk." Joey leaned against the fence, elbows propped on top. More casual than she'd seen him for over a year since the strikes started. The dogs tried to nose him from inside the corral, but he ignored them.

She lowered the shotgun. "Seems a shame to leave one standing."

"Lil, I read your official statement and don't believe a word of it."

Lily popped the unused shell out of the barrel. "This is not something I want to talk about right now."

"Then tell me about Miles Wright. I'm going to check into him, but I want to hear his story from you."

She turned the loaded shell over in her hand. "He's a good man,

Joey. I trust him."

"Should you?" His green eyes sparked. "At the moment, the rumor mill is having a field day. 'Local woman conspiring with armed felons.' I'm worried, Lil."

"Hogwash." Lily shoved the shell into her pocket. "And yes. I would put my life in Miles's hands. You saw how he saved me today."

Joey waved his hand toward the expanse of woods to the north. "Fine, but where does the guy come from? Where did you even meet him?"

She took a calming breath, reminding herself that her twin only wanted the best for her, even if his methods made her crazy. How, then, could she mollify him while still protecting Miles's assignment and her own autonomy? "He lives out east and is here for ... work. And he's a former Marine! I meant it, Joey, you can trust him."

"Well, I don't. I'm still going to check on his background."

"But you trust me." Lily closed her eyes. She wanted to tell her brother everything so he would help her find who kidnapped her. Despite their squabbles, it had always been them against everyone else. She peeked at him, her stomach flipping at his scrutinizing expression. "If I tell you, you promise not to overreact? I want to tell my twin brother and confidant, not a policeman."

"Lil, if you're in trouble—" He pushed off the fence. "If that man hurt you—"

"Miles saved me."

"From what?"

The sharpness in Joey's voice caused tears to sting her eyes, but she blurted the truth. "I was kidnapped, Joey. I didn't disappear. I was kidnapped." Her heart hammering as her brother's mouth fell open, Lily rushed through a brief description of being taken from the diner and held beneath an abandoned homestead.

He braced her shoulders with his firm hands. "And you don't know who did it?"

She shook her head. "That's what Miles is trying to help me find out."

Joey's face went white before blooming into the brightest red. "I'm setting up security for you. I'll camp out here myself. You are not to leave your house without someone with you. Better, let's take you over to Mom and Dad's—"

"Joey!" Lily swiped at tears racing down her cheeks. Pieter and Smokey pressed closer to the fence beside her.

"Listen to me, Lil." He grabbed her shoulders again. "I'm a policeman. Getting the bad guys is what I do. I'll track these culprits down and arrest them. You don't need to be afraid. I'll handle everything."

"That's exactly what I don't want you to do."

He backed away, frowning. "You trust a stranger more than me."

"It's not that." She willed her brother to understand. "Miles doesn't treat me like something fragile that needs to be tucked away. He thinks I'm capable just the way I am. I need resolution, Joey, and I want your help, not your interference."

"Fine." Joey put on a fake smile that did nothing to hide his hurt. "This should be a police matter, but since you don't want me *interfering*, I'll investigate it myself."

"Joey."

"And I'm warning you now, stay away from him before you end up in a jail cell right beside him."

"Joey!"

"I mean it, Lil. I don't trust him, but since you don't trust me, you'll have to learn the hard way. By yourself."

Lily lowered her head. The last time they'd had a fight this bad, she'd been willed Grandpa's farm. Maybe she and Joey hadn't repaired their relationship as well as she'd thought because right now, she felt as alone as she had in that dark hole in the Northwoods.

Miles tried to concentrate on the information his boss had provided for the rescue. A thin file. Thinner than most. Yet, if he could go over the details again, maybe he'd see something the team had missed. That *he'd* missed.

But he struggled to keep Lily out of his head. Should he run over and check on her?

Blithering fool he was, to let a pretty girl distract him.

Perhaps another cup of coffee would help.

Then he could try telephoning his boss again.

Before driving over to Lily's house.

Yes, he was utterly hopeless.

He snapped up his suspenders and buttoned his vest. No one at the Craft Agency knew where Mr. Craft had gone, not even his secretary, and she knew everything. From what Miles could gather, Craft hadn't been seen since the night before, after Miles had informed him of the ambush. Then, Craft's second-in-command, Richard Berkley, and the company lawyer had both left headquarters early this morning. It churned the uneasiness in his stomach.

He paced the small room before stuffing the papers into the bottom of his valise, under his extra set of clothes. Then buckled on his shoulder holster and shrugged on his jacket.

His room was located at the end of the second-floor hall of the boardinghouse. It held one bed, one nightstand, and a large, ornate dresser. Pictures of tea parties and framed doilies covered the walls. The single window was deeply set in the dormer and looked out on a street lined with trees bursting with fall foliage. It'd be lovely for a couple's holiday.

Coffee. That brew, not tea as old Darens believed, solved everything. He'd start there.

Miles felt eyes on him as he entered the dining room. Ah. Mrs. St. Thomas. She peered out the cracked-open kitchen door. He waited until after he poured a cup of black coffee before glancing at her with a smile.

She gave a little gasp and closed the door. Not the same cordial woman he spoke with after service this morning.

Should he let it go? That wasn't in his nature. He knocked.

"I'm busy," the elderly woman called out in a falsely cheerful tone.

"Mrs. St. Thomas? Do you have milk for my coffee?" He disliked milk or sugar in his coffee, but if it got him a chance to talk to her again, he'd suffer through it.

"Oh!" She breathed out the exclamation as he entered, an egg splattering to the floor.

Strange. "I'm terribly sorry I scared you." He set his coffee down on the worn kitchen table where they'd sat together just a couple hours ago. "Let me clean that up."

"It is fine." She reached for an old towel with shaky hands.

"Please." His large hands covered her frail ones.

She pulled away, making herself appear small as she huddled near the hot wood oven. They'd parted on such amicable terms. What changed in so little time?

"What are you baking?" he asked as he wiped up the egg.

"More cookies. Is the coffee … is it still warm?"

He looked up at her, trying to make his eyes kind as he met her gaze. "Am I making you nervous, Mrs. St. Thomas?"

She nodded.

"I know I can intimidate with my size, but I mean no harm."

"I just heard things." She broke eye contact.

Things? "May I ask what you heard?"

"That you're a criminal, a felon, and that's why that man shot at you." She huffed. "My boardinghouse is supposed to be a wholesome place. Not filled with thugs and bad men."

He restrained an unsavory, battle-learned word from his tongue and loosened his grip on the damp towel. "I promise you, I'm not one of the bad men, and I've never been arrested. Perhaps it's my military bearing that has people nervous."

He finished wiping the floor and rinsed his hands in the washbasin, all while Mrs. St. Thomas watched him silently. Finally, he leaned a hip against the table, hoping to appear as relaxed as possible.

"I am glad to hear that." Her shoulders dropped from almost touching her ears. "I didn't want to doubt you. I should know better at my age than to listen to town gossip, but while Lily Moore might come from a respectable family, she isn't always the best influence. She won't marry like a sensible girl."

"Miss Moore is ..." He paused to clear any emotion seeping into his tone. He couldn't let such a statement go undefended, but he had to be careful not to feed the rumor mill further. "I consider myself a gentleman and simply came to her aid as any retired Marine would do."

"Marine?" She brightened, successfully redirected. "So was my Lyle. I knew—"

"Mrs. St. Thomas?" A man's voice came from the entryway a moment before the kitchen door opened. Lily's twin brother appeared, and he aimed a murderous glint directly at Miles.

CHAPTER 15

"What happened out there?" The middle-aged man slammed his fist on his desk, his rage bubbling like a volcano ready to erupt.

The young man cowered as if waiting for the lava to descend—lava that would destroy him if he didn't give the right answers.

"Well? Were you the one to shoot at Lily Moore after I precisely said I need her alive? And at the church!" He let out a string of words that would never be sanctioned within those holy walls.

"It wasn't me."

"Say that again. Louder."

"It wasn't me, sir." The young man swallowed. "I don't know who it was, but it wasn't me."

He blinked at the fool, trying to comprehend this new information. "Then who was it?"

"I—I don't know, sir."

Another swear word and he lurched to his feet. Paced to the bookshelf and back to his desk chair. Bookshelf. Desk chair. Bookshelf. "Can you describe anything that happened?"

"Service had just dismissed. I noticed Miss Moore and the man she came into town with leave the building and tried to follow."

"Tried?"

"Yes, sir, but Mrs. St. Thomas …"

He waved a hand. The old biddy wouldn't be the reason he lost thousands of dollars at a time when every dollar counted. "After you got rid of her?"

"I got outside just as someone shot at them." The young man shuddered. "I scrambled back inside along with everyone else."

"Did either of them get hurt?"

"Not that I heard."

"Did you see any detail about the shooter? Or hear any information that might aid me?"

"No sir. Nothing. Gossip is that Lily Moore is a criminal, and her brother is the maddest I've ever seen him." The young man chuckled. "Madder than the time I greased the bottom of his work boots one particularly icy afternoon before school let out."

He let out a long sigh to discourage further prattle. Then he turned to stare out the window. Someone was infringing on his territory, and he wanted to know who. Before his lucrative pawn ended up dead.

"Miles Wright?" Joey didn't take his eyes off Miles. Measuring. Assessing. Convicting.

"Joey Moore." Miles stuck out his hand and tried to appear non-threatening despite the hostility pulsing from the other man. "Nice to see you again."

Joey grasped Miles's hand. Held it tight. "Stay away from my sister."

Miles attempted to mask any irritation. "Miss Moore?" He needed to choose his words even more carefully than a moment ago. "She is—"

"What?" Joey yanked Miles's arm. Shoved his face against the closed kitchen door. "What were you going to say about my sister before I walked in?"

Mrs. St. Thomas yelped behind them.

Miles relaxed his muscles, not fighting Joey's anger. He could take a lot of pain—he'd let Joey take out his frustration on him. For a moment. As long as the man didn't realize Miles was armed.

"Tell me," Joey hissed. "Tell me why my sister should trust you."

Miles pressed his forehead into the rough wood. He understood the protective anger behind Joey's words and knew the man was beyond a productive conversation even as the words planted doubt in Miles's mind. Why should Lily trust a man who failed his team?

"Say something." Joey wrenched Miles's arm up his back.

Miles cringed. Resisted the urge to turn this into a battle of brawn. It wouldn't help Lily.

"Joey, please," Mrs. St. Thomas said. "Not in my house."

With a huff, Joey released Miles and stepped back.

Miles slowly turned, subtly moving his shoulder to ease the strain.

"Mr. Wright is a paying boarder," Mrs. St. Thomas continued. "With the Depression, I need a full house. This type of action will not help."

"You're willing to have a dangerous man in your house, Mrs. St. Thomas?" Joey demanded.

Miles couldn't deny that adjective described him, but only where bad people were concerned. Or perhaps the heart of a certain green-eyed woman. No, he'd keep her heart safe. It was his that was at risk.

"Dangerous?" Red rose in Mrs. St. Thomas's withered cheeks. "Like you? You carry a gun."

"I'm a lawman."

Miles tilted his head. "Then you should also know better than to charge in here like a bull. How about talking it out like a civilized human being?"

"Fine. Talk." Joey glared at him.

And enter that minefield? Even if he wasn't under orders not to involve the local police, Joey's current mindset did not welcome truth. "Have you spoken with your sister?"

Joey's bluster told him that conversation hadn't gone well. In fact, it was likely the reason for the man's current mood.

"Mr. Wright is a gentleman and war hero." Mrs. St. Thomas wagged a potholder at Joey. "And you assault him. In my kitchen. You better straighten out, Joey Moore."

Shame and anger blotted Joey's face, but without a word, he slammed the kitchen door, then the front door, behind him. Once this ended, the man deserved the full truth and an apology. He loved his sister, and both she and Miles were keeping him in the dark. Miles could only hope he wasn't destroying the twins' relationship by insisting they leave Joey out of their investigation.

Mrs. St. Thomas shook her head. "Those Moore twins have been so much trouble in this town. Even as kids, they never conformed to what anyone expected of them. Their siblings are model citizens."

Miles nodded politely, not wanting to encourage her gossip.

"Their little sister even married the Booth boy. Lovely wedding, it was. Wealthiest family in the county, those Booths. Well, wealthiest family with a son. It's said the Bakers are wealthier, but they have only the one daughter. If Joey married her, he'd likely redeem himself. But it's quite incredible that the Moores are now aligned with the Booths."

"Oh?" Gossip worked both ways, and on this topic, he could use all the intelligence he could get.

"The Moores now own Eagle's largest dairy farm. But that Lily. She never liked working the farm. Spent all her time helping her grandfather, a dear man and gifted gardener. When he passed, God rest him, she inherited what is considered the most fertile land outside town, and what does she do with it? Raises dogs, much to the great disappointment of everyone, but especially her father."

Interesting. "Any idea if Lily knew that when she inherited?"

"Lily, huh?" A mischievous light sparked in her eyes.

"Oh no, no, no." Miles cringed at his over-the-top denial, which said far more about the state of his brain than he cared to explore. "I'm not interested in any relationships right now. I'm only in town for a short while and—" He cut himself off before he dug an even deeper hole for himself. And Lily.

"Of course, dearie." She didn't believe him. Great. "I know just about everyone in town. You ask me anything you want to know. I'm happy to help and glad to have you here for as long as you stay."

"Thank you, Mrs. St. Thomas." And thank you, Joey Moore, for helping change her perspective. "You are a spectacular lady."

Mrs. St. Thomas spluttered as her cheeks turned a bright pink. "Now, off with you. I need to get these cookies in the oven before I'm so tuckered out, I fall asleep listening to the radio and they burn."

Lily set a saucepan on the woodstove and poured in a cup of milk fresh from her family's farm. While it heated, she added the bar of Hershey's chocolate. On her hardest days, hot chocolate set the world right again. Especially when topped with whipped cream.

She pulled the bottle of her family's fresh cream from her refrigerator, poured it into a bowl, added a dash of sugar, and then set to beating the mixture with a whisk. Her forearms burned with the effort, but it effectively drowned out her thoughts.

Just as peaks began to form in the cream and the milk and chocolate mixture began to bubble, her dogs barked. She set the whisk aside and took the saucepan from the stove as the rumble of a vehicle approached.

Her heart raced. She grabbed her shotgun from where she kept it above the archway between her kitchen and the sitting room and loaded a shell into the barrel. Peeked outside. Miles. Her renegade heart sped up even more.

Smokey's howling intensified. Pieter stood at Lily's side, alert. She snapped her fingers, and two noses pointed her direction. She held her hand palm out to them, and two furry hindquarters planted on the hard floor. Then she opened the back door, trying desperately to calm the smile that insisted on popping out. And not because Smokey's obedience was improving every day.

"I come in peace." Miles eyed the rifle. Oops.

"Come in, come in." Heat rushed up her neck. "I'm making hot chocolate. Would you like a cup?"

"I don't want to make you uncomfortable. I just wanted to check on you."

"You deserve some hot chocolate after all you've done for me." She kept her tone light as she beckoned him inside and unloaded the gun, then returned it to its place above the archway leading to the sitting room.

"Lily, before we're interrupted." He reached for her shoulders. "Or before I stick my foot in my mouth or someone starts shooting at us again, there's something I need to ask you."

Dozens of scenarios bombarded her, yet all were overwhelmed by his closeness, his strength, his solid presence that somehow gave her peace even in the scariest moments she'd experienced the past few days. She could sink into it, forget about the trouble chasing her down.

"I need to interview your family."

That snapped her thoughts back where they belonged. "Whatever for? My family didn't kidnap me!"

"No, but since you inherited this property, which I learned is considered prime real estate, it creates another possible motive for whoever might be after you."

Placing the pot back on the burner, Lily added more milk and chocolate. "Okay, but why interview my family?"

"I went back over my team's file." Miles scratched Smokey's ears. "When we were first hired, it wasn't for a kidnapping."

"What?"

"No ransom was demanded, as far as we know, so it was treated as a missing person until my company realized you hadn't just gone missing."

"My family probably hired you to find me." She resumed stirring the milk and chocolate mixture, adding, more to herself than to Miles, "Although Joey would want to find me himself."

"That's the strange part." Miles crossed his arms as he leaned against her kitchen table. "There is no record of who hired us. It came directly from our boss, Karl Craft, and it didn't go through the regular channels as far as my paperwork shows."

"That is odd. Your company didn't question it?"

Miles shrugged. "It's all about the action for us. We follow orders and don't ask why."

"That doesn't bother you?"

"Does now. Especially because I haven't been able to get my boss on the telephone since I called him from your house yesterday."

"I don't like this, Miles." She poured the hot chocolate into two cups.

"It gets worse." He took the pot to the sink and continued as he washed it. "My friend called before I left Mrs. St. Thomas's boardinghouse. You know how everyone thinks the Booths are wealthy? He learned the crash hit them harder than they let on. Significantly harder."

Lily frowned. "What are you saying? Amy never doubted she was marrying into money."

"Her new husband's inheritance is gone, and his father could lose his business if he doesn't turn things around. With another strike in the works …"

"Amy doesn't know?" She paused with a spoonful of whipped cream suspended over one of the cups. "Is that why Andy canceled their honeymoon? Does *he* know?"

"I have no more information. Yet." He dried the pot and hung it from the empty hook on the rack over the stove. "But your father is in direct opposition to Booth with the protests and milk dumping. What if Booth had you kidnapped to make your father bend? He'd target a female, which means either you or Amy, and he wouldn't hurt his son by leveraging his new wife. Plus, Booth might think he can get to your brothers through you too."

"And you think my father hired your boss to find me before any of that happened?" She finished topping the cups of hot chocolate with whipped cream.

"It's what I want to find out. Why I need to interview your family. Your father might know more than he's telling."

"But I've never heard of a Mr. Craft. And why hide me in a hole in the middle of the Northwoods, of all places?" Even as she asked the question, her mind ran through the scenario. Miles's team making their way into the ruins. The explosion. Mr. Craft disappearing. Danger following them back to Eagle …

"Miles?" She choked out his name. "What if you're wrong about Booth and the protests and even about me being the target? What if I'm the bait?"

The well-dressed gentleman glanced around the hotel lobby, lowered the brim of his bowler, and shrugged up the collar of his trench coat before approaching the public telephone. Anonymity was why he'd chosen this place. Even if the operators heard his call, he would be long gone before anyone could find him.

"Is the job done?" he asked when the man picked up the other end of the telephone line.

"No sir."

Astonishment had him staring at the earpiece as if it had dared talk back.

"The police intervened." The explanation floated from the telephone, sounding as flimsy as the excuse.

He jammed the earpiece back against his head and leaned into the wall-mounted receiver to hush his voice. "I want the job done tonight."

"I have a plan in place. Check the obituaries in the morning."

He returned the earpiece to the hook with a smile. That was why he hired the best.

CHAPTER 16

Joey pushed out of his desk chair in the back corner of the station. Today was a rotten one, and he wasn't even supposed to be at work. The shooting had occupied the entire police force, all four of them, for the rest of the Lord's Day.

He'd missed family dinner. His sister wouldn't let him protect her. And then he'd shocked himself with his reaction to Miles Wright at the boardinghouse. Frankly, humiliation had covered him ever since.

"Get outta here, Moore." His boss, the police chief, waved him out the door. "We'll finish the investigation tomorrow."

"Yes sir." Joey shrugged into his wool jacket. The temperatures were chilly by the time the sun started setting. Soon, though, if the clear weather held through the harvest, the winter winds would howl across barren fields. It'd been another dry year, too dry, yet they couldn't afford a wet autumn.

"Might need to call in help." Chief Evermore tapped his pencil against his bushy mustache. "This type of crime is highly irregular."

And Lily was wrapped up in the middle of it, thanks to Miles Wright. After Lily's revelation and his confrontation with Miles, he'd returned to the station to read over the man's statement—the statement of a victim, which Joey didn't believe him to be.

Joey balled his fists. He wanted to ball up Miles's statement too. "I'm sure we can handle it, sir." He'd get answers or die trying.

"I'll think on it." Chief dismissed him with another wave.

Joey kicked a rock out of his way as he crossed the street to his lonely apartment. He shouldn't have lost control, assaulting Miles Wright instead of questioning him. Now even old Mrs. St. Thomas seemed to believe Wright innocent. But how did he figure into Lily's kidnapping?

Joey stomped up the back steps, pounding his frustration into each one until he reached the top. A gust of wind pushed him inside. He closed the door and leaned against it, resting his head on the unforgiving wood. He was a policeman. He had to find all the facts before making a judgment. Could Lily have gotten caught up in something nefarious? Maybe this Miles Wright had only pretended to save her for his own purposes. Joey groaned. Too many wild theories and not enough facts.

He needed to sort out his emotions before going back to his sister with more questions about what happened to her. Maybe a bite to eat would help.

Peering into his empty cupboard, he had a much better idea. He would pay a visit to the one person besides his sister who had the ability to help him see past himself. Maybe then he could figure out what he was going to do next.

"Bait?" Miles stared at Lily, attempting to digest her bomb of an idea. If she was the bait, did that make him the target? By being here, was he putting her in more danger? He pictured the bullet paths and couldn't discern which of them the shooter had aimed at, considering Miles had kept his body between Lily and the gunman the entire time.

"Chocolate first." She slid the hot cup—topped with a healthy dollop of whipped cream—toward him. "Milk and cream fresh from this morning's milking. I ducked into my parents' house before they returned from church, knowing I'd need a cup of hot chocolate after today."

Miles leaned a hip on the table. Her chatter about her favorite treat eased the knot in his stomach until it slowly unwound. It also gave him a moment to study her without danger on their heels. Her hair piled atop her head showed off her long neck. Her loose flannel shirt gave hints of her small frame beneath.

"Growing up on a dairy farm has spoiled me." Lily paused to sip her concoction, leaving a distracting bit of whipped cream on her lip. "We went through at least a gallon of milk a day between the five of us children. Now that our parents have electricity for refrigeration, they keep glass jars filled for Joey and me to pick up, which we do nearly every day. At Christmas, I splurge—splurged, that is—on peppermints to crush and sprinkle on top of my hot chocolate."

"That sounds … perfect." Miles didn't mean to let the wistfulness seep into his words, but they were out before he could stop them. What was he doing? He couldn't let himself go down this path, imagining a home and holidays with Lily. *God, why put this in my path now, when it's dangerous and impossible for me to even entertain the idea?*

Lily ducked her head. "I talk when I'm overwhelmed. Can't seem to help it. And all this" —she waved her hand abstractly—"has me feeling, well … Just stop me if I get to be too much, okay?"

"On the contrary." He smiled to set her at ease. "You've cleared my mind, and I'm ready to talk about why I'm here." Including why she thought she could be bait instead of the target.

"Couch is comfier." Lily led the way, and no sooner had they settled than Smokey climbed into his lap. She smiled at him over her mug. "They like you too."

Too? His heart somersaulted, and he glanced at his feet. Pieter had curled up on his shoes. Smokey nosed his head under Miles's arm, jostling his cup of hot chocolate. He ran his hand over the puppy's back, and Smokey rested his paws on his chest, stretched his neck, and licked his cheek.

Lily gave a soft chuckle. "I can call them off if they bother you."

"I don't mind." Miles swallowed back his emotions. No, he sure didn't mind sitting here as if he belonged—as if he'd found a home with her just as the dogs had.

"They trust you." Lily's voice was quiet. "They don't settle this quickly with anybody but Joey. Especially Pieter."

"And you trust their instincts." The hot chocolate amplified the cozy feeling taking root in his heart.

"Absolutely. Dogs have an innate ability to read humans, and my two are incredibly protective of me. The fact that they not only accepted you into the house without protest but are treating you as one of their own says all I need to know about you."

Didn't that make him feel like a hero? He cleared his throat. Time to get back on track. Miles had come for two primary reasons. First, to check on Lily, and second, because he couldn't get Joey's accusations out of his head. He braced for her reaction.

"Lily, I need to offer an apology."

She set her mug on the table beside her. "For what?"

Miles ran his hand over the puppy's fur, finding it reassuring. "It seems I have, albeit unwittingly, been a part of ..." He blew out a breath. Why did apologies have to be so hard?

"Yes?"

"There are rumors about ... about ..." He cringed. He could face down an enemy, but his fear of losing Lily's respect stole his capacity to speak.

Lily raised her eyebrows, took a sip of her hot chocolate, and returned the mug to the table. "Rumors about us meeting up at a speakeasy, of being criminals, and running illegal alcohol?"

"Something like that." Was she hiding a smirk? Wait. She wasn't kicking him out of her house. In fact, she'd known all that before she invited him inside. Before she offered him the hot chocolate. Before she told him how much she trusted him.

"I heard some whispers as I left the churchyard this morning, and my brother confirmed them." Lily sighed. "I'm the one who should apologize. I'm sorry you've gotten caught up in Eagle's gossip. I should be used to it by now. I'm considered a rebel, so most townspeople don't give me the benefit of the doubt."

"Then they don't really know you. You care for the people around you, and I didn't mean to cause you more distress. I should have been paying more attention. Your brother has every right to be angry with me." *I'm mad at myself.*

"Miles—"

"I didn't come for an apology from you, Lily. You have no responsibility for any of this. It's me. I have not been at my best, and it could have cost you far more than just having to deal with these rumors."

"No. Your actions are the only reason worse didn't happen." Pieter left Miles's shoes to rest his muzzle on his mistress's lap. "You have done nothing but keep me safe, keep me alive from the moment you found me in that hole. If anything, I should apologize for being stubborn and selfish. I don't know what I've done that you so willingly put yourself in harm's way for me." Her voice cracked.

"Oh, Lily, you are worth saving." He clasped his hands between his knees to keep himself from following Pieter's example and comforting her. "You have so much to offer others if they would only let you. I am a better man for knowing you."

She nodded, running a hand over the dog's head.

He wanted to say so much more. Couldn't. Shouldn't. He needed to avoid any more forays into personal territory. Instead, he should make his security assessment, create a plan to ensure her safety, then return to the investigation without Lily's further involvement.

Pieter gave a sharp bark and trotted to the picture window. Smokey raised his floppy ears from his spot curled at Miles's side. Miles's senses went on alert, but Lily offered an innocuous explanation.

"It's their dinnertime." She gathered the empty mugs. Smokey scrambled to the floor to trot after her.

"May I at least see you to the barn?" Trailing them, Miles shoved his hands in his pockets.

"Because you want my company, or because you're worried about me going out there in the dark?" Lily gave him a sideways glance before heading into the back room where she shrugged on a coat and slipped her feet into work boots.

Both, but he'd stay away from the personal. "Well, Pieter did seem to hear something. And we never got to discuss why you think you're the bait." Miles followed her outside. The dogs brushed past and headed straight for the barn.

Lily stayed beside him, her voice quiet. "It's just that the lethal danger started when you rescued me."

The moon that had been so brilliant last night—romantic, even—was now eclipsed by clouds. Darkness covered the fields in an inky blanket. Not even a breeze stirred the corn. The hair on the back of his neck rose—and not because of her observation.

"Come with me." He grabbed Lily's hand and hurried her toward the deepest shadows against the barn wall. "You shouldn't be exposed out here."

"Miles?"

"Just humor me. Call your dogs and stay as quiet as possible while I make sure the barn is secure." He pulled his Colt from his holster.

She gave a gasp so similar to the fearful one Mrs. St. Thomas had uttered earlier that it went straight to Miles's heart. Throwing ramifications to the wind, he placed a gentle kiss on her forehead. Added a whispered prayer for her safety. Then disappeared into the barn.

CHAPTER 17

Lily touched the place Miles had kissed. How was she supposed to keep him at arm's length when he did something so sweet? He had a life to return to once this was over. She must remember that. In no way could she let her heart get wrapped up in his security or kindness.

She crouched, unable to stay upright with the swirl of emotion coursing through her. Pieter immediately came to her side, and she whistled for Smokey to join them. She held the puppy close. Strained her ears for whatever put Miles on alert.

Pieter sensed something, too, given the dog's tense body.

The barn door slid open, and a large shadow slipped out. Pieter's tail gave a single wag. Not a threat.

"Lily," Miles whispered. "This way."

She gave the signal to heel, and Pieter attached himself to her leg. Miles stood sentry, gun drawn, searching the front lawn. This was the intense Miles, the one who'd rescued her from the armed men. The warrior. Her heart hammered against her ribs.

"I need you to find a corner in your barn and stay there until I come get you. If I'm not back in twenty minutes, call your brother and tell him everything."

She grasped Smokey more tightly in her arms. "What's going on?"

He holstered his gun and cupped her shoulders in his large hands, a move that was becoming all too familiar. Warmth seeped through her coat. "There's someone outside. I need you here, safe, so I can do what I do best. Can you do that for me?"

"If you're looking for someone, Pieter and I should come with you."

Miles shook his head. "I can't risk dividing my attention."

"I can't stay here." Lily hated the fear that shook her voice. "I—I won't be locked in the dark again."

His brown eyes melted like the chocolate she'd put into the saucepan.

"I'll leave Smokey here." She bargained with him. "Pieter and I will listen to everything you tell us." *Just please don't leave me alone.*

"Lily." He wrapped her in his powerful arms, Smokey between them, his voice muffled in her hair. "If you get hurt on my watch ..."

"It won't be your fault."

"Yes, it will. Because I could make you stay here."

She recoiled at his ferocity. "You wouldn't."

"No. Because I—" He pressed a finger to his lips. Pulled her into the shadows.

Her dogs whimpered, and she knelt beside Pieter, burying her nose in Smokey's fur. Her face heated at the memory of Miles's chest pressed against her cheek. Her heart pounded. A branch scraped the wall, and wind moaned through the cracks. Miles eased open the back barn door, his bulk a shadow amid the darkness.

Father God, please protect us. Please keep my fear away. Please don't let Miles leave me alone. A tear slipped down her cheek.

"You and Pieter stay right on my hip." Miles whispered the instruction against his better judgment. He tried to convince himself that having Lily with him would be better. He could keep an eye on her instead of worrying about whether or not she stayed in the barn.

At her light touch on his arm, he nearly reconsidered. He needed all his focus on whomever he tracked, not on the beautiful woman he'd held in his arms. But the quiver of breath he heard escape her stayed his decision. He couldn't force her to face her fear alone. He couldn't leave her behind.

Lily secured Smokey in a storage room and grabbed a lead for Pieter before Miles silently led them out the rear of the barn, along the wall toward the dog run, halting at the corner. Voices? He signaled to Lily to keep quiet. She knelt, her arm around Pieter. The dog stood ramrod straight, focused on something Miles couldn't see. He wished he could see in the dark. Then he could find a vantage point and secure the higher ground.

Instead, he eased himself around the corner, gun muzzle first. No one. He searched the deeper shadows. No movement.

Lily tapped his shoulder.

What? he mouthed.

She pointed to Pieter. The dog had his nose to the ground, sniffing by their feet, then using up all five feet of lead to follow a trail. He had a scent.

"Are we following Pieter?" Lily whispered. "I don't like standing still, waiting for trouble to find us."

Her interminable spunk. He admired it as much as it drove him crazy. No. He admired it more. "As quiet as we can."

Lily whispered in Pieter's ear, and he took off. Every few feet, the dog would check that Lily followed. Somehow, she kept hold of Pieter's lead as they ran after the nimble canine across the uneven ground behind Lily's barn.

Miles had never worked with a military dog but had heard about their growing success. It gave him even more appreciation for the work Lily put in to train her dogs. He couldn't help watching her as they raced toward the tree line to the north of her property. She seemed at her best in this moment, as if God had created her for this purpose. To work with her dogs.

Pieter took a hard right, then left, and disappeared into the trees. If only Miles had a map to better understand the terrain. But these were Lily's woods. She knew them. Her dogs knew them. He could trust both and commit his senses to listen for danger. The trees offered a false sense of security. Harder to be seen, but also harder to see.

Out of the darkness, Lily grabbed his arm, stopping all three of them.

"What is it?" he whispered, then bent his head to hear her reply.

The *thwap* of a bullet hitting the tree behind him propelled him into Lily. He pushed her forward, toward some type of cover. Another bullet splintered a branch by his shoulder. He needed a place to hide her. Thicker trees. A boulder. Something.

Pieter swerved back toward the barn.

"We can't leave the trees." Miles pulled Lily the opposite direction.

"I can't stop him." Lily's voice was tense in the dark. "He's not letting this one go."

Even as she spoke, Pieter yanked the lead out of her hand.

"Pieter, stop!" Lily dove into the woods after her dog.

Miles had no choice but to follow, searching the shadows for the shooter. He should have left Lily behind.

Two more missed shots, and they came to the edge of the trees. Pieter stood at the base of a tree, paws on the trunk.

"Pieter, down!" Lily lunged for him, throwing herself over him in a protective covering. "Release, Pieter. Good dog."

Miles raised his gun, following a sight line up the trunk of the tree. The shooter was behind them, so what had Pieter been tracking?

"Miles!"

Lily cried out only a moment before pain radiated across his shoulders, sucking the breath from his lungs. Then his knees buckled, and he crashed to the ground like a toppled oak.

Lily scrambled after the gun that flew out of Miles's hands as the assailant struck him from above. Like a panther, a skinny man in a mask had dropped from the tree Pieter indicated and nailed Miles across the shoulders with a branch.

"Pieter, stay," she commanded before her dog reacted, then aimed the gun at the attacker. "Don't move."

The man raised his hands.

"Not a good idea," said another voice, this one belonging to another man nearly as large as Miles, but with eyes like two dark holes and a malicious grin. Pieter growled as the man aimed his gun at her. "This ends here."

The skinny guy took one look at the gunman and dashed into the trees. His flight drew the second man's eye, and Lily took action. She aimed the Colt at the space between the gunman's shoulder and right ear. Fired.

The bullet flew true and embedded in the tree behind him. The man cursed, ducked. Before he could right himself, Lily aimed for the air beside his left ear. Fired. The man spun, another curse scraping the air. Tremors shook her fingers. Would she have to actually shoot the man to save their lives? Could she?

"Next one is in your rump." She aimed a shot just beside his hip, praying her bluff would buy her time to steady her nerves enough to end this without someone dying.

The man dove for the cover of a tree, his taunt coming a moment later. "Getting tired of missing?"

"Peek your head out, and I'll show you." Her voice didn't shake. *Thank you, Father God!* She could do this. One well-placed bullet would injure, not kill.

She knelt beside Pieter, who lay beside her left foot, and aimed. She might be used to a shotgun, but she was a fowl hunter. She could hit moving targets with ease—in the daytime. Nearness offset the darkness. She studied the edge of the tree. Saw the shadow deepen as the shooter moved his gun out from his hiding spot. Deep breath in. Deep breath out. Pull the—

Two shots split the air, neither from her gun, and a *whoosh* flew past her as the gunman let out a howl to rival one of Smokey's. Lily shrieked and covered her head with her arms.

The next instant, Miles's large body formed a shield between her and the shooter. Brush cracked to their right, and Miles swung his gun—a tiny one in his large hand—toward the sound. Lily held her breath.

"He's gone," Miles whispered.

"I'm sorry, Miles. I'm so sorry." Residual fear and relief tangled in her voice.

Miles wrapped warm hands around her trembling ones, took the gun from her, then pulled her into his solid arms. She let herself sink in the damp leaves, not caring how wet her jeans would get. Miles knelt beside her, one hand pressing her head into his chest. Was holding her comforting him as much as being in his arms was helping her?

"You did good." His voice calmed her, but she detected a quiver in his. "Just please don't ever scare me like that again."

A wet nose pressed her cheek.

Miles chuckled. "Pieter wants a hug too."

Before Lily could oblige, Pieter whirled around with a growl. Footsteps crackled leaves in the open field between them and the house. Miles spun the cylinder of his Colt, then aimed it at the sound, putting Lily behind him as he did. She hissed at Pieter to heel.

Miles whispered over his shoulder as they crouched beside the tree. "If I say run …"

She pressed one hand on his muscled back and gripped Pieter's lead with the other. "I'm not leaving you."

"Lily, please."

"Police! Hands up!"

"Joey?" Lily leaned around Miles, and Pieter's tail thumped against her ankle, his hackles immediately smoothing. "What are you doing here?"

"Hands!" Joey aimed at Miles.

"Easy, Joey." Miles raised his arms, letting the Colt swing by the trigger guard from his right index finger. "Just protecting your sister. There was a shooter. I winged him, and he took off deeper into the woods."

Joey swung his gun toward the trees Miles indicated, his hesitation to pursue revealing just how little he trusted Miles. "Reinforcements are on the way."

Miles slowly lowered his hands, easing his gun into its holster. "There were two—"

"Miles?" Lily cut him off, blinking at her hand, the one that had been on his back. Her heart pounded in her ears. She edged back, her ankle twisting on a tree root.

"Hey, there." Miles caught her before she tumbled. He raised her hand to the filtered moonlight. "That's blood."

Joey was beside them in an instant.

Lily's stomach roiled as she met Miles's concerned gaze. "I ... I think it's yours."

CHAPTER 18

Miles refused pain medicine while the doctor stitched up the three-inch gash on his left shoulder blade. He'd been hurt far worse and in much less favorable conditions. The blow of the branch against his back hadn't left any internal physical damage. Just humiliation. Here he was, supposed to be Lily's protection, and a single knock to the rear had caused his diaphragm to seize up. Admittedly, it might have rebruised a few ribs too.

"Care to tell me what happened?" Joey rested his hands on his holster belt. He had insisted on following Miles into the doctor's exam room, much to the physician's annoyance. The room was small, but not claustrophobically so, with a black-and-white-checked floor and green walls. Much better than the frontline tents in which Miles had been stitched up during the Great War.

"Don't you think you're too close to this?" Glancing sideways at Joey, Miles winced as the doctor pushed the needle into his back with cold hands. "You obviously can't keep your emotions out of it."

"And you can? I see the way you look at her."

Great. Now his personal business would be all over Eagle. No, make that Lily's personal business. His inability to keep his emotions in check was going to cost her reputation for good.

Miles blew out a breath that coincided with another needle prick. "This covered under doctor-patient privilege, Doc?" he asked the older man.

The doctor peered at him from over his reading glasses. "What's that you say, sonny?"

Uh-huh. The man was pleading the fifth.

"I took an oath." The doctor stopped his work to stand between Miles and Joey. "The Oath of Hippocrates. What you say here will not leave this room because of me."

His implication clear, the man returned to his work. Miles studied Joey—a man torn between his job and his family. Miles had never struggled with that dilemma. Now, however, he found himself torn between his job and his heart. With Craft's insistence on the men in his employ remaining free of any attachments, it left him with no room to maneuver.

Joey rubbed both hands through his hair, ruffling it so that it stood up like rooster feathers. "Just tell me my sister isn't mixed up in some kind of trouble."

Ha! Trouble? Lily Moore was at the center of a whole lot of trouble! Not a point he needed to explain to her brother. "She's an innocent, Joey. If you believe nothing else, please believe that."

"And you?"

He should be drawn and quartered for how the night went down. "It's my fault she was in danger tonight. I take full responsibility, and I won't let it happen again."

Joey's nostrils flared.

"All done." The doctor patted Miles's good shoulder. "Got some muscles on you, son."

Sure, but all the brawn in the world hadn't helped him keep Lily safe. He hadn't anticipated a two-pronged attack with two very different methods. The branch to the back caught him by complete surprise. Had Lily not acted so quickly, they'd both be dead.

"Some scars, too," the doctor continued. "I heard you saw action in the Great War."

And in Central America, but he wasn't proud of those years. They were the reason he left soldiering. They haunted his dreams as much as they propelled him to stand between a victim and a perpetrator. And they left him, a man who lived by his gun, with the conviction that he would never kill again unless he had no other recourse.

"Miles? Joey?" A voice that was becoming all too dear floated down the hall. Quick footsteps came toward them. She'd taken her dogs to her friend's house, was supposed to stay there with her ankle up while he and Joey figured this out. Obviously, she hadn't followed the plan. His and Joey's plan.

Joey flung open the exam room door with contained force. "What are you—"

"I couldn't sit still knowing you were planning to interrogate ..." Her eyes widened and cheeks pinked as she appeared in the doorway and took in Miles's shirtless state.

Joey grumbled. "He's fine. Doc said so."

Usually, around other soldiers or medical staff, Miles thought nothing of carrying on a conversation while half bare and getting stitched up, but not so in front of Lily. He quickly hopped off the exam table and snatched his shirt, easing it on with a grimace.

"Did you finish giving your statement?" Joey recaptured her attention, giving Miles a chance to tuck in his shirt and snap up his suspenders.

"Yes, and as I keep telling everyone, neither of us did anything wrong."

Joey's chest puffed out. "Doc, give us a moment?"

Dr. Holland held up a finger in front of Miles's face. "If it shows signs of infection or you develop other symptoms, I want you back in here. Understood, soldier?"

"Yes sir." Miles shoved his hands in his trouser pockets while the doc closed him in with the twins.

Joey turned to Lily. "Were you almost kidnapped again?"

Again? He knew?

Lily explained what she'd told Joey. "But, no, this didn't feel the same. This was ..." She blew out a shaky breath.

No need to mince words. Miles completed her sentence. "This was meant to be lethal."

"How have you two become targets twice in one day?" Joey stared down Miles. "Is this because of you?"

Guilt snaked down Miles's sore back.

"Joey, why didn't anyone report me missing?" Lily fingered the cuff of her coat. "Everyone thinks I just took a trip somewhere. Even you."

"I didn't until enough people saw you leave town."

"What?" Lily echoed Miles's reaction.

"I looked into your disappearance, asked around. Once I weeded past the ridiculous idea that you ran away, all indications said you went out of town to meet someone about a dog."

"Proof?" Miles demanded.

Joey focused on his sister. "Eyewitness statements and a vague note you yourself left on your kitchen table."

"But why didn't I make arrangements for Pieter and Smokey? That should have been proof enough I didn't leave of my own accord!"

Red infused Joey's face. "I thought I'd forgotten you asked me to watch them."

"Oh, Joey." Lily wrapped her brother in a hug.

Miles turned away to give them a moment, processing this news. Who were these witnesses, and why had they thought Lily left on her own?

Joey didn't give him a chance to ask. He speared Miles with a glare over Lily's shoulder. "Your turn. Who are you, really?"

"Joey!" Lily pushed away from her brother. "He's the one who rescued me."

Miles rubbed his neck. Craft would not approve of this conversation, and Miles still felt uncomfortable telling Joey everything, such as how he'd lost his team. He needed to finish his own reconnaissance before he defied orders and fully trusted someone he didn't know. Even if that someone was Lily's brother.

"Then why do you two keep getting shot at?" Joey said, reverting to a policeman.

"I wish I knew." Miles huffed out his frustration. "But I'm not the threat to your sister. I'm here to protect her."

Joey met him stare for stare. Two men who'd pledged to protect innocent lives, especially ones they most cared about.

"Yoo-hoo!" Lily waved a hand between them. "I don't like being talked about while I'm standing right here."

Joey laughed, cutting the tension in the room. He gave her shoulders a quick squeeze. "Fine. Then I'll tell you directly, I want you to stay with Katy for a while and let me do my job."

What now?

"Katy, huh? You keep calling her that." Lily crossed her arms. Uh-oh. Miles was beginning to recognize that stance meant her stubborn streak would emerge.

Miles held himself in check. This wasn't about his battle with Joey. He needed to act in Lily's best interest. Was this it? He tilted his head and dared to ask, "Who is Katy?"

"Our local vet and a good friend of mine. And she's always been *Dr. Wells* to him. Until tonight." Lily narrowed her eyes at her brother.

Red flushed Joey's cheeks for the second time.

"Ah-ha!" Lily shook her head. "You've been secretly seeing my friend, and neither of you told me."

"We'll talk about that later. For now, I've told her you need a safe place to lay low, and she's expecting you." He met Miles's eye and gave a nod. "You've got five minutes to say whatever you need to say."

Lily looked between them. "Five—"

Joey kissed his sister's cheek and left the room.

"We're not done, Joseph Moore," Lily hollered after him, then rubbed her face and ran her fingers over her hair, which was still in disarray. In fact, she had a couple twigs and leaves sticking out of it. Miles suppressed a chuckle as she continued grumbling. "He jumps down my throat because I haven't told him everything, but he's been keeping his relationship a secret too. We never used to keep secrets, and even our fights felt more like teasing. Until I moved onto the farm after Grandpa died."

Miles stilled. Joey had given him five minutes, and he wanted to make the most of it. If Lily needed to talk, that's what he would let her do.

"Why can't a woman live alone? Own property and conduct business?" She looked at him with shining green eyes. "Why is my only option to be a good little wife? You know, I overheard the latest rumor—that if I were married and home where I belong, no one would have shot at me. Can you believe it? I just want someone to take what I say at face value, regardless of whether I'm a woman or unmarried. I want someone to believe me for no reason other than that it's my story."

"I know, Lily." He drew her to himself. *I believe you.*

"Just because I refuse to get married, even my family thinks I'm crazy."

His heart stumbled at her words. *Refuse to get married.* He couldn't have a relationship in his current job, so it was good she was so adamantly unattached. Right? Then why did it feel like the piercing of a blade?

"I'd probably feel better if I could go home." She rested her head against his chest. "Only, it doesn't feel safe anymore, and I'm weary of being frightened. I keep repeating the verse from Psalm 46 about how God is 'our refuge and strength, a very present help in trouble.' But it is not enough, Miles. It's not tangible. I can't feel it."

"I know." Miles closed his arms around her, as if that could banish all those fearful thoughts. Only God could do that, so he would pray. Better, get Gio to pray. "Maybe we did bring trouble back with us, but right now, you should listen to your brother. You'll be safer at your friend's house. No one expects you there, so you can sleep restfully. There's nothing we can figure out right now, anyway. We'll go back to our investigation tomorrow. Your home will be your refuge again."

"You're right." She took a shaky breath but didn't sound convinced.

If only he could hold her until she felt safe again, but his five minutes were up, and he wouldn't take advantage of Lily's vulnerable state.

And if only he felt confident that God would hear his prayers, he would intercede for her. Fervently.

Instead, he escorted her out to her brother, giving the man a silent *thank you* for the moment alone with the most captivating woman he'd ever met. A woman who didn't know she held the power to crush his heart. If she did, she wouldn't be so afraid.

Why was there a knocking at his door at this time of night?

The middle-aged man pushed out of his armchair, where he'd been dozing over a glass of smuggled whiskey, and shuffled to the front hall, tossing open the door. Apprehension cut through his grogginess. "Why are you here?"

The young man fidgeted on the porch in a rumpled black suit. "Sir, I have unfortunate news. Somebody tried to shoot the girl again tonight. He tried to kill me too."

The middle-aged man tuned out the rest—something about an injury. He needed to think on this more. The shooter had come after his leverage again. What must he do to keep his deal alive?

"Do you know who the shooter was?" he asked even though he already suspected the answer.

"Got a good look at him this time, and he's not from around here."

"*You* didn't get identified, did you?"

"No sir." The young man pulled himself up straight. "Of course not."

"Very well." The middle-aged man scowled. "Observe my target for the next twenty-four hours and report back."

The boy actually looked pouty. "I didn't get to implement my mischief for tonight. I've been looking forward to causing that bluenose more trouble."

"Fine." He waved his free hand. "Do whatever you want, but

information is my priority. Find out who the shooter is, and don't get caught. Got that?"

"Don't reckon I wanna see the man again."

"Then I have no more use for you." He moved to slam the door.

"All right!" The young man's desperate voice stayed his hand.

He smiled. "You'll get me my information?"

"Of course, I will. Sir."

"Good night. And don't call here again."

The young man disappeared, leaving the street quiet, but the town would be busy once word spread of another shooting, Lily Moore once again at the center of criminal behavior. A part of him relished seeing Bill Moore's daughter humiliated. It reflected on her father. And that was a thought that brought intense satisfaction.

Yes, he would revel in their misfortune for another few minutes. Then he would need to take care in how he handled his knowledge of the incident. He could manage outrage, indignation. He couldn't let on that he'd found out about it from a source who'd witnessed the attack firsthand. That would destroy everything he'd worked so hard to achieve.

CHAPTER 19

Dawn crept over the horizon as Lily stood on the grass between Katy's house and the barn that served as her veterinary practice. Her breath appeared in white puffs, and she rubbed her mittened hands together. She would have stomped her feet, too, but her left ankle ached. She hadn't mentioned that it hurt to either Miles or her brother last night because she didn't want them to baby her, so Katy had bandaged it after she set up a cold tub for Lily to soak it in.

Pieter ran over to Lily before trotting back to join Smokey, sniffing all the smells that came from being on an animal doctor's property. They seemed no worse for the excitement of the last few days, and Lily found that no small mercy. God had protected them just as He had her and Miles.

She could almost feel the hug Miles had given her last night. It had been a balm, yet her heart still felt bruised. Too many people had stomped on it the past few days, not to mention how her emotions had been an indecipherable tangle since being thrown into that hole. It was enough to have her safety threatened, but to have people blame her only refueled her determination to prove them wrong. She'd find the people who'd kidnapped her. She'd return her home to the sanctuary she intended. And she'd show her neighbors an unmarried woman could be as much an asset to Eagle as if she made a proper match.

"Mornin'." Katy interrupted Lily's mental speech as she emerged from the house with two steaming cups of coffee. "Joey rang. You can go on home, if you're pleasin.'"

Lily had taken an instant liking to this shy woman the day they'd met at an animal husbandry lecture in Chicago several years ago. Lily had convinced the dark-haired Irishwoman to return to Eagle with her, and their friendship had only deepened since Katy hung her shingle. Or so Lily had thought.

"Ya know, you can stay with me for as long as you're needin.'" Katy took a sip of the potent brew in her cup. The woman made her coffee strong. "Joey, he's a keepin' an eye on me house, so you're safe here as anyplace."

"Speaking of Joey." Lily grasped her cup with renewed determination to confront her friend. "Why didn't you tell me he was calling on you?"

Katy turned bright red but didn't look away. "Right. Joey, he didn't want you to feel poorly with all the marryin' going on."

"And you?"

"I'm right sorry, Lily. Really, I am." Katy teared up and Lily felt horrible. "I didn't want to keep it from ya, but Joey, he asked, you know. Then you disappeared, and I didn't know if I'd ever be tellin' you about us. I told Joey right then, I wanted to tell you just as soon as I got a chance."

Lily sighed. She understood, she did, even if it hurt more than she wanted it to. "I'm glad it's you Joey is calling on."

"Ya are? I was scared you wouldn't be approvin.'"

"Of you?" Lily gave her friend a hug with her free arm. "My twin brother is courting my best friend. It doesn't get much better than that."

Katy giggled through a shrug. "C'mere, what about that handsome man? Miles, right? You've takin' a likin' to him, have ya?"

"Oh no." He had a life elsewhere, and now she had something to prove as an unmarried woman. Yet she flushed despite herself.

"Hollyhocks." Katy laughed. "Are you tryin' to pull the wool over me eyes? Right. Or … You poor girl, ya really don't see it?"

"See what?" Lily crossed her arms, coffee cup resting on her opposite elbow, as if that action could defend her heart. Pieter appeared at her knees.

"See how much you like him."

"I do not!"

"Right. You do, Lily Moore." Katy took another sip of coffee, only partially hiding her grin. "And Joey thinks Miles likes you too."

Lily would never admit it, but those words warmed her more than the coffee. Thankfully, a dark-blue motorcar, sleek and shiny with a brown roof, pulled into the yard before Lily came up with an answer. Miles sat behind the wheel, but she didn't recognize the woman beside him. In an instant, it was as if someone dashed through her heart, slamming all the shutters to keep out the danger.

Pieter and Smokey ran up to Miles as he exited the car. Lily hated the giddiness she felt at seeing him here with a freshly shaved face and clean, pinstriped suit. He looked refreshed too. As though he'd slept.

Miles cast her a smile before he opened the passenger door and helped out the most gorgeous woman Lily had ever seen. Her red dress flowed along every curve, a belt at her waist showed its narrow contours, and her black heels raised her to nearly Miles's height. They looked perfect together. As though they belonged to one another.

"Right. Who is that?" Katy whispered to Lily as Miles ran his hands over Pieter's back.

Lily slowly shook her head, dread pushing hope over the precipice. Was this the type of lady professional Miles preferred? And how accurate a read could she really have on the man? She'd no knowledge of him outside his job of protecting her.

With a woman like that in the picture, what chance did Lily have of Miles ever pursuing a farm girl like her?

"She's very quaint, darling." Agnes smiled with artificially red lips as she patted Miles's cheek with her gloved hand. "Frankly, I'm surprised you're so attached."

Miles squelched the feeling of protectiveness that rushed over him as he waved Lily closer. She wore her customary flannel and jeans, hair in a messy pile at the crown of her head, and Miles thought she looked like a cup of hot cider. Warm, welcoming, and a taste of home.

"So you are the alleged kidnapping victim." Agnes held her fingers out for Lily to grasp, calculating eyes barely hidden behind the veil of her hat. "Agnes Fillery. Lawyer at the Craft Agency."

"Lily Moore." She accepted Agnes's outstretched hand but sent her unspoken question through a glance at Miles. *Can I trust her?*

After she surprised him by showing up at the boardinghouse that morning, Agnes wanted to return to the hotel where she'd set up a field base. Miles had insisted on picking up Lily first. She was part of this investigation, whatever anyone said, and Miles wanted to keep her as close as possible.

"Lily." Miles stuffed his hands in his pockets and rocked on his heels in an attempt to quell a strange nervousness in his stomach. "Would you join us? We need to discuss the investigation, and there are a few people I'd like you to meet. My boss arrived in town early this morning with Agnes and his vice president. This is our chance to get answers."

Lily toyed with the cuff of her flannel as she glanced at Agnes. The woman who'd faced down a gunman last night was nervous? Because of Agnes? She had no reason to be.

He tugged Lily out of Agnes's earshot. "Gio will be there too. He's a good friend I've known for over a decade. He's seen more poverty, violence, and destruction from a young age than any child should, yet he has a foundation of faith that doesn't ever seem to shake. We trust each other implicitly, and that's why he left everything to come here. It would mean a lot to me if you came."

Lily wasn't quick enough to hide a smile behind her cup. His heart warmed. She'd wanted to know whether his invitation was personal or professional. Well, he'd crossed that line last night when he'd lain awake tormenting himself over what he would have done had she been hurt.

His body still ached, and his shoulder throbbed, but it was a small price to pay for the sorry excuse of a protector he'd been.

"Oh, for heaven's sake. Either get in the car or stay here. Bank's closed." Agnes spun on her heel and headed for the driver's side of the Chevrolet—a replacement for the car Miles had appropriated from the ambushers, which Agnes had managed to return to a rental company in Milwaukee from which it was originally stolen.

"I'll need a few minutes." Lily retreated toward her friend, who watched the goings-on with eyes that saw beyond the surface of things.

"I'll wait for you." Miles returned his hands to his pockets and leaned against the hood of the car, keeping Agnes from driving away. Honestly, if he had another form of transportation, he wouldn't hesitate in putting distance between himself and Agnes. He could only manage her company for so long before he wanted to toss her into the nearest freight car that would take her miles and miles away.

Thankfully, it only took a few minutes for Lily to settle her dogs with her friend and change into a bright blue skirt, tan coat, and matching beret. Miles helped her slide into the back seat of the car before sitting beside her. Right where he wanted to stay.

What if he gave up the job to fulfill that wish? He'd been a sharpshooter his entire adult life. He didn't know how to be anything else. If it meant having a chance with Lily Moore, could he take the risk and step into something new?

He let the jostling of the car as it hit a bump in the road jar him back to reality. He couldn't let his thoughts carry him away. Why would Lily want to associate with someone who failed so miserably at protecting her? As it was, she huddled in the corner of the car, looking decidedly uncomfortable.

"How are you holding up?" He shifted his large frame enough to face her.

"I slept, so that was good." She gave him a small smile.

"We're about to get the answers to some of our questions. I'm looking forward to introducing you to Gio … and my boss."

Like a butterfly emerging from a cocoon, curiosity pushed away Lily's reticence. She sat forward, gloved hands clasped in her lap. Her head tipped at an angle, making her beret slip to the side. "Have you found out what kept him from answering your call?"

"Not yet. Agnes is notoriously tight-lipped about things that matter. It's the lawyer in her, I'm sure." He hesitated, then dove into the apology he'd been thinking about since he woke up. "But I will figure this out, Lily. I promised you I would protect you, and it seems I'm failing miserably at that job. I'm sorry. If you can't count on me to protect you, then I hope you will believe me when I say that my team and I will do whatever it takes to find whoever is doing this and put an end to it. You deserve that much. And more."

"Miles." She surprised him by placing her hand over his. "We're in this together, remember? You didn't fail to protect me last night, so please stop beating yourself up. You carry too much guilt about your brothers-in-arms already. You've sacrificed so much for me." Her fingers tightened around his. "And you're right, we're going to find out who did this. But we're going to do that together."

Miles turned his wrist to capture her hand in his, clearing the emotion from his voice. "You are a remarkable woman, Lily Moore. I wish people could see what I see in you. Somehow, you take the wrongs done to you and turn them into purpose. You inspire me, Lily. You make me believe …" *Believe that I'm a good guy, maybe even a hero, despite the mistakes I've made.*

"I don't know about all that." She laughed away a blush. "But I do know you have a good heart. It's why my dogs welcomed you into our pack."

And why I did too.

He heard her unspoken words, read them in her eyes. Welcomed into her family. He rubbed his chin to combat the emotion building behind his eyes.

Agnes cleared her throat, glancing back at them. "Pull it together, people. We're here."

Miles straightened. Showing his soft underbelly to Agnes hadn't been on his agenda, nor the smartest move he'd ever made. But Lily had a way of reaching into his heart and pulling out what was good and tender. Or maybe, rebuilding the ruins there.

CHAPTER 20

As Lily exited the motorcar, she pushed thoughts of Miles out of her head. Hard to do when he stood so much larger than life. His eyes flicked from her to the surrounding area, a hand resting over the gun he kept holstered under his left arm. The other hand he pressed to her back, guiding her ahead of him, his body a massive wall guarding her back. She bit her lip, hiding the pain in her ankle and anxious for what she was about to step into.

Agnes led them through the double doors into the four-story, square building that housed the Paradise Hotel in Hillway. She'd never been inside and stopped to gawk at the ornate decor, from the brown-and-ivory tile floor to the red carpeting covering the curved staircases that ran up both sides of the lobby. A crystal chandelier hung from above. Brass banisters lined the stairs. And directly before them stood a massive oak reception desk.

Miles gently urged her toward the right staircase, where Agnes tapped her foot. She belonged in a place like this. Frankly, Miles did, too, with his square shoulders, dashing smile, and confident stature. Lily didn't. Her coat, though her going-out coat, not her work coat, was worn about the elbows, cuffs, and along the buttons. Her shoes were sturdy Oxfords, not elegant pumps like Agnes's. She'd taken only minutes to pin up her hair and didn't feel anywhere near dressed nicely enough for a place like this.

With Agnes before and Miles behind, Lily had no choice but to march onward, careful not to draw attention by limping. She tried to remember her resolution to prove herself, but the hotel atmosphere wasn't her usual sphere. Give her a field or a lake with her dogs, and she could prove plenty. But here?

Agnes veered off on the second floor, leading down a hallway with doors on either side. Stopping before one, she knocked. "I have them," she said in a singsong voice.

The door opened, and first Agnes, then Miles were dragged inside, Miles pulling Lily with him before the door slammed shut behind them.

"Thank you, Agnes." A bald man in a tailored suit stood before them. He came nowhere near Miles's size or strength, but the presence he exuded stifled the room.

Lily stepped closer to Miles.

"Mr. Craft." Miles held out a hand. "After I didn't hear from you, I wasn't expecting—"

"I know." The man waved him off while shaking his hand. "There have been developments. This is Miss Moore?"

"Lily Moore, meet my boss, Karl Craft."

"A pleasure, Miss Moore." Mr. Craft lifted her fingers five inches shy of kissing her knuckles. Releasing her hand, he smoothed the lapel of his suit coat. "This is my vice president, Richard Berkley, formerly of the BOI."

Lily glanced at Miles, and he leaned down to whisper, "Bureau of Investigation." A government man. Ex-government man. Who could also be Mr. Craft's twin, only lighter-skinned as if he avoided the sun. He was well-dressed in a blue-checked suit, with confidence that rivaled Mr. Craft's, and he nodded at Miles before glancing over Lily to give Agnes a full perusal.

"Meet Miles's acquaintance, Giosue Vella." Mr. Craft motioned another man forward.

"It is good to see you, *mi amico!*" Gio embraced Miles in a crushing hug, and Miles laughed as he returned it with equal enthusiasm. Gio was stocky and thick, with hair as black as Katy's and as curly as Pieter's. He wore a brown vest with a faded shirt that made his skin darker than any farmer's she'd ever seen.

Miles drew Lily forward and introduced her.

"*Giglia! Bellissima!*" Gio opened his arms as wide as his smile.

"He called you a beautiful lily," Miles whispered.

Stunned into silence, Lily tentatively offered her hand. Gio snatched it, only to pull her close and kiss both her cheeks. Then he clapped his hands on both of her shoulders, the warmest, most welcoming light turning his dark eyes into starlight.

"The pleasure, it is all mine, *Signorina* Moore." Only he pronounced her last name *Moor-ray*.

Miles clasped Gio's shoulder with a smile. "He's a charmer, this one."

Mr. Craft cleared his throat, stopping Gio's reply. "Sit, we have much to discuss." He waved them to a small table tucked into the corner of the room. The room also contained two couches with a low table between and a door likely leading to a bedroom. Two other men stood to the side, dressed in black suits with revolvers on their belts. Security?

Miles held out a chair for Lily, then sat beside her. Gio settled to her left, Mr. Craft and Mr. Berkley across the table, and Agnes off to the side.

"Good so far?" Miles whispered.

She nodded even though she felt entirely overwhelmed.

"Miss Moore?" Mr. Craft beckoned for her attention. "Berkley has several contacts at the BOI that, since Congress passed the Federal Kidnapping Act, specialize in kidnapping investigations."

Mr. Berkeley straightened his jacket. "When I mentioned the hallmarks of your case to them, they admitted there were no signs of kidnapping."

Lily gaped. "But I *was* kidnapped."

"Other than your word for it, we have no proof." Mr. Berkeley looked down his nose at her, and she instantly disliked him. "Everyone thinks you ran away, so you could be making up the story—"

Miles practically growled. "I found her in a hole."

"I heard your story, Wright." Mr. Berkley squared his shoulders.

"Then how can you say she wasn't kidnapped?"

"Were her hands tied?" Mr. Berkeley shot back. "Was she gagged? Did—"

"That's enough." Mr. Craft slammed his hand on the table. "There is more here than a simple abduction, whether she was in on her kidnapping or not."

In on it? Lily fought to keep her composure. This was worse than in Eagle. At least, there, when people didn't believe her, they shook their heads in pity. Here, it felt as though spears were striking her heart, leaving her nowhere to hide.

Miles rested his elbows on the table, taking up a full quarter of the space. "Not only was my crew murdered when the booby trap went off, but Miss Moore and I were shot at several times upon arriving in Eagle. The question isn't whether Miss Moore was kidnapped but whether the ambush has to do with Elite Company or Miss Moore."

"Valid question." Mr. Craft steepled his hands against his mouth. "On my way here, I detoured up north to see to the location personally."

Lily blinked back her surprise, nerves crawling. "You saw where they … where they … kept me?"

Miles pulled his hands to his lap, tension easing from his shoulders with a slight release of air. "What did you find there, sir?"

"I saw to the recovery of the bodies but found nothing helpful regarding the perpetrators." Mr. Craft leaned back in his chair. "We will focus the investigation here. On the living. Especially since it appears you've attracted unwanted attention."

"And makes me consider, Miss Moore," Mr. Berkley said, intensity radiating off of him as his gaze pierced her. "Did you say anything to anyone about your so-called kidnapping? Does anyone suspect you didn't leave town of your own volition? Have you told anyone of Craft Agency involvement?"

Lily felt exposed and confused by his hostility. She hadn't even told Joey the whole story yet. So what did Mr. Berkley think she'd done? Gossip around the entire town of Eagle? To what end?

"I sincerely doubt—" Mr. Berkley was interrupted by a knock at the door.

Craft nodded to one of the sentries. "That will be the final member of our party. The man who originally hired us to find Miss Moore."

Lily leaned around Miles's bulk to have a better view. Could finding the answer to at least one question be so easy? The door opened, and the silhouette of a man with broad but slumped shoulders stepped in from the hallway. He wore his best suit and held his hat in his hands.

Lily stared. "Dad?"

"Miss Moore's father?" Miles hissed at Craft. How could they not know he was the one who'd hired them to find Lily?

"You didn't know?" Lily looked at him with hurt in her eyes.

"No." Miles grabbed her cold hands. "I swear, I would have told you."

Lily blinked, the mistrust washing away. She believed him. *Thank you, God.*

"Karl." Mr. Moore stomped into the room, waving his hat at Lily. "What's the meaning of this?"

Lily returned Miles's grip as if he were her anchor. Miles wished he could step between her and her father as Mr. Moore stood toe to toe with Craft, something few would dare. Silent sparks flew between the two men until Berkley pried them apart. Rather, Craft stepped back, and Moore held his ground.

"Sorry, Bill." Craft seemed genuine in his apology. "I didn't know she'd be here."

Didn't that make Miles feel worse? He'd given in to his desire to have her with him only to put her in the middle of this mess. He squeezed Lily's hand in apology, and she pursed her lips.

"We were supposed to have a quiet reunion at your headquarters. After the strike." Moore's hands flailed.

"I know, Bill." Craft never used the placating tone he attempted on Lily's father, and it wasn't working now, given the red rising in Moore's face.

"No, you don't know!" Moore shouted. "Because you didn't follow my instructions, we have the entire town involved in female hysterics!"

"Hysterics?" Lily squeaked, yanking her hand from Miles's grasp as she stood. "I was kidnapped, nearly blown up, then shot at. Twice."

Gio's hand on his arm kept Miles from entering the fray—a good thing, considering he had no control over his emotions right now. Anger and shame whirled into a cyclone, ripping at his heart.

"I am well aware." Craft kept his voice calm, showing why he was the boss. "The situation is no longer a simple rescue. The loss of my men is highly concerning. What we need are answers, particularly to the question of whether these additional attacks are targeting Miss Moore."

"Do you think I brought the danger to Eagle with me?" Miles had to ask.

"And who are you?" Moore faced him down.

Still sitting, Miles had to look up at the man. Not acceptable if he wanted Lily's father to have an ounce of respect toward him. Not that he deserved it right now. But he cared about Lily, and he wouldn't give her father any more ammunition against him if he could help it. Miles rose to his full stature and held out a hand. "Sergeant Miles Wright, US Marines, retired, sir."

"Dad, this is the man who saved me." Lily stepped near. "Saved me every time."

"He should have taken you to headquarters so he only had to risk your life once."

Miles's face heated. Lily touched his arm, and even through the sleeve of his suit coat, he could feel her calming effect. It gave him just enough breath to whisper a prayer.

"I'm not convinced any of this is related." Berkley sharply ended Miles's moment of peace. "Unless you're a threat to someone, Miss Moore."

"Honestly, Mr. Berkley," Lily snapped at him. "Why would someone kidnap me, then try to kill me? Isn't that counterproductive?"

"That may be the question of the hour." Agnes spoke for the first time, tapping a perfectly manicured nail on the worn table, having discarded her gloves. "You have been with Miles at each shooting."

"You're the one my son told me about?" Moore glared at Miles—an identical match to the way Joey Moore had looked at him.

Before Miles could respond, Berkley edged toward Lily. "Have you a reason to want Wright dead?"

"Me?" Lily turned a shade white.

"Lay off, Berkley." Miles tucked Lily against his side.

"Getting kind of personal there, Wright?" Berkley sneered.

"I agree." Moore balled his fists.

Lily pushed away from Miles, putting herself between him and the other men. "Mr. Wright has been the one person who believed me when I said I was kidnapped. He's kept me safe through every danger so far. So don't you dare malign him. Any of you. He's been perfectly honorable and a gentleman."

Miles froze. Emotion he hadn't let himself feel in seventeen years strangled his throat. Lily—the woman he was supposed to protect—had inserted herself in the line of verbal fire to defend him. He hadn't had a champion since he buried his parents and went to war. Since his world changed forever and he determined his life was only worth what he could give to save someone else. And yet she dared protect him despite how he'd failed.

"Enough." Craft's command sliced into the room, effectively reinstating Miles's soldiering facade. "Until we have actual intelligence, I want Miles in Eagle. No objections, understood?" He didn't wait for agreement. "Wright, next step?"

First, assuring himself Lily's house was safe enough for her to return. "Interviewing the last people who saw Lily before she disappeared." And the witnesses Joey talked about.

"I'm going too." Lily folded her arms.

"Absolutely not!" Moore.

"I don't think—" Berkley.

Lily stared both of them down better than even Craft had done. "I don't need anyone's permission to do as I see fit. This is my life at stake. I will not stay in the background to let someone take from me again. I am going to track down the person who kidnapped me whether I have your support or not." Lily took her coat from where Miles had laid it on the back of the nearest couch. "I know what happened to me. I was there. My clothes are still stained with the dirt from the hole in which they left me. My ears still ring with the explosions. And my skin crawls with how close those bullets came to hitting me. I want the person who did this. Who killed the men who came to save me. Who nearly murdered Mr. Wright because of me."

The men were silent, looking at anything but her. Except Miles. He couldn't look away. Lily's beauty shone like a bright beacon, her strength a harbor. Jiminy, he liked her.

"We've never allowed a victim to participate in an ensuing investigation." Agnes's silver tongue felt like hot iron. "We should not start now."

"Then there is no more reason for me to stay. Miles, I'd like to go home."

As if on quaking ground, Miles walked unsteadily to gather his things by the door.

"Stay away from her, Miles." Agnes's voice followed him as he escorted Lily from the room. "She could get you killed."

If that's what it took to keep Lily Moore safe, he'd gladly make the sacrifice. For the first time, however, death felt like a loss because dying for her left him with one regret—not living long enough to see where a relationship with her could take them.

CHAPTER 21

The entire drive back to Eagle, Miles wracked his brain for something to say. Lily stared out the passenger window with her arms across her body until they reached the outskirts of the town proper.

"Can we pick up my dogs before going home?" she asked, glancing at him for the first time since he helped her into the vehicle.

"Of course." Miles frowned as she turned away again. He briefly touched her arm before returning his hand to the shifter. "Lily, I know what happened at the headquarters was hard for you. Are you all right?"

Tears glittered in her green eyes when she looked back at him. "To hear your bosses doubt everything I went through—my father, too—it wears a woman down, and I don't know who to trust. I know I said we'd be in this investigation together, but maybe it's not worth it. Maybe you should listen to Agnes and stay away from me."

"Not a chance." Miles squeezed her clasped hands.

"I can't be the reason ..." Her voice choked, and she tried to pull away. He held on for a moment longer.

"We're in this together, Lily. You were right. I need your help just as much as I want to protect you."

Lily swallowed.

Miles slowed the vehicle as they drove past the church. He tapped his left thumb on the steering wheel. "Something about the shootings has been bothering me. Maybe you can help me sort through it."

"You really want my help?"

"Absolutely."

She took and released a huge breath. Miles held his.

"I'm glad." She raised a shoulder, shy hope sparkling in her eyes.

He grinned, not sorry at all that he'd only told her one of his motives. He wouldn't admit he simply wanted to stay in her presence a while longer.

Miles parked on Main Street two blocks from the church so their destination was not obvious.

"You're positive it's safe to do this?" she asked as they emerged from his Chevy.

"I don't think anyone will expect us to be here today." Miles snatched his binoculars from his gear bag and locked the car before they set out on the plank walk that ran in front of the stores along Main Street.

When they paused in front of the church, Lily shifted her weight onto one leg. "So what exactly is bothering you about the cemetery incident?"

Miles raised his binoculars, scanned the tombstones. All seemed quiet. "Can you sit exactly where you were when the first shot was fired on Sunday?" The shooter had stayed behind the trees on this side of the church.

Without a word, she worked her way toward the statue. Miles kept his eyes moving—until he spotted her limp. She hadn't said anything about her ankle bothering her, nor had he seen her favoring it. Had she hurt it worse last night than anyone thought?

He raised his binoculars to get a better look at her, troubled to see relief on her face when she finally sat on the bench and waved. He acknowledged her. Studied her beautiful face. Freckles dotted her nose. The sun caused light brown streaks in her hair. He shook himself, moved the binoculars beyond her to the grave marker chipped by Sunday's first shot. He'd address her ankle later.

The chip was high and to the left. Had the shooter stepped out of the trees, he would have had a cleaner shot and a better angle, the risk being exposure. Which is why a good sniper used only one bullet to finish the job. Because once that first shot was fired, secrecy didn't matter. Everyone would hear the gunshot.

Only, Miles hadn't heard it. Not the first one. Now he knew what was bothering him. The sound. The muffled pop so opposite the sharp report he usually heard when he fired his Springfield. There could only be one reason for that. The shooter had used a silencer.

A cold feeling swelled in his gut. There was no doubt in his mind that first bullet should have killed one of them, a silent, deadly shot bringing death without warning. Then why did it line up with Lily's left shoulder?

Miles closed his eyes, pictured where he had been sitting. Nausea spread. The shooter hadn't aimed at Lily. That bullet was meant for him.

"Will you tell me why you look a little green?" Lily asked as Miles accelerated out of town and toward Katy's to pick up her dogs. She'd tried to get Miles to talk as they went from one bullet hole to the next, but he stayed tight-lipped, and she struggled to keep her irritation at bay.

Miles scrubbed the stubble beginning to show on his chin, making a chaffing sound against his callused hand. "I think the shooter aimed at me."

"You?" Her astonishment ripped her attention from the curvy road. She brought it back just in time to direct Miles on where to turn.

"Now that I figured out he used a silencer," Miles said once they bounced down the dirt road between two cornfields that would eventually lead to Katy's house. "I'm confident the shooter last night was the same as Sunday."

A shiver ran down Lily's spine. "He wanted to kill you?"

"Yes." It was a word loaded down with so much meaning. So many questions. If Miles was the one the shooter aimed at on Sunday, why hadn't he just shot Miles while he was lying on the ground last night? Or break into the boardinghouse to finish the job? Or kill him any other time Miles was alone? Why include her as a target? To muddle it?

Lily stifled a sigh. She wanted to help Miles, not add to his worry. "Did seeing the cemetery help you make sense of the shooting?"

"It made it worse." Miles rubbed his thigh before returning his hand to the shifter as if he couldn't sit still. "Confirming it was the same shooter as in the woods gives me the ability to compare the instances, see the similarities."

"That sounds like a good thing."

"Except that now I'm fairly certain as to the identity of the shooter. If I'm right, he's a second-rate army sniper who boasts about how much he enjoys using a Maxim Silencer. Like President Roosevelt did. The former one, I mean. Old Teddy. But Charles Wade made his name doing what an honorable commander would never ask of his men. He might as well be an assassin."

"A what?"

"A trigger man. Wade also wanted to be a sniper with the Craft Agency. Only, Craft hired me."

"Does that mean you think this Charles Wade still wants your job? He's already been denied once, so how would he be sure to get it? Even if he ... removes the competition? Unless ..." Lily swallowed hard as the idea that there could be an inside man within the Craft Agency sank in. One high up in leadership who could make hiring decisions. "Are you sure you should keep your boss informed of your investigation?"

"You mean we should trust your brother more than Craft?"

Lily tried to forgive Miles's tone. "I didn't exactly mean that, but, yes, maybe we should."

"I'm worried about your dad, Lily."

So was she. Especially since he was the person who connected Lily to the Craft Agency. "What do we do, Miles? Who do we trust? How do we stay alive?"

Miles took such a long moment to consider her question that Lily knew the words he spoke were not meant idly. "First of all, we can trust each other. We're in this together. I mean that, Lily. I trust you."

Lily nodded, wanting to verbally agree wholeheartedly yet afraid of getting her heart broken.

"Second, we can trust Gio. He's not tied to my company, and I would put my life in his hands without a second thought. Even more, I trust him with your life."

"I feel that way about Joey too. He already knows I was kidnapped. Why not tell him about Dad and your job and the agency? Maybe he can help."

"Can I think on it?" Miles squeezed her fingers. "Craft's policy against working with local police, especially in rural towns, has good cause. Ineptitude has cost lives more than once. However, I'm willing to break that rule if I know Joey won't compromise us."

"He wouldn't."

"He's an officer of the law, Lily, and I think he's an honorable one, which means he's going to follow the rules. It may not be wise to put him in a position where he has to choose between his morals and your safety."

"You think he'd have to make that type of choice?"

Before Miles could answer, the cornfields gave way to Katy's property. Miles pulled to a stop beside the vet's farm truck. Lily waited for Miles to apply the brake before putting her desire to trust to the test. The words were quiet, but she forced them out. "I'm scared, Miles."

"I know." Miles gripped her hand, a cascade of emotions in his eyes. Lily wished she could read them all, but they moved too quickly to latch onto even one.

CHAPTER 22

Charles Wade stared at the young man his employer insisted he track down. Standing here at the edge of a half-harvested field of corn wasn't worth his time. But he wanted the money promised for the job, and the only way that could happen was to follow his employer's directions by meeting with the kid.

"My boss needs Lily Moore alive." The kid puffed out his chest as if he were someone important.

"My employer says he and your boss are not at odds. The dame is merely collateral. Acceptable collateral." They wouldn't even be having this discussion if Wright hadn't leaned forward just as Wade had pulled the trigger in the cemetery.

"You want the bodyguard." The kid bounced like a jackrabbit. "Getting rid of him would make my job easier."

As if that were Wade's sole purpose here. "Then we have an understanding. You'll stay out of my way."

"Whoa, whoa, no way. We need leverage, and I already have a plan to make that happen. You stay out of my way. Then you can have the big man."

Wade narrowed his gaze. He could clip this kid and be done with it, but it was messy. No need to bring the coppers looking too close.

"You ruined my plans last night, so I want tonight." The kid sounded annoyingly petulant. "With the Farmer's Holiday Association determined to strike again, my boss needs Miss Moore in a particular frame of mind."

Wade tapped his thumb against his leg. If the kid's plan worked, it would distract Wright from Wade's real goal. The man had been glomming what rightly belonged to Wade for far too long, and it was time to put an end to it. Permanently. Another day of patience wouldn't kill Wade. In fact, it may be better to let Wright face the humiliation of publicly failing before sending him into a deep, deep sleep. The thought made Wade smile.

∽∾

"That's my dad's truck," Lily said as they turned into her drive, bringing Miles back to reality.

The past fifteen minutes as they drove from Katy's to Lily's home had been the most enjoyable he'd yet spent with Lily. They'd shared companionable conversation, the dogs poking their noses between the seats, with the backdrop of a beautiful fall afternoon. Golden sun had reflected off brown cornstalks swaying under a dark-blue sky. Red leaves had floated down the curving road while a hawk soared high above them.

"What should we do?" Lily's voice trembled.

"Do you want to talk with him now?"

"I don't see how I can avoid him, so I might as well get this over with."

"Do you want me to talk to him first?"

Lily shook her head. "I need to do this. I'll get us answers."

"So you'll invite him in?"

"No. I don't want him staying that long."

"Then put yourself between his truck and the house." Miles gently squeezed her wrist. "I'll stay by the car, but I'll be close if you need me."

Lily nodded, then raised her chin and straightened her back.

He parked the car facing the road for an easy getaway, a habit he hoped he wouldn't need to act on in Lily's case. Hand on his weapon, he scanned the area as she freed her dogs from the back seat. No sign of Wade or any other danger. He felt Mr. Moore's scrutiny but ignored it. He'd honor Lily's wishes and save his own questioning of the man for later.

Moore paced between his truck and the house until Lily reached him. She tucked a strand of hair behind her ear. "Hi, Dad."

"Why were you at the meeting today?" Mr. Moore ran his hands through brown-gray, wavy hair. "Why didn't you go to Craft's headquarters right after that man of Craft's found you, as you were supposed to?"

"Why did you hire Mr. Craft?" Lily somehow managed to keep the frustration out of her voice.

Tension hung in the air as Moore continued to pace. Miles leaned against the Chevy, gaze roaming the yard along with the dogs, arms crossed to keep his right hand near his Colt. No intuitive warning bells sounded.

"Before you were taken ... had you really run off somewhere?" Moore came to a stop in front of Lily.

Miles kept a tight grip on his emotions. Why did everyone think Lily ran away?

"No, Dad. One minute, I was eating at O'Reilly's. The next, I was stuffed in someone's trunk."

"O'Reilly's? What were you doing there?"

"It was a business meeting. Why hire Mr. Craft's people to find me if you weren't even certain about my ... leaving?"

"Karl Craft is an old acquaintance of mine. He did this as a favor. The timing of your disappearance bothered me. He promised to look into it. Your mother suspected you left because of Amy's marriage, and, well ..." Moore waved his hand as if that finished his sentence. "I wanted to believe that, too, but ..."

"What aren't you telling me?" Pieter and Smokey must have sensed their mistress's unease because they both trotted back to her.

Her father shifted his weight and sighed. "I think I may be the reason you were kidnapped."

Miles stepped forward, barely holding himself in check, torn between respecting Lily's wishes and wanting to shake answers from her father.

"What do you mean?" Lily lifted Smokey into a tight hug. Pieter sat on her foot.

"It's better if you don't know the details, which is why I hired Craft to find you and expected you to go straight to his headquarters. Whether your mother was right or my fears were, his men could take you to safety."

Had Miles made a mistake in allowing her to return home? He wouldn't have forced her to stay away, but had he exhausted every form of ethical persuasion? Or had he allowed his grief —or worse, his regard for her—to keep him from making the right decision?

"Were you given a ransom demand?" Lily set Smokey free to romp once again, and Pieter lay beside her feet.

Mr. Moore shook his head. "As I said, nothing felt right about your disappearance. We can't lose you, Lily." Her father's emotion pricked Miles's heart. And conscience.

"I'm not going anywhere." Lily flung her arms around her father's neck. "Miles is going to make sure I stay safe."

No pressure there.

Mr. Moore barked a harsh laugh. "Miles, huh?"

Lily rested back on her heels, an adorable grin on her face. "He did save me, you know."

Yeah, he did. Despite everything.

"Just remember, that was his job. He was paid to do that."

True. And didn't that throw cold reality at him?

"I don't want to see you hurt, Lily. Because of my decisions or because of his."

Neither did Miles.

Lily stepped away from her father. "Then tell me what's really going on."

"I came to persuade you to go to Craft's headquarters in New York. At least until all of this unrest passes."

"Dad." Lily shook her head.

Mr. Moore cast Miles a look that had Miles standing taller. "Craft will cover expenses, and Mr. Wright can escort you."

Miles's mind raced. He'd received no such order. Then again, he hadn't yet returned to the boardinghouse. Of course, he would take Lily wherever she wanted to go—he'd proved that much already—but what about their investigation? What about finding Lily's kidnapper, his team's killer?

"I'll tell Craft you can leave within the hour." Mr. Moore opened the door to his truck.

"Dad." Lily caught his arm. "I'm not going to New York."

"I insist, Lily. Take the dogs with you."

"I—" She looked over at Miles as if seeking permission. Permission to stay. He'd come to know that much about her. She wouldn't give up this investigation any more than he would. But standing up to her brother was one thing, whereas disobeying her father ...

Miles stepped forward. "If Miss Moore desires to stay—"

"You'll defy a direct order?" Mr. Moore demanded.

Miles raised a shoulder. "I already have once, on this exact matter."

"I'm staying, Dad." Lily crossed her arms, her voice trembling. "I refuse to run away. Not after ... I can't cower. I won't."

Mr. Moore tapped a finger on her nose. "You always were too self-reliant for a woman. I blame your grandfather."

"Dad."

"I know when I'm beat." He climbed into his truck. "You stay safe, Lily, hear me?"

Lily's shoulders sagged. "I love you, too, Dad."

CHAPTER 23

"Lily, wait!" Miles barely held his watchful stance while Mr. Moore drove away before dashing toward Lily as she trudged for the back door of her house. He pressed her shoulder as she pulled open the screen. "Let me."

Without looking at him, Lily stepped aside. Miles rested his right hand on his Colt while turning the knob. It moved easily under his hand.

"Stay here." He left her in the mudroom as he looked in every nook, starting with the lower level. Pieter and Smokey trailed after him as he moved to the kitchen and sitting area and then into the bedroom he discovered through the doorway under the stairs. A quilt covered the bed, and dust coated the dresser. He gladly left the stuffy room behind.

Up the steps and down the hallway, he went alone, the dogs waiting at the bottom of the steps. The first rooms on the left and right were empty. At the end of the short hall, he found Lily's room. Her personal items strewn about a dressing table, clothes tossed atop a tangled quilt, the sweet scent of her lingering, raised too many questions in his mind. Such as, what would it be like to come home and join her here?

He huffed out a breath as if someone punched him in the gut. He had no business letting a thought like that enter his mind, especially at a time like this. Anyway, that life was not meant for him, no matter his daydreams.

He finished checking the room and made his way back downstairs. The dogs followed him back to the mudroom where he found Lily waiting as he'd asked. "It's safe. I'll go check the barn."

A few moments later, Lily met him in the yard, the turmoil from her dad's visit washed from her face. "All good?"

"Yes, thankfully." Miles let the tension he carried in his shoulders slip out with a sigh.

"I'm ready for the next step in our investigation. When do we interview people?"

With a chuckle, Miles held up his hands in mock surrender. "I'd like to make sure we keep you safe, first."

"You checked the house. What more can you do?"

"I'd like to bring Gio over here. He's an expert with a radiotelegraph … something or other. I can't begin to explain it, but he can, and it would make me feel better if he set up security for your home."

"He can do that?" She rubbed the cuff of her coat.

"Not just can—he would be delighted to do so. And then maybe you could make hot chocolate for us?"

"I'd like that very much." Lily rewarded him with her brilliant smile, and his heart took wing. How was he supposed to walk away once this was over?

While she waited for Miles to return with Gio, Lily put an apple pastry into the oven, already anticipating its warm, autumn scent wafting through her house, spreading comfort and peace. Her ankle throbbed, but baking gave her a sense of normalcy, even if she lacked sugar these days. She would need to put a compress on her ankle before bed tonight. Especially since she kept jumping at every little noise. Miles had reluctantly left her alone while he rendezvoused with his friend in an attempt to keep their meeting hidden from Miles's employer. She hoped their cloak-and-dagger worked.

As usual, the dogs heard the motorcar before she did. She wiped her hands on a towel, then reached for her shotgun before peering out the picture window. Miles's car. At least, the one he and the lawyer had used that morning. The anxiety swirling in her stomach changed directions. She tried to tell herself it was due to the dangerous situation she—they—were in, but this new feeling only appeared when Miles Wright was around.

Miles spotted her watching out the window and gave her a quick grin while driving the car around to the back of the house. The man with black hair she'd met at the hotel rode in the passenger seat.

Miles glanced at the shotgun in her hand when she met him in the mudroom. "I see you have your friend. That's good. Can't be too careful."

She peeked around Miles's bulk to Gio behind him. "Welcome to my home."

"*Grazie*, Giglia. It is good to see you again."

"Come in, please." She snatched up Smokey before leading the way into the kitchen.

"Something smells good." Miles reached out to Pieter. The dog's tail went from calm to gale force as he rammed his head into Miles's hand. He dragged himself across Miles's legs, spun back around, and plopped down on Miles's feet, looking up at Miles with what amounted to a smile.

"That's puppy love if I've ever seen it." Lily laughed.

She put the shotgun back on the hooks that held it over the archway between her kitchen and sitting room. Gio still stood in the mudroom, bushy brows low over dark eyes.

"Gio," Lily asked, "are you comfortable around dogs?"

"I have not known many." Gio dragged his newsboy cap from his head while keeping his eyes fastened on Pieter.

"If you don't want their attention, either turn your back to them or simply say *no*."

Gio gave a single nod.

"They're friendly." Miles gave Pieter a solid pat. "Hold your hand out and let them sniff."

"Like this?" Gio extended his hand, palm up. Pieter nosed it. Man and dog looked like a matched pair—short, stocky, and topped with a mop of curly black hair.

"That's good." Lily opened a jar on her shelf and pulled out a handful of kibble she used as dog treats. She gave a few to Gio. The sparkle returned to his brown eyes. She could see why Miles—anyone—would want this man as a friend. His mere presence exuded a warm welcome.

Miles winked, causing her heart to flip-flop as he snagged a treat. He slipped his to Smokey, his arm brushing against Lily and making her stomach act as unruly as the dog in her arms.

Gio held one of his treats out to Pieter, using his thumb and three fingers to pinch it.

"Put it in the palm of your hand." She demonstrated, giving a treat to Smokey.

Gio squared his shoulders and followed her direction. Pieter gently took it, and Gio smiled, his entire face breaking into lines that showed how often that expression appeared. "He is *gentile*." Gentle? An apt description of both man and dog.

"Thank you." Lily scratched Pieter's ear. "Please, come in and make yourselves comfortable. Cake will be ready shortly, then I can make hot chocolate."

"You've outdone yourself." Miles seemed much more relaxed than he had when he'd left earlier. Gio's effect, no doubt.

"I would like to begin my task, if I may?" Gio gave Pieter his last treat as if they had always been the best of friends. "However, I will break for the cake. *Il pasticcino*, it is my ... what is the idiom?"

"Achilles' heel?" Miles offered.

"*Si, si.*" Gio waved his hands. "It is as you say. The Achilles' heel."

Miles laughed and patted his belly. "Mine, too, mi amico. Mine too."

Lily's gaze bounced between the two men like a tennis ball. They seemed so comfortable with each other, even as Gio switched languages more rapidly than she could discern the meaning of the lyrical phrases.

These moments gave her a tiny window into their real selves. And it was a show she wouldn't tire of anytime soon.

At Gio's prompting, Miles followed Lily out to the barn to feed her dogs while Gio plied his trade inside. Gio made it sound as though he was kicking them out while he worked, but Miles knew better. His friend was a romantic at heart and had been matchmaking for as long as Miles knew him. This once, Miles didn't mind.

"What is Gio going to do?" Lily asked, securing the dog run gate behind them.

Besides attempt to create a romantic setting? "Install a private, temporary radiotelegraph alarm system." Miles leaned against the fence. Long shadows stretched out before him as the afternoon waned. "He's a brilliant radio man, and I don't pretend to understand it. He will set up a command post of sorts nearby and will be able to relay messages to me from you."

"I don't even own a radio. How—"

"Don't worry, he'll teach you." He smiled to hopefully ease her discomfort. "We'll use coded Morse, but all you need to know is how to send an SOS. Perhaps we'll set up a less urgent code as well. That way, if you're feeling any nervousness at all or your dogs sense something out of the ordinary, tap it out, and I will be here in minutes."

Her cheeks reddened. "I don't need you barraging into my house."

"No, of course not. I'll scout any potential dangers before knocking at your door."

Lily stayed quiet as she picked up two piles of dog droppings.

"Is that a good plan for you?" It would certainly make him sleep better, knowing she had some type of security.

Lily threw the offending piles into the covered garbage bin in the corner and stuffed her hands into the pockets of her heavy coat as she wandered into the corral area, dogs following. He spotted her limp again, would have spoken up, but it seemed she wanted to disguise it.

Miles searched the expanse behind the barn as he joined her. The late afternoon held the warmth of the setting sun even as a cold wind drifted across the fields. One or two stars blinked in the pinking sky. Lily stopped in the middle of the corral and stared up at them.

"Do you hunt?"

Her question surprised him. "Hunt?"

Lily nodded.

"I do." He leaned his elbows on the fence beside her. "Did. Haven't for a long time. You train hunting dogs and are a good shot, but I don't see you enjoying the sport."

"Pieter loves fowl season." She pointed to a flock of birds flying over the trees in *V* formation.

"Spaniel, you said he was. What does a dog like that do to help a hunter?"

"The American Water Spaniel is specially designed to both flush and retrieve. Pheasant, duck, quail. I take my dogs hunting because it lets them use their innate skills. Pieter is teaching Smokey how to track what I shoot down and bring it back. Out on the marsh, the two of them are in their element, doing what they were bred to do."

Her gaze left the flock to watch a squirrel climb up what looked like a hitching post twenty-five yards away. It chattered at the lone tin can, drawing the dogs' attention. Smokey raised his paws on the fence and barked.

Lily laughed. "You won't get it from here, boy, and I'm not setting you loose. Let the squirrel gather its food for winter."

"Your dogs aren't the only ones in their element," Miles said.

"I grew up on a farm, so I have great respect for the circle of life." Pieter brushed up against her legs, and she ran a hand over his curly back. "The Conservation Committee's use of tags and stamps for hunting is a part of balancing out the sport, as is the development of wildlife refuges. If a species is decimated due to overhunting and overfishing or a drought such as we've been experiencing, it can have a devastating impact on the whole area. I've already noticed a drop in the number of birds on my lake."

"Besides tags and stamps, what else can be done?"

"This year, there is no open season in Wisconsin. They needed to take such drastic action because hunting is no longer about provision. I still do not like to consider it sport, even though many do nowadays. In my view, taking a dog like Pieter hunting gives him an opportunity to ply his craft while also providing humans their food. Tagged hunting also keeps species that could overwhelm an area at healthy population levels, which then protects the topography, which, in turn, provides shelter and food for all creatures. I know it isn't perfect, but it's my way of being a good steward in the place God has planted me."

Her voice faded, and Miles dared not move. He didn't want her to stop speaking.

"Sorry. I didn't mean to ramble on like that."

"Please don't apologize. I like to hear about what you're passionate about." He reached for her hand. Thought better of it.

She patted the worn wood of the fence. "You know, I've always considered my home my retreat, my refuge from the gossip and rumors. Now it feels isolated. As though the shadows are creeping ever closer." She shivered.

Miles fisted his hands to keep himself from pulling her into an embrace. It was one thing after nearly being shot, but here? In the golden sunset? He wouldn't give in, couldn't overstep.

"I just don't understand. I live a quiet, peaceful life. What possessed someone to kidnap me? Why would someone want to kill us?" Her voice cracked.

"Hey." He grabbed her shoulders so she faced him. "Don't lose hope. We've got the agency behind us now and Gio here. With their help, we'll get this sorted out soon so you can get back to doing what you love."

She nodded and leaned forward so that just her forehead touched his chest. Miles's heart melted. He pressed a hand to the back of her head and wrapped the other arm around her shoulders. She wasn't sobbing, but he could feel her ragged breaths. With each one, he prayed he could keep his promise.

The stillness was broken by her dogs' barking from the other side of the corral, their tails wagging. Must be Gio.

"Sorry." Lily pulled away, swiping at her eyes, her cheeks as red as the tree in front of her house. "I love my home, and I hate not feeling safe here. I guess it all tumbled out."

The oaf that he was, he again didn't trust his words not to ruin the moment, so he simply pressed his hand to her cheek. She closed her eyes and leaned into it. If he hadn't heard the sound of a vehicle, he would have pulled her close again. Maybe given in and kissed her.

"Stay here." He pried himself away and jogged around to the back of the house where Gio met him in the mudroom.

"It is Joey Moore," his friend said, sleeves rolled up and some sort of radio part in his hand. "If my guess is correct, mi amico."

"Stay inside. There's too much evidence of our visit—"

"I won't invite him in." Lily appeared at his elbow, rubbing away the evidence of emotion left on her cheeks. Even with a red nose, whether from the cold or tears, she was beautiful. "Miles, it's time we told him. He needs to know my dad hired you."

"I'll go with you." Miles braced for a showdown with her brother. "My car is already in your driveway, so he knows I'm here."

"Thank you, but this is family. I need to do this alone." She sent her dogs inside with Miles and Gio, then squared her shoulders and marched toward where Joey was parking his car beside Miles's Chevy.

Miles tamped down the urge to follow her and run interference. She trusted him with her safety. He had to trust whatever decision she'd make about sharing the truth with her brother.

CHAPTER 24

Lily hurried out to meet Joey, her emotions tumbling over each other like raging rapids. She shouldn't have shared so much with Miles. Right now, however, she had to shut him out of her thoughts, or Joey would read everything right there on her face. She didn't want to have to explain that to him too.

"What is he doing here?" Joey slammed the motorcar door. He drove the police one today, with the Eagle seal painted on the side. Which meant he was in full policeman mode. Just what she needed.

"Are you asking that as my brother?"

"Where is he?" Joey stomped toward the house. "Unchaperoned. I'm rescinding—"

She blocked his path. "Joey, I'm sure you didn't come here to fight about Miles."

"Maybe I did." He threw up his hands. "Can you blame me? I haven't been able to find either one of you all day. Here I thought he skipped town, but now I find his car here at your place. Again. And you keep getting shot at, as much when he's around as when he isn't. I'm scared for you, Lil."

"Miles is protecting me, Joey. He's a retired soldier. I'm in good hands."

"Not if he is in your house alone with you."

"I trust him, Joey. He's proven himself. Now you need to trust me."

"I'm trying here, Lil." He snatched her hands. His were not nearly as comforting as Miles's. "What do you really know about Wright? How did he find you after you were kidnapped?"

Joey's insistence cut deep, making her eyes burn and her voice rasp. "Why can't you trust my judgment?"

"Lil."

"No." She sniffed. Squared her shoulders. "If you want to know more about Miles, then go talk to Dad. But until you can trust me, I don't want you here."

"What?" Joey stared at her.

"You heard me." A tear escaped her control. "Go."

"What am I supposed to tell Mom?"

"To talk to Dad! He knows more about this situation than he'll tell me." Which bothered her more than she could admit. Lily hugged herself. "There's something bigger going on, and somehow, I'm in the middle of it."

"That's all the more reason you need me at your side."

"Oh, Joey, you don't get it. I need you on mine."

Miles waited until he heard Joey's car drive away. Even with the door closed, he could make out most of the conversation. He wanted to go out there, offer himself up, but that would only make things worse. The dogs raced past him when he opened the back door. Lily knelt, wrapped her arms around them, and let them lick her. Miles stayed back, watching them comfort her. Wishing he could too. It twisted his stomach to see her pain.

"I almost complete the transmitter." Gio appeared behind him like a phantom. "I must attach the antenna, then all will be finished."

"It will transmit clearly, without interference?" Miles confirmed.

"Si, mi amico."

"You don't trust his security measures?" Lily watched Gio round the back of the house.

Miles snapped on his professionalism. "It's not that."

"But it is." Those green eyes met his. "You don't think it will give you enough time to save me."

How could she know that was his fear? But no. He couldn't give in to his anxiety where she was concerned. This was why he'd asked Gio to come. He must trust the security system his friend put in place. Trust God to keep her safe.

Before he could find the words to assure Lily, assure himself, Gio reappeared. "*Finito.* All is complete. We should celebrate. *Il pasticcino* smells *benissimo!*" He kissed the tips of his fingers with a dramatic flair and swung them toward her kitchen.

Lily's cheeks pinked as she laughed. "I should check to make sure it's done. Then you can teach me about the radio?"

"*Bene, bene.* This plan, it is good." Gio wrapped Lily's hand around his arm like the incorrigible flirt the man could be. Why did it bother Miles so much? Probably because his friend had planted too many romantic notions in his head.

Lily laughed again, her limp more pronounced as she ascended the stairs, the dogs traipsing after them. Miles stalled on the doorstep to observe the outside longer than necessary. To give his mind time to get out of the clouds and return to reality.

When he finally pushed inside, the smell of apple struck him in the stomach, which responded with a low rumble. Smokey and Pieter welcomed him. Gio gave him a snarky smile. Lily looked up at him, a telegraph transmitter in her hand, eyes worried.

"Miles, this is really too much. I can't ask you to be at my beck and call just because I'm scared of mice in the attic."

This woman wouldn't be scared of mice in the attic. Rather the opposite—she'd wait too long to call for help. "Just promise me you will use it if the dogs are acting funny or if you have a nervous feeling. Don't wait until there is actual danger."

She raised a finger of protest.

Miles crossed the room in an instant and clasped her shoulders, silencing her even as he urged her to hear him. "You aren't asking for me to be at your call, Lily, I'm insisting. Please. Do this for me."

Green eyes melted his insides. "If you're sure."

"Absolutely."

"The silence. The solitude." She stepped away to include Gio in her statement. "Grandfather knew that's why I loved this place. It has long been my refuge."

"And now it has a security system," Miles said.

Lily nodded, but Miles could tell his words didn't touch the root of the problem.

"Giglia." Gio held his hands out, palms up. Gone was the flirt, the romantic. Here was the man Miles trusted with his life. "When I was a boy, I hate God for what I thought He did to *mi famiglia*. One day, a new famiglia become our neighbors, and they … they reintroduce me to have this relationship with *Dio*, with God. Before I left for the Great War, they give me this." Gio lifted a pendant necklace over his head, a pendant Miles had never seen his friend remove. Ever. "It is a—how you say?—*Santo* Christopher."

Lily held out her hand with wonder in her eyes. "And you wear it always?"

"It represent many things, but to me … to me, it is reminder of *la protezione,* that is, God … His … what is word?"

"Protection?" Miles whispered, emotion clogging his voice at the kindness of his friend.

"Si, si! It will honor me, Giglia, if you keep until safe again."

A tear slipped down Lily's cheek. "Gio, I couldn't."

"*Per favore.*" He let it drop into her palm, then sandwiched her hands together in his for a long moment. His friend was praying for Lily, and the emotion Miles barely held in check spilled out in a silent prayer of his own.

Shame humbled him that his friend offered more spiritual comfort than Miles had even thought to extend—the type of comfort that was a balm to a wounded soul. Miles knew that firsthand. So why hadn't it crossed his mind to share that with Lily? He'd shared his grief with her—part of it, at least—but not everything. In fact, if he was honest with himself, sharing his grief with her had been an impulse, something that slipped out because she tugged at his heart. Not something he ever intended to do.

Now, standing in Lily's kitchen, watching tears drip down her cheeks as Gio's silent prayer moved to a whispered one, one spoken in the language of the man's heart, Miles had a decision to make. A personal decision. He could no longer deny the distance he'd allowed to creep in between himself and God. His struggle with the Almighty had begun the day his parents died. He'd blamed war, then his job as a sniper, but standing that close to death—holding its power in his hands—had kept him from walking away from God entirely.

He could no longer deny his feelings toward Lily. Whether she harbored the same emotions or not, he didn't know, but this decision wasn't about her. Yet. First, Miles had to decide whether he was willing to let his heart crack open. First to God, then to Lily. The two were related somehow, the one dependent upon the other. His ability to care for her as she deserved could only come from a right relationship with God. Only then could he see if she returned what he felt toward her.

Gio ended his prayer and smiled at Lily as he patted her hands. Lily returned his smile with thanks in her eyes. A smile Miles longed to have turned on him. Which led back to the decision he had to make. He'd do whatever it took to be the man she deserved, so, of course, he'd open his heart wide. He only needed to remember this moment to have the courage to do so.

"*Il pasticcino*, it is ready?" Gio rubbed his hands together.

Miles caught his eye before Lily looked up. *Thank you.* Gio nodded, winked. His friend had likely discerned the battle Miles had just waged. In fact, if Miles wasn't mistaken, neither this scene nor his prayer had been entirely for Lily's benefit.

"You both have done so much for me." Lily fingered the St. Christopher before glancing between them. "What can I do to help you? Serving you baked goods and hot chocolate doesn't seem enough."

"*Il pasticcino*. It is enough." Gio rubbed his belly. "I clean up and be ready."

Lily chuckled as Gio disappeared outside.

"I prepared this for you." Miles handed her a card he'd stashed in his coat pocket earlier that afternoon. "It has the numbers for where Gio, Agnes, and I am staying. If you have questions or need help ... or simply want to talk. I, uh ... well, uh, don't hesitate to use it. I'll cover any charges. Just—"

"Call." Lily swiped at the remnants of her tears with her wrist, an embarrassed blush rising on her pretty face. "Thank you, Miles. For everything."

He pressed a kiss to her cheek. "You're welcome." He wanted to give her so much more.

CHAPTER 25

Lily stoked the blaze she'd started in her fireplace. Autumn nights set a chill in the house that only a fire could eliminate. Silence weighed heavy around her now that the men had left, doors and windows secured, a light breeze tossing the leaves outside. She couldn't push away the fear that rested on her shoulders, so she planned to sleep on the couch tonight, the dogs beside her. An easy escape route planned. The radiotelegraph thingamajig nearby.

She curled onto her couch, snuggled in her flannel nightgown, a compress on her ankle, another cup of hot chocolate in her hands. Good thing Hershey chocolate bars were affordable even during the Depression. She pressed the cup to her cheek, remembering Miles's kiss. Of the few men who'd tried to kiss her over the years, none had ever given her such a sweet one. Miles's touch made her feel protected. Treasured.

She shook the butterflies away. What did she really know about Miles? It didn't matter. She trusted him. But that trust was threatening to offer her heart on a platter. Miles had a life beyond Eagle. When all this was over, Miles would leave, and she'd be stuck here, watching Joey court Katy. Sure, she was happy for both of them, but if she was truly honest, she felt left out. Especially since she and Joey usually shared everything. Or, at least, they used to. She missed him. Terribly.

But that wasn't the only reason she felt left out. Having watched her little sister get married a week ago and now watching the last of her unmarried siblings pursuing a courtship, she realized just what it meant to be unmarried. Alone. She'd always insisted she preferred it that way, and, honestly, she believed she still did. The idea of always having another person around made her feel claustrophobic. Why else had she chosen to live in such an isolated place?

Yet Miles's comfort and protection the last couple of days …

No, she needed to be realistic. Once this was over, he wouldn't remember her. Better not grow too comfortable with his presence. Even if it filled a need she hadn't known she had.

Lily stirred, suddenly aware of the cold. Had she fallen asleep? She blinked in the darkness to gather her senses. Smokey and Pieter shared the couch with her, the compress in a lump on the floor. Not even red embers remained in the fireplace, so the flame must have died out hours ago. Then why did she smell smoke?

She scrubbed her face. Squinted at the mantel clock. In the dim light from the picture window, it read three in the morning.

Light from the picture window?

Another whiff of smoke passed under her nose. Unease rolling through her body, she sniffed … followed the smell to the front door. Pieter trotted after her, Smokey watching from his comfortable spot on the couch. She gave Pieter the command to wait and cracked open the door she never used. A red glow came from the barn. It was on fire!

Running to the kitchen, she tapped out the SOS code on Gio's contraption. Then she snatched the earpiece to her wall phone to herald the night operator to ring the fire brigade. Having sent both messages, she stuffed her bare feet into her work boots and wrapped her coat over her nightgown before racing out the door, forcing her stiff ankle to cooperate and leaving the dogs inside.

Flames crackled against the west side of the barn, the side closest to her father's cornfields. If the wind shifted, the fire would rapidly consume the dry stalks, taking out a significant portion of her family's harvest. The drought, the economic depression, *and* losing half a crop? Not enough feed alone had a domino effect on a dairy farm. Could put them out of business. She wouldn't let that happen.

The closer she jogged, the more nausea turned her stomach. The smoke seized her lungs, but it was laced with the overwhelming smell of pork. Bacon, more accurately. *Bacon?* She looked closer. Someone had created a campfire under a tin of bacon fat, creating a grease bomb to set her barn on fire!

Knowing this was no accident sent a surge of energy through her. She held the collar of her coat over her nose and shielded her face from the heat as she dashed past the fire. With a bound, she scaled the corral fence. The fabric of her nightgown ripped, and she nearly tumbled when her ankle gave out upon landing.

Smoke poured out of the barn as she fought her way inside. Growing up on a farm, she kept all the old kibble sacks in her storage room, just in case. Lily snatched a handful of them. Outside again, she hauled in air, but smoke followed her, and she bent double, coughing. She must keep going. Couldn't wait on the fire truck.

Covering her mouth again, she dunked a sack in the repaired water trough. Then a second one before draping them over her shoulder as she scaled the fence again. The fire had grown, licking at the pine that stood fifteen feet from the barn, between it and the field. She'd considered asking her brothers to chop it down for just this reason but hadn't been able to bring herself to lose such a beautiful tree. Now, if the dry needles at its base, the pine cones, let alone the tree itself, caught a spark, the tree would erupt in a towering blaze.

Coughing through the smoke, she flung the wet sacks at the base of the wall, trying to smother as much of the fire as possible. Taking a moment to clear her lungs, she jumped the fence and dunked two more sacks. She covered the pine needles. Beat at sparks that threatened to spread toward the tree and cornfield. Her efforts did nothing to slow the fire as it consumed the grease-splattered west wall.

"Lily!" Miles's voice reached over the crackling flames.

She waved the sack she held, then returned to beating the sparks.

"Lily, please." Miles pulled her away from the flames. "It's not safe."

She shook her head. "Have to save the corn."

"Oh, you amazing woman." He wrapped her in a hug. Coughed.

"We need to get you away from the smoke. Fire brigade is on the way."

"Not fast enough. Need to—" A fit of coughing nearly forced her to her knees.

Miles wrapped her arm around his neck and swept up her legs. Her *bare* legs, with naught but the fabric of her flannel nightgown between them and his arm. Despite her embarrassment, her lungs relaxed the farther from the smoke he took her. She leaned her head on his shoulder. The safety of his arms allowed reason to push through to her consciousness.

"Someone set the fire on purpose," she choked past the emotion building in her chest—emotion not caused by Miles.

He set her down against the trunk of the old oak. "The dogs didn't hear anything?"

"Not that I know of." The words scraped past her raw throat as she stared at the smoke billowing into the starlit sky. "I would have heard them. I slept downstairs."

"On the couch? Lily—"

"We need to get back over there." She tore her eyes from the destruction to meet his. "We have to smother the fire before it spreads any farther."

An old-model Ford bounced its way to park beside them, Gio at the wheel.

"On purpose, you said." Miles recaptured her attention. "Lily, let's not wait for Joey to talk to your dad. I think it's time to bring your brother in on everything we know."

She gaped at him. If Miles suggested that now, how bad did he think things were about to get?

A bell clanging through the night startled Joey awake. It took him two shakes of the head to clear the sleep from his mind before he realized it was the fire bell. He might be a police officer, but he was also a volunteer firefighter, as were most of the men in town in a community so small.

He was dressed in a minute and pounded down the exterior steps from his upstairs apartment as the fire chief drove out from behind the police station across the street. Six other men converged on the roofless fire car, and they all grabbed onto the long ladders attached to its side as the chief accelerated out of town.

"Where's the fire?" one of the volunteers asked.

Others shook their heads, but a sour pit began to form in Joey's stomach. They were headed toward his family's farm. Toward Lily's place. Sure, there were other farms out this way, but with the events of the past few days, he knew her property was the one in flames.

Why had he left her with tension remaining between them? Why had he been so hard on her in the first place? Why did he have such a problem with someone courting her? Especially someone who'd saved her life.

Until you can trust me, I don't want you here.

Joey's heart pounded against his ribs as the cold night air slapped his face.

What if this afternoon's fight was the last time he would ever see her? He didn't understand where she had gone and why she wouldn't tell him anything. Couldn't comprehend why she trusted a stranger over her own twin brother. But right now, none of that mattered. He'd believe anything she wanted him to believe as long as he got one more moment with her. They had to get there in time for him to say he was sorry.

"What can I do?" Gio asked, securing a cloth around his mouth and nose.

"Water pump is beside the windmill, and we need more sacks from the barn." Miles removed his own cotton shirt, tying it over his face. The stitches in his back protested the rough movement, but he ignored the pain as he snapped his suspenders back in place on bare skin and stowed his Colt and holster in his motorcar.

A quarter of the barn, the area where the kennels used to be, was already in flames. Miles didn't know how much of the barn they could save, if any, but stopping the fire from spreading was the priority. Then he would find the answer to who did this. Who would destroy Lily's business and risk fire spreading to fields and woods, all ripe for burning from the drought?

Miles slammed open the barn door facing the front yard. Time was short, and he needed to expend his agitation, or he'd make a careless mistake. If he was home, he'd run until his mind was clear, miles and miles if he had to. On a mission, he'd funneled his energy onto his target, into reconnaissance and stealth and strategy, and in so doing, he could remain unmoving for hours.

Here, however, his target was a phantom assailant, or two, and he cared too much about what harm could come to a certain brown-haired, green-eyed beauty for logic to stay at the forefront.

Through the hazy smoke, they followed the directions Lily had given. The fire hadn't reached the east side, but it would in moments. Urgency driving them, Gio grabbed an empty bucket beside the door where Lily told them they would find more feed sacks.

Miles wiped his forehead with his bare arm before piling the empty sacks over his uninjured shoulder. "We need to look for what isn't there."

"You thinking that now?" Gio grabbed the bucket of dog food and the rest of the sacks.

"Why burn her barn down and not her house?"

"Si, si."

"I just think ..." Miles huffed, the heat and smoke taking his breath as he headed for the back exit that led toward the corral, Gio close behind. "Maybe he wanted me to know ... he can get to Lily ... no matter what I do ... because ... he's as ... well trained ... as me."

"You know who this is."

"I—"

A thundering roar exploded through the barn. Boards dropped from the roof. Flames shot into the night sky. Miles and Gio dove for cover. Miles wrapped his arms over his head as a beam crashed toward him. Would he live through this to see Lily one more time?

CHAPTER 26

Midway through wrapping the torn hem of her nightgown around her ankle so she could get back to fighting the fire, Lily spun as the night lit up behind her. The pine tree flamed like a torch. The barn creaked. Then the west wall collapsed in a plume of dust and smoke.

"Miles!" Lily ignored her ankle and the makeshift bandage and raced for the barn. Fire ate at the wooden structure. Smoke billowed from the entrance. Lily covered her mouth with her sleeve and pushed inside the open door.

"Lily, get out of here!" Miles's choked voice came from near her storage room.

Her eyes burned and watered. She blinked away the moisture. Crawled toward where she'd heard his voice. Gasped when she reached him. Miles lay with a charred beam across his back. Gio leaned on a blackened board, trying to leverage enough space for Miles to claw his way out.

"What can I do?" Lily stopped beside the crossbeam that had once secured the roof of her barn. The structure couldn't be salvaged, but the fire was escalating out of control. Soon, depending on sparks and wind, even her house could be in danger. Why was it taking so long for the fire brigade to arrive?

"Lily, please." Miles reached for her, desperation tinging his voice. "It's not safe."

She clasped his dirty hand. "We're going to get you out of here." She would have hope for both of them until there was no hope left to be had.

"Giglia. *Aiuto*." Gio swiped a mixture of dirt and sweat from his brow, smearing it down his cheek.

Miles held on tighter. The warrior faded into a terrified boy before her eyes. His sides expanded and contracted faster and faster. Blood seeped from his shoulder.

"Look at me." She bent over so that her head was beside him in the dirt and he had no choice but to meet her eyes. "We're getting you out of here. You hear me. Whatever Gio says, you listen to him." She pressed a kiss to his forehead, then scrambled up beside Gio.

"Lean here on three." Gio indicated where on the board. Sweat poured down his face.

Lily heaved in as much of a breath as she could, then, shoulder to shoulder, she and Gio put their whole weight on the board. The beam creaked but didn't lift. The fire overhead burned hotter, brighter.

"Gio, leave it," Miles's panicked voice pled. "Just get her out."

Gio shook his head, met Lily's eyes. He was going to try something. She didn't know what, but she nodded. She'd do whatever she could.

With a grunt, Gio made the board a vault, using the force of his jump to land hard on the end. Lily leaned in with all her strength, and the beam lifted. An inch, but it was an inch that they hadn't had a second ago.

"Amico!" Gio shouted. "Move!"

Miles hauled himself from under the beam just as the board cracked in two and the beam crashed back to the dirt. Lily threw her arms around him, barely registering his bare chest or solid muscles as they knelt together in the dirt and he held her with a desperation that threatened to take away what little breath she had left.

Joey's feet faltered at the sight he found just inside the barn door. His sister, dressed only in her nightgown and a coat, was plastered against the bare-chested body of Miles Wright. Worry, rage, fear—it all came out of him in a growl. He yanked Lily away from Wright and sent a right hook toward his chin.

Another man pushed Wright out of the path of Joey's fist, causing Joey to flail for balance. The next instant, his feet were kicked out from under him, and he landed on his back, staring up at the burning remains of the barn's roof.

A knife pressed to his throat, and Joey froze.

"Gio!" Lily grabbed the man's wrist. "It's my brother."

"I know." Gio, if that was his name, didn't take his eyes off Joey.

"Let him go. I can't carry Miles on my own. I need your help."

Joey darted a glance at his sister. She wasn't looking at him. She was staring this Gio down. Something odd and nauseating pooled in his stomach. Was Lily more concerned about Wright than she was about her own brother?

Gio gave a nod. The knife vanished, and so did Lily. Gio gave Joey another dark look and then wrapped Wright's arm over his shoulder. Wright leaned heavily on him, but Lily was attempting to support the man's other side too. Blood dripped down Wright's shoulder, and small welts were forming on his back.

Smoke billowed into Joey's face, and he coughed as he stumbled to his feet. The fire chief hadn't bothered trying to keep Joey from racing into the burning building while he directed the other men in containing the fire, but since Lily had left with Wright and Gio and there was no indication of anyone else present, he staggered back into the fresh air.

Neighbors had begun to arrive, including his own family, but Lily was nowhere in sight. It didn't matter now. Joey had no idea what to say to her. Instead, he turned his attention to keeping the fire from destroying the rest of his family.

Charles Wade watched the fire slowly die. At first, he'd thought the kid's idea was idiotic. Then just plain crazy. Until he watched Wright race into the barn. Perhaps Wade wouldn't have to put a bullet in him, after all. Not that he didn't relish the idea.

Of course, Wright emerged from the fire alive.

Wade attached the Maxim Silencer to his rifle. He'd use the distraction of the fire to finish off the man.

If he could get off a clean shot.

Which he never managed to line up. The doctor arrived, and Wade lost Miles amid the crowd of neighbors.

So maybe the kid's plan had possessed potential, but Wade couldn't capitalize on it, which frustrated him and made him want to go after the kid instead. But his employer wanted him at the hotel, an order he'd already put off to come here. Hunting Miles Wright would have to wait until tomorrow.

Miles lay on his stomach. Pain radiated with each shiver that shook his body. His back felt as if it were still on fire. Then cool hands lay cool cloths over his shoulders, followed by soothing words. The pain deafened his ears to the actual words, but the tone eased his discomfort like a balm.

The cloths were removed and heat seared, only to be brushed back by a cool touch.

"It'll be all right, Miles." The words became a voice. Lily's voice.

Again the cold left. More heat, then cold.

"I know it hurts."

He grabbed onto her words as the relief left once again, giving way to burning heat.

"Doc says to keep cleaning and cooling the burns," Lily said as she covered his back with a wet cloth.

"Where?" The word rasped out, scraping his throat.

"Miles?" Lily's face appeared in his vision. "Don't move. You're on my couch."

Miles inhaled, and his lungs rejected the breath. Pain reverberated through his body as he coughed.

"Gio?" Anxiety filled Lily's voice.

"Here is water." Gio supported Miles as he put a cup to his mouth. "Doc, he want honey?"

Honey?

"I don't have any, but a farm on the other side of town has bees. Doc will know where."

"Si, si. I go." Gio eased Miles back onto his stomach. "Doc, he is outside."

"Thank you, Gio. We'll be fine."

A door closed as the cloth again covered Miles's back.

"Doc said to use cool water to clean the burn, then he'll make a salve for it," Lily said. "The beam left bits of charred wood and other debris on your back. Doc removed most of it before he went to check on any others who may have been injured."

"Your barn," Miles gasped, the memory of the fire returning with the heat in his back.

Lily lay another cool cloth on him. "Lost, but the fire didn't spread. We saved all but a couple square feet of corn."

Thank you, God. "There were other injuries?"

"Nothing serious." Lily replaced the cloth, wiping at his skin as she did. If it didn't hurt so much, he might enjoy it. "The wind picked up, blew sparks, but it helped keep the pine from igniting the corn."

Silence stretched between them until Lily cleared her throat. "I thought ... I ... you ..."

He caught her hand as she removed the cloth. "This is not your fault."

She pulled away and continued her ministrations. "You wouldn't even be in Eagle if I hadn't insisted on returning."

"Still not your fault." Miles propped his forehead on his hands to avoid burying his face in the couch cushion. "I chose to go into your barn. I chose to come to Eagle. And I still choose to help you."

"You were so scared." The words were a whisper, yet they brought back his fear like a whirlwind. The panic as he lay trapped under the beam. The heat scorching his skin. The smoke choking his breath. The memories that threatened to wash him away in a flood of pain.

"Lily." He pushed himself up to his elbows. Heat seared through his back and lungs, and he tucked into himself as a coughing fit ripped through him.

"Lie back down, Miles." Lily met him with a cup of water that eased his throat. "It's too soon for you to move. Doc said so."

He let her help him onto his side but fixed his eyes on hers.

She knelt before him, ash sprinkled in her hair, grime on her face. "Can I get you something? More water?"

He reached for her, running his hand down her arm until he caught her fingers. She wore a dress the color of autumn leaves, and he could imagine walking through the woods with her by his side, danger behind them, a future ahead.

"Are you feeling worse?" Lily placed her free hand on his forehead. "Doc said to pay attention for fever. You don't seem warm."

"Lily, I want to tell you something." It was time.

"No need for confessions, Miles. You're going to be just fine." Her light words belied the fear that flashed in her eyes.

"All the more reason to tell you. To explain why I was ..." *Terrified.*

Lily made a show of relaxing beside the couch. He realized then that he hadn't seen her dogs, but he couldn't get sidetracked. He'd ask after them later. They were alone, and he needed to share his story before he lost his nerve.

Lily offered him a smile.

Right. "Springtime, my seventeenth year, my family helped with a barn raising. Ma brought a blackberry pie." His voice rasped, a combination of emotion, smoke, and pain.

Lily held the cup of water to his lips. He wanted to forget the past, focus on the sweetness of being with her, but he'd opened the door, and the scene replaying before his eyes wouldn't be blinked away.

"To this day, I don't know how it happened. Ropes frayed, beams slipped, the barn toppled, crushing six and injuring a dozen." He squeezed Lily's hand, the only tie he had to the present. "I lay under a beam, helpless as I watched my mother die."

Tears welled in Lily's eyes, but she didn't move, didn't speak.

"Lost my father too. As soon as I was fit enough, I sold everything and registered as a soldier, and a year later, found myself in the trenches of the Western Front. That's where I met Gio. He'd left Italy as a boy but ended up going back to fight alongside his countrymen under a different flag. I was rash and angry yet somehow survived, thanks to him. At some point, the anger became determination. Being a sharpshooter was something I could use to protect my fellow soldiers. Until we were used against civilians in Central America. Then I joined Craft's agency."

"You've never gone back home?"

Miles shook his head. "I didn't have one of those any more. Didn't need one."

"Didn't?"

Don't. The word died on his tongue. Because for the first time since he was a lost and hurting seventeen-year-old, his heart wanted more than to beat simply to keep him alive.

CHAPTER 27

Tuesday, October 17, 1933

"There you are." Miles found Lily out behind her house the afternoon after the fire. Or better said, the dogs led him to her. While she looked like a summer afternoon with her hair knotted at the back of her head, wisps escaping, no hat, flannel sleeves rolled up to her elbows, and jeans tucked into her work boots, he felt like a scrap heap. Bandages covered his back and wrapped around his front, hidden by his cotton shirt and vest. He'd forgone his customary suspenders as the doctor suggested. However, no matter the pain, he wouldn't give up his shoulder holster and Colt.

Lily's green eyes lit up when she spotted him around the corner, and every sacrifice he made to be here felt worth it.

"Are you all right?" She shouldered her shotgun and trotted up to him. "I was so worried when the doctor insisted on taking you to the clinic last night."

"Merely precautionary." Miles gave her an easy smile. In truth, the burns had required additional treatment—including something for the pain—to avoid infection. Now his back and shoulder ached worse than any bullet he'd ever taken, but he refused to tell anyone, especially Craft, about this latest injury, lest he take him off the case—or worse, use Miles's weakness against him. Instead, he nodded toward Lily's gun. "Nervous?"

"Practicing."

Miles cocked his head. With a grin, she pointed to the muzzle where she'd tied a flashlight. Then she deftly raised the gun to her shoulder. Feet spread shoulder-width apart, she swiveled at her hips, and the dim light followed the shadowed roofline of her house.

"It helps calm me." She lowered the shotgun. "I have to consciously slow my heart to steady my hands. It forces me to focus on a single point."

Did she know how true that was for him too?

"Being alone in nature helps me think, too, and, well …" She gazed to the east, over the expanse of a large garden, smokehouse, and cellar doors that protruded from a short hill. "I can hardly look at what's left of my barn."

"I'm so sorry. I should have been able to stop it."

"No. No." She clutched his forearm. "Do not take responsibility for what happened. It was bad enough you and Gio went inside to get those empty sacks and risked your lives. The police know it was arson, so they'll be doing what they do."

"Did you talk to your brother?"

Lily shook her head. "My whole family helped fight the fire, of course, along with half the town, but after Doc took you into town and assigned Katy to look after me, she wouldn't let anyone inside, even Joey—except Gio, of course, because, as I'm sure you know, Gio could sweet-talk a cow into giving him her milk without the effort of milking." She didn't sound too unhappy about how the rest of the night had gone, which eased Miles's worry some.

"Gio enjoyed his time with you." In fact, Gio had greeted him early this morning with his thoughts—not about the investigation—but about Lily being a good potential wife for Miles. The question was, did Lily know she'd not only passed Gio's matchmaking assessment, but she'd exceeded his expectations to such a degree, Gio was ready to drag both of them to stand in front of a preacher before sundown?

Lily chuckled. "He told me how you two met. He stumbled on your sniper spot?"

"I nearly killed him." Miles laughed. "He was a messenger for command and had gotten turned around. Good thing he ran into me.

Another hundred feet, and he would've been behind enemy lines. The man can still get his directions confused, even if he is the best at finding anything you need. Which reminds me, he's exploring some options this morning to give you better security."

"I don't know if it's worth it."

"Your safety is definitely worth it."

"That's not what I meant. I have to rebuild before I can take in dogs again, but rebuilding takes money." She raised her eyebrows, letting Miles fill in the blanks. Needing money during a depression meant trouble. "I don't want to give up my home, but I don't know how I'll afford to live without my job."

Against his better judgment, although Gio would be cheering if he knew, Miles wrapped his good arm over Lily's shoulder. His left shoulder had required restitching last night as well and ached nearly as fiercely as his back, especially if he moved it away from his side. Lily leaned toward him, and he soaked in the feel of having her tucked close. Safe. Where he could protect her.

"Before the Great War, I was rather handy," he said before he thought it through. "It's been a few years, but I tinker around between cases. What if I helped rebuild your barn?"

She looked up at him. "You'd do that?"

"Building things is what I planned to do with my life before …" He let his train of thought trail off. She knew the story now, so he didn't need to say more. "I'd be happy to help any way I can."

As she scrutinized him, he expected her to voice the questions she hadn't been given the opportunity to ask last night. Instead, she said, "I need to train Smokey today. He's lost significant ground this past week, and if I don't work on those skills soon, he'll lose them completely, and we'll have to start over. It just means taking the dogs on a short jaunt into the woods."

"It's not safe for you to be in the forest by yourself."

She grinned. He'd been had. She'd known that was exactly what he'd say.

"Lily, somebody kidnapped you, blew up my buddies, shot at us, and burned down your barn. I can't in good conscience let you wander in the woods, even with my protection." Could he protect her well enough with his injuries? He held her closer. "I don't mean to scare you."

"Yet you do." The green eyes she turned on him weren't accusing. They were vulnerable and hit his heart like the blast of a mortar attack.

"If we run into trouble, you'll let me do what I do best? No protests?"

"Thank you, Miles." She reached up on her tiptoes and kissed his cheek.

And there went his heart, waving a little white flag.

"I'll grab Smokey's lead, and we can go." Lily ducked into the house to hide the warmth spreading up her cheeks. Seeing Miles almost die— again—and then hearing about his heartbreaking loss, caused her to give her own heart more leeway than was prudent. But she didn't care. Not today. She simply wanted to spend non-case time with him. And Smokey did need training. He was developing some less than desirable behaviors.

In no time, she'd closed up the house, then fitted a harness over Smokey's wiggling body before attaching the lead rope. "Fortunately, I keep all my training gear by the pond. It's easier than lugging it out there every day."

"What type of gear do you use?" Miles looked up from where he squatted beside Pieter, giving the dog the attention he craved.

"Besides my boat, I use pelts, decoys—"

"You use decoys too?"

"Yes, wooden ones. I refuse to use live decoys."

Miles slowed and massaged his left shoulder as they passed the remnants of her barn. She pursed her lips, remembering him lying under that beam. The welts and burned flesh on his muscled back. Now she understood his fear too.

"Maybe this is a bad idea. You should rest in the house. Training Smokey won't take long."

Red slunk up his cheeks, and he rubbed his stubble. He hadn't shaved since she saw him yesterday, and it reminded her of the first time she saw him. He lowered his head. "I'm sorry you had to see that side of me."

"That side of you? Oh! No. No. I don't think less of you for what happened last night. I—" *I wanted to throw my arms around your neck and—*

"Being stuck under that beam made me feel as though I was back home again when the barn collapsed. Until you showed up." His voice cracked.

The warrior broke before her, and Lily opened her arms. Together they stood there, outside her charred barn—the ruins of her business, her dreams—holding each other as if the world couldn't hurt them as long as they had each other.

CHAPTER 28

Lily loved this spot by the pond in the woods. The still water perfectly reflected the blue sky above them, and a chill breeze rustled the tall grasses. The scent of pine mingled with the smell of fish and frogs. It was an island of tranquility, especially with Miles sitting on a fallen log nearby. Only the slight throb in her ankle reminded her of the danger they'd faced.

"Do you come here often?" Miles surveyed their surroundings with an appreciative expression.

"Nearly every day, especially if I'm training the dogs." Lily pointed across the lake. "My sister lives on the other side of the trees now. She and her husband are staying with his parents."

"Your sister, Amy?"

"They were supposed to go to Milwaukee for a couple days after the wedding, but Andy canceled the trip." If she hadn't been avoiding her family, perhaps she'd already know why.

Smokey darted after a rabbit, yanking the lead out of Lily's hand, something he hadn't done in over ten days. When on the lead, he was supposed to wait for her command ... like Pieter, who—despite not having a lead—swung his head between Lily and the path down which Smokey had vanished, his body quivering with the desire to follow.

Lily held up a finger to Pieter. "Wait." She'd send Pieter after Smokey and hope the puppy followed the older dog back to her. Otherwise, this could be a long afternoon chasing her wayward dog.

Grabbing a small sack filled with pebbles—quail feathers securely attached—she waved it in front of Pieter's nose, then side-armed it deep into the woods in the direction Smokey had run off. She gave Pieter the retrieve command, and the dog bolted into the trees.

"How much of Pieter's response to your commands is instinct, and how much is training?" Miles stretched out his legs in front of him, crossing his ankles.

"It's a mix of both." Lily shrugged. "The American Water Spaniel was bred not just to retrieve and flush out, but to withstand Wisconsin's frigid lakes. Their medium size also allows them to join a hunter in a boat. They can leap into the water without knocking the hunter in as well."

"Why does it sound as though you know this from experience?"

Lily laughed. "I've been dumped into the water too many times to count."

Miles shook his head. "Where did you learn how to do all this?"

Lily ducked, the warmth of pleasure and embarrassment slipping up her neck.

"And how do you trust them to always return?"

"I don't, at first." Lily looked toward the woods. It seemed to be taking Pieter longer than usual to find the peasant feather sack. "That's why I use the leads. It gives them a sense of freedom, but I still have the ability to pull them back as needed. We also work on commands. If I need them to recall immediately, I whistle. Unladylike, but it's the clearest call. Once I have their attention, I slap my thigh. Like this."

She let loose a shrill whistle, waited a beat, then slapped her thigh once. A rustling came from the trees, and then Pieter bounded toward her, the peasant sack held loosely in his jaws. He pranced around her feet, and she knelt to praise him. Little Smokey appeared next, stumbling over branches with his gangly legs, and pushed his way onto her lap. Pride in her dogs swelled in her chest.

"Such good dogs." She hugged Smokey tightly. He may have lost some of his discipline, but he still responded to one of the most important commands. Yes, her dogs would always come back to her.

Miles carefully leaned against a tree. Sitting in this secluded spot, watching Lily train her dogs, caused tension to seep out of his muscles and eased the pain in his back more than medicine had. He needed this recovery time, and, frankly, he wanted the time with Lily too. So he rested on his sniper training, keeping ears and eyes alert to suspicious sound and movement, though Lily's joyful smile kept wrenching his concentration away from her safety.

"Pieter and Smokey have earned playtime in the water." Lily dug in the metal box anchoring her small boat and lifted out a wooden duck. "Want to toss this decoy about four feet into the lake? I'll send Pieter first. Once he comes back to me, you can toss the other three in just as far."

"Why one first?" Eager to participate, Miles took the decoy. It was painted like a Mallard duck, with a green head and brown body, wings spread.

"Dogs learn well by watching each other, so I have Pieter show Smokey how it's done."

Miles followed Lily's instructions, tossing the decoy underhanded to reduce the pull on his bandages. She recalled Pieter to her side, then sent him in after the wooden decoy. The dog bounded into the water with abandon. Birds flocked out of the grasses. Smokey tugged his lead. Lily waited for Pieter to return with the decoy before giving Miles the nod to toss in the rest. Then she gave Smokey and Pieter the command to heel, which must mean to sit by her side because that's what they did. She unhooked Smokey, then released them. The dogs flew over the ground and leapt into the water with giant splashes.

Lily laughed, her eyes alight. "I love how excited they always are."

"They're not the only ones." Miles couldn't take his eyes off her face. He'd noticed her beauty multiple times, but seeing her now, animated by her passion in life, put every other time to shame.

"You okay there, big guy?" Lily patted his arm with humor dancing in her eyes.

"Really impressed." *And in love?*

"By the dogs?"

"The dogs?" Could she not know how amazing she was? "No. I mean, yes, of course, but I meant I'm impressed by you."

She turned a bright shade of red and looked away.

"I didn't mean to embarrass you." He reached out to her, once again feeling like the big oaf that he was. His hand engulfed her shoulder.

She flinched at the touch, and when she looked back at him, tears welled in her eyes, cutting him deeply.

"What did I say?" He snatched his hand away.

"No, no." She grabbed his hand before he knew what to do with it. She held it between her small ones, studying it as if she'd discovered a fascinating rock.

"Then what?" He tried to bend down enough to see her face.

"I've never impressed anyone before."

"What?"

"I'm a middle child, a twin. My siblings always got more attention than me, especially since they followed everyone's expectations." She continued—seemingly absently—to run her fingers over his callused hands, distracting him terribly.

He wanted to hug her but forced himself to stay perfectly still, knowing even a twitch would make her dash away like a deer.

"As a child in school, I looked so much like a boy, none of the boys paid me the attention they did the other girls in my class. So one year, I purposefully fattened myself up like an animal going to slaughter, thinking I'd get curves like the other girls." She blinked, sending two quick tears down her cheek. "I got attention, all right. Not the good kind."

He fought to keep his hand relaxed while the rest of his body coiled at the anger coursing through him.

"It took me the rest of the following school year to return to my normal size, but I did. Guys started paying attention to me, but I couldn't forget how they'd treated me. The names they'd called me." Her cheeks flushed again. "I refused to go out with a single one of them. Instead, I spent even more time with my grandfather and discovered my refuge and my dog training business." She shrugged, finally looked him in the eye. "That's why I have the answers to all your questions about the dogs. I spent all my time learning."

"Lily …" He lifted his free hand to touch her cheek, hoping she'd understand the words he couldn't form.

A tear dripped onto his fingers, and he pulled her into his embrace. He held her tightly, yet carefully, as she sobbed. His heart hurt for her, for the pain she harbored, while also admiring how she weathered it all. No wonder she'd responded to the kidnapping, the grenade, the shootings with such strength.

"Sorry." She pulled away, her cheeks the reddest yet. "You must think—"

"That you are one of the strongest, most compassionate, most incredible women I have ever met?" He clutched her shoulders. "That's what I was just thinking about you."

"Really?" Clearly, she didn't believe him.

"I don't know how I can prove it to you, but yes, really."

Pieter slipped between them, and Smokey sniffed around her shoes. She cracked a smile.

"They're worried about me." She knelt, moving out of his reach and wrapping her arms around Pieter, then Smokey, whispering soft words of comfort.

His heart was in deep trouble. He cared about this woman, cared what she thought of him, hated to see her experience any type of pain. What would happen when he found the people who'd killed his friends? When Lily was safe again? When he had to go back to the work that took him to dangerous places all around the country—work that demanded he have no family, no attachments? He wouldn't just leave a piece of his heart here in Eagle—he'd end up leaving the whole thing.

"Ready to get back?" Lily looked up at him, much more composed but with an openness in her eyes he hadn't seen before. She reached a hand out to him, let him help her up instead of standing up on her own, which he knew full well she was completely able to do. What did that say about the risk to Lily's heart?

CHAPTER 29

Gio leaned against the bumper of the old motorcar he'd driven last night as Lily and Miles returned from their walk. Lily smiled as her dogs dashed up to greet him.

"Careful, they're wet," she called.

Miles's chuckle rumbled beside her. Something had changed between them, and it simultaneously made joy bubble and butterflies dance. Would it end when they stepped from the enchantment of their nature walk? Or did it have a chance for lasting much longer?

"You go swimming?" Gio stepped back from the dogs even while patting Pieter on the head with a flat hand. Smokey shook, and Gio spun away from the spray.

"Sorry." Lily reluctantly released Miles's hand and hurried closer, whistling for her dogs. Of course, Pieter came at once, but she had to snatch the lead to gently direct the puppy to obey.

"It's a good look, Gio." Miles was laughing.

Gio scowled down at his water-splattered clothes.

Lily cringed. "I can wash—"

Gio held up a hand, and when he raised his head, a twinkle emerged in his dark eyes. "No, no. Do not worry. Mi amico, he knows I do not like to swim."

"What are you talking about? You *hate* the water!" Miles hadn't stopped laughing yet.

Lily glanced between them, unsure what to make of their banter.

"And you, you are *il pesce*, the fish." Gio's hands waved through the air like a conductor's. "*Pietro*, you shake water on him for me, si?"

The dog cocked his head. And Lily felt a smile rising.

"You know Pieter likes me better." Miles wiped at his face. Was he laughing so hard he was crying?

Gio snorted. "Because he sees *il cane—*" He cut off his words by snapping his fist closed.

Miles doubled over.

Gio clasped his hands together as if he prayed to Lily. "*Mi scusa, bella Giglia. The Italiano*, it does not translate to *Inglese.*"

"No, what you almost called me certainly does not translate well in mixed company." Miles's chuckling finally tempered. "Sorry, Lily. We can't help teasing one another."

Lily let her amusement show. "How about we bring this good mood into the house so I can make hot chocolate? I always need a cup after a long walk, and I suspect Gio didn't come just to tease you."

Gio took her elbow, eyes alight with expectation. "The *cioccolato* you serve yesterday ... it was *molto bene!*"

"Chocolate is Gio's weakness." Miles clapped his friend's shoulder before walking on Lily's other side. "I'll have a cup as long as you promise to put a compress on your ankle."

"Si, si, signorina. You must sit. I will be your hands."

Before Lily could blink, the two men had her ensconced in one of her high-back chairs, moved from her other room into the kitchen, with her foot on one of her kitchen chairs and a compress on her ankle. The dogs sprawled out on the floor, exhausted from their training. Gio rummaged for utensils, then added wood to the stove. And Miles rested his forearms on the table, observing her with a faraway smile.

A long-ago memory finally managed to squash the butterflies swarming in her stomach. She hated to ruin this moment, but she'd ignored the mental image long enough. "Something's bothering me about the fire."

As she anticipated, Miles's demeanor changed. Though he physically didn't move, his smile vanished, and his eyes searched hers with the same intensity as when she'd first met him.

"Out by the marsh today, it triggered a memory from my school days." She fingered Gio's St. Christopher, which she kept around her neck. "I hadn't thought of it for years, but I think it might be relevant."

Miles leaned forward. "Start from the beginning."

"On the last day of class one term, our teacher planned a picnic. She made a fire outside to cook up bacon before adding it to beans for lunch. One of the students helping build the fire added too much pine, and the fire erupted. Our teacher doused it with a bucket of water—only, she got some in the bacon pan, and a tower of flame flared several feet into the air."

"That attracted the boys, didn't it?" Miles frowned.

"Yes. I don't know how they did it, but they ended up with a tin can full of meat fat, so when the teacher instructed the boys to put out the fire, they stoked it instead. With the can of fat in the center of the fire, they added water and—" Lily used her hands to illustrate the fireball they had created.

"*La latte*, the milk, it bubble," Gio interrupted. "What is next?"

"While stirring, add the chocolate to the milk."

"Si, si." He did as she instructed.

"You think someone replicated that incident last night?" Miles returned to her story. "Can you give me a list of those children? The boys, in particular. I'll look into whether any of them would target you now."

"That's just it." Lily took a shaky breath. "The story became legend. Everyone knows it. But the instigators from that picnic were my brother-in-law, Andy, and his friends, Alex and Harry."

Miles let the clanking of Gio beating the cream shake up the thoughts rolling through his mind. Andy, Alex, and Harry. They were back to those three and their connection to Lily's kidnapping. Alex and Harry were the last to see Lily before she disappeared, and Andy's dad owned the dairy processing plant that would be affected by Mr. Moore's strike.

"The other attacker that night in the woods," Miles said as Gio stopped mixing, the whipped cream ready. "The one who hit me with that branch. He wasn't with the shooter."

"I can see what you mean," Lily replied as she scratched behind Pieter's ear as he sat beside her, "but what are you thinking?"

"I'm not sure yet …" He couldn't get his words to cooperate with his thoughts. If he could just get them to line up, he might break the case. It was there. He could sense it. He just felt too addled to figure it out.

"This will help." Gio slid a cup of hot chocolate across the table with a grin at Lily.

"It does." She grinned back before casting a shy smile at Miles that melted his knees.

Focus, Wright. Your distraction isn't helping keep her safe. "Let's back up. Instead of lumping everything together, let's look at each incident separately."

"*Prima.*" Gio pointed to Lily's ankle. "The compress, it should have reduced swelling."

"Of course!" How could he forget? Miles gently lifted the damp material from Lily's ankle. Before he could help her, she was on her feet, taking the compress from him.

"The hot chocolate is exceptional, Gio. How do you say *well done* in Italian?"

Gio beamed. "*Complimenti.*"

"Then, complimenti, Gio."

Warmth filled Miles as he watched the exchange. The woman wedging herself into his heart and his best mate, comfortable together, accepting of one another, even though their backgrounds differed to a great extent. Instead of jealousy that his friend would get along with the woman he wanted to consider as his girl, it mattered more that any sweetheart of his would blend with his friend who was more like a brother. He never thought he'd find a girl worth settling down for, but watching Lily and Gio now, longing crashed into his heart like a battering ram. He wanted this. He wanted her. Wanted to come home.

"Yoo-hoo." Lily waved a hand in his face, bringing him back. "You disappeared on us."

Focus! "Sorry."

"Miles." Lily caught his arm before he could move. "Are you all right?"

He cupped her face with his free hand. Memorized the feel. Pulled away. "Let's solve this case, okay?" Then they could explore the future.

She studied him for a moment before nodding. "We haven't had a chance to get our feet under us before the next attack has come."

"True, but reconnaissance time is over." He shoved fisted hands into his pockets. "We'll review our information and make a plan to go on the offensive."

"I take notes." Gio took a pad of paper from his satchel, stuck a pencil behind his ear, and sat at the table, a cup of cocoa before him. "What is first incident?"

"My kidnapping?" Lily took the chair her foot had rested on and tucked her legs under her. "Alex and Harry were the last to see me at the restaurant. Then I was taken up north."

"Next?" Gio scribbled like an attentive student.

"Lily's father called my boss." Miles returned the high-back chair to the other room, then settled into his chair at the table, carefully leaning back, then deciding against it. Pieter lay beside Lily's chair, but Smokey curled up on Miles's feet. "My team tracked Lily to the ruins. A bomb killed my team during the rescue, and several people threw a grenade at us and shot at us as we escaped."

"The bomb, it target both?" Gio glanced up, brow furrowed.

"Maybe." Miles rubbed his chin. He'd forgone shaving this morning, and already, his beard grew. "I'm confident it was an ambush. Whether they targeted Lily as well, I'm not as sure."

Lily worried the cuff of her flannel. "But I could have died."

"Doesn't mean you were targeted." Miles squeezed her shoulder, hoping to take away some of the trepidation he heard in her voice. "Next came the cemetery shooting. We were together, but the trajectory of the bullets suggests he aimed at me."

"Like the ambush?" Gio jotted down the information.

"Correct. Lily may not have been targeted, but she would have been collateral damage."

"What about the instances in my barn that morning?" Lily asked. "The food bag and trough breaking?"

"At first glance, it doesn't seem to fit." Miles turned the cup of hot chocolate in his hands. "That's why I want to go over this again, incident by incident. What if that break-in has nothing to do with any of this or is related only to your kidnapping, not the ambush or shootings?"

"I suppose, but why commit what could be seen as simple mischief? It's a far cry from kidnapping."

"Reconciling the answer may be the key to figuring this out," Miles took a sip. "Since the kidnapping didn't work, what if they tried a different tactic? Your father said he was afraid your kidnapping had to do with him. What if the mischief, as you call it, was aimed at him through you and the shootings aimed at me?"

Lily cocked her head, and by her absent expression, her thoughts wandered far away from the kitchen.

Miles let her think, turning back to Gio.

"The man, the one with the branch?" Gio's inflection turned the statement into a question.

"And who burned down my barn?" Lily jumped back into the conversation.

"I don't know about the man with the branch." Miles rubbed his beard again. "But the barn burning has me thinking there is still a significant part of this situation that is about Lily. They must not want to kill you, or why not burn down your house?"

"It does destroy my business."

"And threaten *la famiglia* as well?" Gio twirled the pencil in his fingers.

Lily rested her chin in her hand, elbow on the table. "Why?"

The word wheedled its way through Miles's mind like a burrowing mole until the answer popped up to the surface. "Coercion."

Lily and Gio stared at him.

"Your father would do anything to keep you safe."

"I don't doubt that."

"Exactly. But they lost their leverage on your father when we rescued you."

"So why not kidnap me again? Why go through this charade of ruining my work?"

"Because your fear would be a more potent voice in your father's ear. If it's about your father, it's about business, and as Gio said, if the fire got out of control, it would have burned your father's fields first. Lily, I think you are a pawn in a ruthless man's game. He has no concern for you, your life, or your work, and he's using you to control your father."

Realization washed over Lily's face. "The strike. Is it someone pushing my dad into the protest or away from it?"

"I don't know, and that's why we need to talk with your father."

"Of course, but Miles, what does the strike have to do with you?"

Miles glanced at Gio. His friend was digging up information on Miles's coworkers the way only Gio knew how. For now, they had nothing but suspicion. He sighed. "I don't know how it ties together. If it even does. But your protection is my priority. Let's follow that lead first."

CHAPTER 30

As the late-afternoon sun sank in the western sky, Miles joined Lily in the front seat of his car, cranking the engine, then turning to her. "I want to talk with your father alone."

Her heart stuttered. She hadn't spoken to her father since their argument after the meeting with Mr. Craft.

Miles worked his jaw as he eased the car out of her yard. "It's not that I don't want you there. I think he'll be more honest if I speak with him alone."

She could see his point. "You should have left me at home, then."

Miles was already shaking his head. "Gio couldn't stay, and I don't want to leave you alone. Not until I have a few more answers. I'll let you off before we pull into their drive. As long as you stay within shouting distance, you should be safe. Just stay hidden. I will be able to reach you instantly if something goes wrong."

Lily tried not to shudder. "You've thought this through."

Miles quickly squeezed her fingers. "Always."

The familiar drive took only a couple of minutes but felt even shorter, so occupied was Lily's mind—whether from Miles's touch or her fear at Miles's warnings, she didn't know. Maybe anxiety over Miles talking with her father alone. Her father was definitely hiding something. Would Miles be able to get him to talk?

"It'll be all right." Miles covered her hands with one of his large ones as he stopped at the edge of her parents' land. The warmth settled her, and she breathed more easily. "Hop out and get as close to the house as you can. I'll be right back."

Lily followed his instruction. Mature pines lined the drive up to her parents' house on the north side, creating a solid windbreak and deep shadows. She should go unseen as long as her father and brothers weren't working the north field. This late in the day, nearly milking time, they shouldn't be.

She peeked from behind a tree as Miles exited his car, skirted the house, and headed for the barn. He must have heard her father there. The windbreak didn't reach that far, but with everyone focused on evening chores, Lily risked leaving the pines and darting to the smokehouse, then around to the chicken coop. The hens clucked at her, but they clucked at everything, and their noise should hide her presence. She crouched out of sight and strained her ears as Miles greeted her father.

"Hello?" Dad's voice filtered out of the barn. "Oh, it's you."

That didn't sound promising.

"Yes sir. Miles Wright, sir."

"Karl said you're one of his best." Dad sounded as though he didn't agree.

"My company was, sir."

Lily's heart tugged. *So are you, Miles, so are you.*

"Sympathies on their loss."

Miles cleared his throat. "Sir, are you still of the opinion that your daughter ran away?"

"Why do you want to know?" Hard and impatient. *Ease up, Dad. None of this is Miles's fault.* He fired off another question. "Are you courting my daughter?"

Lily's pulse skyrocketed, and her cheeks burned.

"Sir, I'm attempting to find the persons who killed my company and nearly murdered your daughter." Anger radiated from Miles's voice. "Are you going to give me the answers I need, or are we going to keep dancing around whatever problem it is you have with me?"

There was the warrior she'd come to know.

"My problem is that you did not follow instructions." Dad wasn't backing down. "You brought my daughter home instead of to your headquarters. You brought her into danger."

"I wasn't about to hog-tie her just to bring her to headquarters." Miles practically growled his response. "She had just been kidnapped, for heaven's sake. I wasn't about to put her through that again."

"And because of it, she's still in danger."

Lily pressed a hand against her throbbing heart. She hated this. Wished she could jump out from behind the coop and make the two men she cared about talk civilly to one another. But maybe they needed to battle it out to come to a mutual respect on their own terms. If she stepped in, it could make things so much worse.

"Will you tell me what you know?" Miles's voice had quieted, as if he'd regained some form of levelheadedness.

Seconds ticked by, and Lily held her breath, waiting to see what her father would say.

"This farm has been in my family for generations," Dad said. "My father, my grandfather, now two of my sons, all dairy farmers. I won't sell the land no matter how in debt I become."

Debt. Because of all the advancements Dad brought to the farm. Just because they had the largest, most productive farm in Eagle didn't make the money follow. Not during a drought and an economic depression.

"Someone is putting pressure on you. What do they want?"

"To stop the strike. But I won't do that. I can't do that. Milk prices are too low and have been for too long. Just because some new president has a new deal that's supposed to help us, it isn't putting food on the table or keeping the electricity running so I can milk my cows today. At the current price of milk, I lose money by driving it to the processing plant, and I'm certainly not paying to have it picked up. If that's the case with my big farm, how can little farms survive?"

It was all about the milk strikes. Lily held her breath while Miles remained silent.

"If we don't strike on Saturday and force the powers that be to give us a fair price for our milk, it will put me and my sons out of business. What else can I do but be a dairy farmer?" Dad sounded more tired than Lily had ever heard him, and for the first time, she wondered if she should have let Miles take her to Craft headquarters instead of insisting on returning home for her own selfish reasons. If only she'd known her actions could cost her family the farm.

What else can I do but be a dairy farmer? The question reverberated through Miles. What else could he be but a sniper? Simply conducting this investigation revealed his way of operating. He needed time to think, to plan, before acting. Without it, things went wrong.

Miles scanned the barnyard. The chipping paint on the wooden, top portion of the main barn. The grazing field full of lowing cows. The John Deere tractor parked behind Mr. Moore. The faded siding on the farmhouse. Even the chicken coop looked as tired as the man standing before him with more gray hair than he'd first realized.

"Who is pressuring you to stop the strike?" Miles spoke quietly but firmly. This was the answer he needed most.

"I received a letter this morning confirming what I suspected." Moore let out a humorless chuckle. "Andrew Booth. My youngest daughter's new father-in-law."

Andy's father.

"He owns the dairy processing plant, and all our dairy funnels through him. He can't afford the strike. I borrowed from the bank to improve the farm, whereas rumor has it that he borrowed from a loan shark to pay his gambling debts. When Lily disappeared, I could hardly believe it was because she couldn't watch her baby sister get married. What a bunch of hogwash. Lily is one of the strongest people I know. She built her own business from nothing. She …" His voice broke.

"You're proud of her." Miles shifted, his throat thickening.

"Of course, I am. I'd do anything to protect my daughter. And that's why I hoped she actually had run away. If she hadn't, that meant something far worse … that's why I hired Karl to find her. Discreetly."

Miles's stomach churned. "Sir, I was not told the entirety of the situation. I would not have put her in additional danger by bringing her back to Eagle if I had known." Not that he would have been able to stop Lily even if he had the needed information.

"Don't you people communicate?" Moore's demand caught Miles off guard, and he took a step back.

"You told Craft why you needed him to find Lily?"

"Of course!" Moore flung his arms wide, and his eyes bulged. "I told him everything."

Miles's breath quickened as his mind began firing off like a barrage of bullets. Did Craft withhold this information purposefully, or was it something he didn't think they needed to know? And, for heaven's sake, why?

Moore's brows furrowed. "What is it?"

Miles closed the distance between them, nervous energy vibrating through his body. "Does Booth know Craft?"

"I don't think so. Why?"

"While rescuing your daughter, my team was ambushed, set up." Miles scrubbed the stubble of his beard. "Someone knew we were going to be there to save Lily and didn't want us living to finish the job."

"You're suggesting a conspiracy."

Miles wouldn't have used that word exactly, but his mind was weaving a dark web.

"I thought perhaps I was wrong when Lily returned, but this morning's note threatened to find more leverage if I don't back off the strike, especially if I tell the police."

Miles swallowed. "Like going after Lily again?"

"Booth won't hurt Amy because she's now his daughter-in-law, but Lily—my sweet Lily—has no protection from him. But if I stop the strike, I won't be the only one who will lose everything. My sons will lose their farms. So many others could. Even Pritchard, who lives on a tiny plot of land on the other side of town and still takes his milk to the dairy plant in a horse-drawn cart. We might lose everything, anyway, and if we do, what's left of a town built around its dairy farms?"

The truth ignited Miles's protective instincts, and he let out a slow breath to regulate his pounding heart. "You have my word, Mr. Moore. Anyone will have to go through me to get to her."

Moore cocked his head as Lily was wont to do. "She's not just a job to you, is she?"

"No sir." Might as well be honest with her father. "I'd give my life for her."

"Son"—the older man laid a hand on Miles's shoulder—"I believe you would."

Andrew Booth, senior, paced behind his desk, his shoes sliding along the plush carpeting. Already it was Tuesday night. If the Farmer's Holiday Association got their wish, the strike would happen on Saturday. He needed Bill Moore to put an end to it. To at least stop Eagle's farmers from participating. If milk didn't come in, his company would make no money. Without money, he couldn't keep the creditors off his back.

He'd seen the signs of national economic hardship coming years ago. He didn't invest in stocks and took his loans from people instead of banks. Problem was, the economic depression still came, and he still needed to pay back those loans. Only now, instead of the banks seizing his property when he defaulted on his payments, his creditors wanted his life. It left him with few options, but making a deal with the visitor who had just driven up in a shiny new car could save him.

The businessman escorted into Booth's office wore an expensive suit, not a worn one like Booth's. He tossed his hat and cane onto a chair beside the desk and lowered himself into the other. Gloves followed the hat before the man leaned back and steepled his hands.

Booth summoned all his business acumen. If he wanted to beat his creditors, he had to raise his level of risk and reward, and that meant doing business with this man from the East.

"My man tells me you need Miss Moore alive." No greeting, just straight to the point.

"I need leverage." Booth sat at his desk. "If my leverage is dead, what good does she do me?"

"Then we are indeed at cross-purposes."

Booth shook his head. "I believe we can work together to accomplish our mutual desires. There is one person standing in the way of both of our goals ... Miles Wright."

The man sat forward ever so slightly. Booth squashed a grin. He'd hooked him.

"From what *my* man tells me, you need Miles Wright dead. Since he is making it difficult for me to get to Miss Moore, I propose we work together to eliminate him, solving both of our problems at once."

"I would agree, but the kid you have working for you is not allowing my man to solve our mutual problem. What do you have in mind to fix that issue?"

Booth suppressed a smirk. "The kid, as you say, has further information that will seal our deal. It seems your Mr. Wright is sweet on Miss Moore."

His guest's eyebrow arched. "I have already heard the same information."

"Then Miss Moore could be useful to both of us. If the kid lures her to me, you can use her as bait for Mr. Wright. When her father sees that Mr. Wright has failed to protect her, I'll have the leverage I need to stop her father from ruining me."

The man gathered up his gloves, hat, and cane. "My men will execute the plan. Once they have Miss Moore, you are free to manipulate her father however you choose while I use her to bring Wright to me."

"We are in agreement." Booth reached out to shake on the deal.

But the handshake left Booth feeling as though he might have been left holding his own noose.

CHAPTER 31

Lily was sure her heart would hammer itself right out of her chest by the time Miles returned to the car. A cacophony of emotions overwhelmed her.

I'd give my life for her.

She stood out of sight, in the pines, waiting for him, unable to listen to any more of his conversation with her dad. Panic shot pinpricks through her body. She couldn't let Miles make that sacrifice.

A car motor derailed those thoughts. She stepped into the deepest shadows as the Eagle police motorcar came into view. It rolled past without Joey noticing her, but she could see the concern etched into his features. The wall of anger shutting out her brother cracked. He was her twin. She needed to reconcile with him.

Before she could step out of the shadows, Miles's motorcar blocked her way. She slipped into the front seat. She'd find Joey later.

"You look sad." Miles's voice floated into her consciousness as he drove them away from her parents' farm. "Was it seeing Joey? I saw him drive up to the house. Have you talked to him since the fire?"

She shook her head. "Joey hasn't pushed to see me after I asked him to leave."

"I meant what I said last night." He glanced at her, then back to the road. "I think it's time we tell him everything, especially after what your father said. And yes, I know you were hiding behind the chicken coop. The situation involves your family. Joey will make the right decision."

She should be surprised he'd spotted her eavesdropping but

decided to focus on the rest of what he said. "Why the change in your perspective?"

"I'm the reason there is a wedge between you two, and that is wrong of me. I have Gio to watch my back. That's all Joey has wanted to do."

I have you too. But she shouldn't lean on him, especially not if he was willing to die for her. She could never ask anyone, especially someone she cared about, to give that much of themselves. "Our argument wasn't your fault, Miles. Joey has always been overprotective of me, and I simply wanted him to trust me."

"Understandable. Alex and Harry—we need to talk to them next. What did you think of them prior to your disappearance?"

"Immature," she answered quickly to hide her breath of relief. She wasn't ready to talk about what else Miles had revealed to her father—that he'd be willing to trade his life for hers. Not yet. Not when the fear of losing him outweighed the gallantry of the offer. "Joey thought so too. They interact some socially since all three are bachelors. He said all they talk about is money and girls."

"Can you tell me about the day you were kidnapped?"

Lily hugged herself tighter. This was nearly as hard as imagining Miles dying for her since he almost had while rescuing her from that hole—none of it anything she wanted to remember. "Why now?"

He covered her hands with one of his. "Please."

Lily blew out a breath. Watched the darkening landscape flash by the window. "They were interested in hiring me to train a couple new hunting dogs of theirs. I doubted the sincerity of their plan since they didn't actually own the dogs yet, but they insisted they needed my help finding the dogs they planned to purchase. I didn't feel comfortable meeting with them at my house, so I suggested a public place. Alex put the whole plan together, including picking the restaurant."

"Alex initiated?"

"Uh-huh. It was a place I didn't know, so I didn't mind when he offered to drive, especially when he said my brother planned to join us. They picked me up, but Joey wasn't with them. They said something about work, and he was sending Andy in his stead, but Andy would have to meet us there. I didn't feel as though I could back out without making a big deal. I was grateful when they took me to a nice, reputable restaurant instead of a speakeasy. Being kidnapped never crossed my mind in a place like O'Reilly's."

"And why would it?"

"Exactly." She swallowed. "Andy wasn't there when we arrived, so Alex left to telephone Andy's house, and Harry went to ask the hostess if she had seen Andy. Next thing I knew, I had the most nauseous feeling. I made a run for the powder room but don't know if I made it."

"You were drugged."

"When I woke up, I was in the trunk of a car." Her voice quivered. "I was so afraid of what they'd do to me."

Miles squeezed her hands. "Hang on just a bit longer, Lily. We're getting closer to figuring this out. Putting an end to it. I never want you to feel unsafe again."

Please, Father God. Neither do I.

Miles forced himself to focus as he and Lily walked up to the front door of Alex and Harry's boardinghouse. Anger at what Lily had suffered strung his muscles as taut as a catapult. He couldn't let it cloud his judgment. These two may not be involved. Someone else could have drugged Lily's drink, made a show of helping her, and dragged her out the back door. Though if he were a betting man, he'd put a wager on the likelihood Alex and Harry were up to their necks in this mess. How telling would their reaction to Lily's presence be?

The electric light beside the front door illuminated the porch, and a golden glow spilled from inside, as did jazz music. He knocked hard and stood to the side, pulling Lily behind him.

"Howdy!" A grinning young man swung open the door. Brown, shaggy hair, medium height, and maybe weighed a hundred-fifty pounds. Suspenders pinned his shirt to bony shoulders.

"Harry Williams?" Miles asked.

Looking past Miles, Harry wagged his eyebrows at Lily, and Miles's hackles went up. "You'd look better in that dress you wore to dinner."

"Mr. Williams." Lily didn't sound amused.

"You here to take me up on my offer of a good time?" Harry crossed his arms and leaned on the doorframe. "'Cause the offer still stands."

"Of course not." Lily took a step back.

"You need to lighten up, you know. You're in need of—"

"Enough," Miles growled. How could Lily have patience with this kid? "We need to talk with you a minute. Can we come inside?"

Harry shrugged but shoved the screen open. Miles stepped in first, protective instinct stronger than chivalry.

Lily caught his arm. "Let me talk to them," she whispered.

Miles clenched his jaw. He didn't like it, but he trusted her instincts.

Harry led them into a room filled with mismatched couches surrounding a radio, the source of the jazz. "Alex, Amy's sister is here with her bodyguard."

"Oh yeah?" Alex propped himself up on an elbow, flinging long, sandy hair out of his face, a bottle in his hand. "Hello, doll."

"I do hope both of you are drinking legal beer." Lily looked down on the pair like a judge, adding in a mumble, "Although, I doubt it."

"Nothin' against drinkin' the stuff." Alex raised his bottle but froze as Miles stepped from behind Lily, arms crossed. Even if the motion caused the damaged skin on his back to scream.

"In your fog," Lily continued, "do you remember inviting me to O'Reilly's a week ago?"

Miles was sure he spotted a change in skin color on both men.

"Yeah, I remember takin' you there." Harry fell back on the couch. "Told you we're lookin' for some huntin' dogs."

"You're the last people to see me before I *left*."

Miles glanced at Lily, who clenched her fists.

"So?" Alex attempted to chug the rest of his beer. Choked on it when he spotted the gun Miles allowed to peek out from under his suit coat.

"I'm worried about what rumors could be started," Lily said.

Alex frowned. "Why does that matter?"

"Why should we care?" Harry rolled his eyes. "What's done is done. You're here now, so it's old news. I think you should leave unless you wanna dance with us."

"I don't. Last time I went to O'Reilly's with you two, I didn't leave there on my own."

"What do you mean?" Alex sat up. Gaped at her. "We didn't do nothin' to ya."

"Look, I don't care much for the gist of your questions, so either dance or go home." With quick, jerky movements, Harry headed for the front door and pulled it open. "Either way, the bodyguard has to leave."

Lily shook her head, lacing her hand through Miles's elbow and tugging him toward the exit. "We're going. Any girl deserves much better than either of you."

Lily sat in the passenger seat of Miles's car, willing her hands to stop shaking. Alex and Harry were involved. At least, Harry was. She might not be the best at reading people, but even she could see Harry wouldn't answer her questions.

"I already have Gio digging into both Harry and Alex." Miles broke the silence as if he'd read her mind. "There has to be some type of trail between them and Booth. Neither is smart enough to have done this on his own."

Lily nodded. Didn't trust herself to speak.

"How about dinner?" He nodded toward a small diner on the edge of town. It was a quiet spot with a pleasant proprietor who wouldn't gossip all around town if she was seen in a public eating place with Miles. Apparently, everyone now thought he was her bodyguard.

She didn't stop shaking until the food warmed her stomach. Miles kept the conversation light, seemingly unconcerned that it was entirely one-sided. His tales of growing up on a farm in Minnesota elicited fond memories of her own childhood. And it was with much more composure that she let Miles escort her back to his car at the end of the meal.

He paused, his hand resting on the closed passenger door, as he studied her.

She pulled back at his scrutiny. Felt exposed.

He grasped her hand before she could pull away entirely. "When this is over"—a hitch deepened his voice—"will you allow me to call on you, perhaps take you to dinner? Socially."

She couldn't catch her jaw before it popped open. Of all the questions she expected, that wasn't one of them. A cold breeze swirled around them, but Miles didn't move. Her stomach twisted with a mix of fear and excitement.

Yes bubbled up, but doubt clogged her throat. What about his life back at Craft headquarters? Wouldn't he prefer to date someone like Mr. Craft's lawyer?

"You can say no, and I won't think less of you." His words might be true, but Lily heard the hesitation, the slipping of his hope. Before she could gather her courage, he opened the car door.

Lily clutched her purse as she settled in her seat. Why could she be brave in other areas of her life, but when it came to relationships, she faltered? Miles was a really great man. One she could trust and wanted to be around. Maybe it was for the best. Saying no would save him the heartache later. No need for him to find out how ordinary she was. She was a loner and got along best with dogs for a reason. Anyway, he had a life somewhere other than Eagle.

They drove in silence for a little over a mile before Miles pulled off on a road similar to the one where they'd stopped that first night after he found her. Stars now filled the sky, and darkness surrounded them. The moon cast an eerie glow over the shadowed cornfields. He left the car running, not explaining why he stopped. The awkwardness between them grew. She needed to say something, but what?

"One of the things I like about leaving the city," Miles said, "is the great expanse. The openness. I miss that about living in Minnesota—and it's like that here amid the cornfields and pastures."

Lily stared at him. What was he saying? When he stopped at that, leaning back and gazing out the windshield, she ventured, "Miles?"

"Hm?" He turned his head without lifting it off the seat.

"What happens when this is over?"

He shifted to face her. "The honest answer is that I don't know."

Then how could she say yes to even one dinner with him? She couldn't put herself out there, even a little bit, just to get crushed. She'd been humiliated too many times to risk it again.

"But that doesn't mean we can't talk about it." His warm hand lifted her chin to make her eyes meet his. "I like you, Lily Moore. I'd like to get to know you better. Where that leads us, only time can tell. But you are someone I want in my life."

Lily's heart hitched. "What if you don't like what you see in the monotony of normal life?"

He ran his thumb over her cheek. "You know how you knew you could trust me because you trust your dogs?"

Lily nodded.

"I watch how you are with them, the way they are with you. Their complete care rests in your hands. Instead of abusing that power, you hold their hearts gently. You care for their needs. You make them better at what they do. And you love them with your whole being. If you care about them like that, I can only hope that perhaps you'll see a bumbling mutt like me the same way."

She gave a scoffing laugh. "You don't bumble! You're strong and skilled, with an awareness of others that puts the average person to shame. You say I don't abuse power. You're the one with great power. Physical and mental power, but you let people think whatever they will of you. You seek justice, seek to protect those who cannot protect themselves. It is you, Miles Wright, who hold hearts so gently in your big hands."

Before she could take a breath, Miles closed the distance between them and kissed her. Quickly and confidently. He pulled back, keeping her cheek against his palm. Lily touched her lips. Whatever the future might bring, whether they saw each other again after this case was over or not, Miles wouldn't crush her purposefully. The risk was worth whatever might happen.

She leaned forward, giving him permission to kiss her again.

He drew closer, his breath on her cheek, but just before their lips met, a car horn sounded behind them.

Lily jerked away.

Miles sighed, eyes closed.

Headlights shone through the rearview mirror, and fear tightened a fist around Lily's throat as Miles reached for his gun. He opened his door.

"Mi amico," Gio called, reaching Miles as he exited the car.

"How did you find me?" Miles leaned an arm on the open car door. "And why track me down out here? What couldn't wait?" Did he sound more than a bit impatient?

"I knew you go to see Alex and Henry, I consider time of day and *la luna romantico,* and I drive the country roads looking for you."

"Gio." Miles's voice held a warning, and Lily's cheeks warmed.

"Part is true—I saw you leave the diner. And it is good I found you. I have news."

What now?

"Your rooms, I think there was a break-in."

Miles's reply—"You're sure?"

"Si, si."

A chill skittered down Lily's back.

"I'll take Lily home and meet you back there."

"Of course," Gio said.

Miles returned to the car and jammed it into gear, gravel flying from spinning wheels. "You heard?"

Lily nodded.

"I hate leaving you alone." Miles barely glanced at her as he raced the vehicle along the dark road. "But I need to go."

"I know." The man she was beginning to care deeply about, so willing to give his life for hers, would continually confront danger, even after her case was solved.

She shivered. *God, please end this before it comes to that.*

And if God didn't answer her prayer?

"Keep your doors locked and stay inside." Urgency sharpened his tone. "Please."

"I will. And about calling on me?" She laid a hand on his as he shifted the gear stick. "My answer is yes."

CHAPTER 32

Miles met Gio in the shadows outside Mrs. St. Thomas's boardinghouse. "What did you find?"

"I think they are gone." Gio's darker skin made him nearly invisible in the shadows.

Miles removed his Colt from its holster under his arm but kept it low by his thigh, hidden in case he ran across someone who didn't need to know he was hunting a criminal. Gio followed close and to his left as they circled to the rear of the building. Gio made quick work of the lock, and they slipped into the dark kitchen. The house was quiet, unusually quiet. He crept up the stairs, avoiding the creaks, Gio stepping in his footsteps. Miles had made sure to note the noisy spots each time he ascended and descended for just such an occasion.

At the top, he listened again. All was still quiet. None of the other boarders made a sound. It wasn't that late in the evening yet. Was everyone out? Even Mrs. St. Thomas?

He reached the end of the hall and leaned his good shoulder against the doorjamb leading to his room. "Stay back and watch the hall."

"Si, si." Gio stood flush against the wall. Unlike Miles who made his living with a rifle, Gio refused to carry a gun after leaving the Marines. Nevertheless, Miles had no doubt about Gio's ability to handle himself.

Miles tried the doorknob. Locked. Just as he left it. He inserted his key. Twisted it. With a breath, he shoved the door open and raised his gun, squelching his reaction to the searing pain that shot across his back. He searched the room. The pillow sat flat on the bed instead of upright the way he'd left it, his satchel unlatched and a drawer on the dresser not fully closed. Whoever had disturbed his belongings was no longer there.

"It's empty." Miles waved Gio inside and locked the door behind them. "How did you know someone was here?"

"I watch the room. See the light. You are with Giglia. Then who is here?"

"They were discreet but were obviously looking for something. I need to check the rest of the house."

Miles confirmed the boardinghouse was empty. Beside the plate of cookies Mrs. St. Thomas had left in the dining room, a note that explained she would be at the church, and if boarders needed anything, they were to leave her a note in return. He snagged three cookies before returning upstairs.

Once settled in the window seat tucked into the dormer of his room, he tossed Gio one of the cookies and bit into his second. He'd considered going to Mrs. St. Thomas's kitchen to pour milk to go with the cookies, but what he really wanted was a cup of Lily's hot chocolate. Her company too.

"You have not told me why you stopped on the road, mi amico." Gio's eyes danced as if reading Miles's thoughts.

Heat rose. "What did you find out about O'Reilly's?"

Gio finished his chuckle at Miles's obvious avoidance before he replied. "It is respectable on outside. In back, it is speakeasy."

Miles sighed.

"You are worried."

Miles left the window seat to pace. Electric light spilled around a curtain covering a window on the lower level of the house across the street, casting a shadow showing a family sitting down for dinner. The scene spoke so strongly to the part of him he'd buried that his longing for home rose like an erupting volcano.

God, please. I need to be strong for Lily's sake. His parents' deaths had nearly destroyed him. He'd let anger consume him until Gio's friendship got his attention. From then on, he'd determined to protect others so that no one else would experience the loss he'd felt. What he hadn't expected was someone awakening the man he was before his parents died. The one who still had hope and a future before him.

He couldn't revert to that man. Wouldn't. Lily needed the soldier, the sniper skilled at reconnaissance and protection. Only once she was safe could he consider the past. And the future.

"You trust me, mi amico?" Gio. He was still here, witnessing Miles fraying right before his eyes.

He cleared the emotion and shame from his voice before speaking. "Of course, Gio."

"Then go protect—" His friend stopped speaking abruptly. "Someone is downstairs."

Miles slipped down the steps as he grabbed his Colt from its holster. He reached the first floor as Agnes slipped inside. She wore a black dress more suited to a speakeasy than a business meeting.

"You can put the weapon away." She waved a gloved hand.

"What do you want?" His impatience melted as the porch light shining into the hall allowed him a clear view of her expression. His heart flipped. Agnes Fillery was terrified. "What's wrong?"

"An attendant told me the hotel received a telephone call from Charles Wade. He was calling one of our people."

Wade. He was right. "Which person?"

"He didn't say." She pulled a file out of her handbag and pressed it against his chest. "I'm getting out, Miles. It's too dangerous, but I know you, what you'll sacrifice. Be careful, won't you?"

His protective instinct rose, and he pulled her into an embrace. She leaned into him for just a moment. In that moment, however, as pain sliced through his back at the motion, he had a flash of clarity. The difference between this seductive lawyer and the beauty that shone from Lily was like artificial light versus the noonday sun. Agnes was like ice, intricate, sophisticated, but cold and hard. Lily was unassuming, like the flower that bore her name. Simple, gentle, and pure. His sign of spring, of hope. And he'd give up anything to be near her for always.

Back in his room, he handed Gio the file and paced while he ran scenarios through this head. The trap that killed his men could have been for anyone coming to rescue Lily. She was present during each shooting. The mischief, the fire. Again, all aimed at Lily. Then why did someone search his room? And what did Wade have to do with her? Unless Booth and Wade were working together?

Dread oozed through him as he sank to the bed and stared at Gio. "If Booth isn't the only one targeting her—if Charles Wade is, too—Lily is in serious trouble."

"We will keep her safe, mi amico. You and me." Gio rested a hand on his good shoulder and bowed his head, whispered Italian words forming a prayer Miles could not understand. It wrapped around him, causing his own prayers to lift toward heaven.

Please, God, I only ask that you not let me fail again.

Lily settled on the sofa in her nightgown, a cotton one since her flannel nightgown was now in the rag pile. A fire crackled in her fireplace, and the two dogs curled around her. She took a sip of hot chocolate and cracked open her book. This particular one was a history of the evolution of poodles. She'd read of two women hosting a dog obedience trial out East after one of them trained the other's poodle in agility maneuvers. Fascinating.

She tapped a finger on her chin. Could she do more than teach hunting dogs to hunt? Other breeds had other skills, so why couldn't she work with them too? Perhaps help her father by training cattle dogs. Although dairy cows didn't go all that far from the barn since they needed to be milked twice a day.

Pieter nudged her.

She absently placed a hand on the dog's head. "Need to go out?"

Pieter's tail wagged, and he headed for the back door.

On a night like this, she didn't want to go out into the dark, but she had no choice. Pieter, she could let out on his own, but Smokey needed her to walk him to the dog run. A wistfulness surrounded her like a patch of fog. If Miles were here, he'd go with her. And just like that, she wished he would appear, unbidden, as he had the first moment they'd met.

Lily stuffed her arms into the sleeves of her coat, which still smelled of smoke from the barn fire. "We're going outside, then it's bedtime."

Both dogs' tails wagged, but Pieter nosed her leg.

"I'm okay, boy." She lied to ease his concern. She most certainly wasn't okay. Her barn was destroyed, her business in tatters, her life in danger. She blinked away the tears that threatened and sank to the kitchen floor to wrap her arms around her dog. Pieter rested his head against her, patiently letting her hug him. Smokey reached up to lick her face.

"It's hard being strong for so long, but what choice do I have?" She ran her hand over Smokey's curly fur. "Falling apart won't solve a thing. Never has and never will. I've gotten by relying on you dogs—and the Lord, of course—so why should that change now?"

Because Miles had worked himself into her heart. She trusted him. Wanted someone else to lean on when her own faith felt weak. He'd said to call when she felt this way. Dare she now?

Headlights flashed in her front window. Pieter and Smokey left her feeling bereft as they attacked the front door, barking their greeting— or warning—at whoever dared enter their domain. Lily jumped to her feet and peeked outside. No car.

Prickles raced down her back. Hackles rose on Pieter's back.

Lily dialed and asked the operator to connect her to Mrs. St. Thomas's phone. Would Miles even be there?

He was!

"Lily, what's wrong?"

The emotion she'd been fighting clogged her throat at Miles's urgent voice. Pieter's barking intensified as an otherwise eerie silence descended.

"Sweetie?" Miles spoke again, his endearment bolstering her. "Can you tell me what's wrong?"

She gripped the telephone's earpiece and forced her voice to work. "Someone is here."

"Who?" Miles demanded. "Lily?"

"Come quickly, Miles."

The line went dead.

The electric light above her snapped off, plunging her into darkness and her heart to her toes. "Pieter. Smokey. Pantry. Now." She pointed to the only inner room in her house as she issued her command. Pieter responded only slightly less reluctantly than usual. She practically shoved Smokey in after him and secured them inside. She could hide with them and perhaps keep them quiet.

Before she could turn away from the pantry, the glass of her picture window shattered. Her front door flew open. The back door too. Her body went numb. Her brain slowed.

Please, no. She sank back to the floor, hands in the air.

Five men surrounded her, each with a rifle aimed at her chest.

CHAPTER 33

"Lily!" Miles shouted into the telephone. When the operator asked if he'd like her to reconnect the call, he declined and raced up the steps to get Gio and his gear.

Gio was silent as Miles accelerated the car through town. The wheels bounced over ruts and holes as he pushed it to its limits. In Lily's yard, he didn't bother cutting the engine or closing the door but raced for her house. The front window lay in pieces. The front door hung from its hinges. He drew the Colt .45—a semiautomatic similar to the handgun he'd carried as a soldier—from its belt holster. He hated the feel of the grip in his hand, but in this situation, it was the weapon he needed.

With a breath, he pushed into the house.

Darkness except for the flickering flame from the fireplace and the barks of Lily's dogs greeted him. He should have grabbed a flashlight. Corner by corner, he searched the lower level. No sign of Lily or anyone else. He aimed his gun up the stairs, then silently climbed. The second floor was empty too.

He dragged a hand over his face, wrestling with a cocktail of pain and emotion. Lily needed him to keep his head. He pounded down the steps and found Gio at the back door, calling out to the dogs to quiet as he studied the ground.

"They took her." Miles nearly shouted over the yelps coming from behind the door beside them.

Gio dropped to a crouch. "I count five sets of footprints."

"Any indication which way they went?"

Gio raised his eyebrows as the sound of a car reached them.

"Watch the back." Miles crept to what was left of the front door. The dogs howled even louder.

Footsteps crunched on the stones leading to Lily's front door. Miles pressed his back against the wall beside the open door, teeth clenched against the pain. He raised his gun.

A large, dark form stilled just outside the doorway, but Miles caught the glint of metal.

In a single movement, the man stepped inside and swung his revolver at Miles's face. Miles knocked the gun aside, kicked at the person's legs, and yanked a muscled arm behind the man's back, pressing him to the ground, gun aimed at the back of his head.

"Don't move," Miles hissed.

"What do you think you're doing?" Joey Moore.

Miles collected Joey's Smith and Wesson as he released his grip. "All I saw was the gun."

Joey rose, equally as wary, as he stood opposite Miles. "Where's my sister?"

"Promise not to shoot me?" Miles holstered his own weapon and held Joey's out to him.

He snatched it. "My sister?"

"Kidnapped. No evidence of blood. No body. I believe she's alive." For the moment.

"She said you were protecting her." Joey's voice was hard.

"You insisted I stay at the boardinghouse."

"Fine. Fill me in." Joey folded his arms, sarcasm undisguised.

Miles rubbed his beard. "I'm only going to tell you this as Lily's brother, not as a policeman." He cut off Joey's protest. "You're in way over your head here, Moore."

"Enlighten me. How are you involved? Why didn't Lily come to me from the beginning?"

"Because I told her not to."

The electric light in the kitchen snapped on as gravel crunched in the front yard. Both men grabbed their revolvers and stood to either side of the door.

"S'pose you won't let me handle this," Joey muttered.

"I'm going to let you help me."

"Gee, thanks."

Miles peeked around the splintered doorjamb as the dogs' barking grew more incensed.

A set of hands rose from the shadows. "Mi amico?"

"Giosue Vella, do you want me to shoot you?" Miles slammed the .45 into its holster. "He's with me."

Joey opened his mouth, then closed it and holstered his weapon.

"I found something." Gio indicated they should follow. In the backyard, he pointed to the footsteps again. "Giglia, her boot prints. She is alive."

"And walking on her own." Miles could exhale for the first time since he'd heard the fear in Lily's voice over the telephone.

"I'll follow it," Joey said. "And find Lily—"

Gio held up a finger. "I make telephone call first."

Miles grabbed Joey's shoulder as Gio disappeared inside the house. "We can't go after her without a plan. Since she's still alive, that means she's leverage and they won't kill her until they get what they want."

"Then I need to go to the chief."

"Jiminy! Get it through your head. You do this wrong—you get her killed. That's why I didn't want her to include you in the first place."

"I'm a police officer!"

"You're her brother first."

Gio returned, interrupting the stare down between Miles and Joey. "Craft, he is gone. Berkley, he, too, is gone. I call my contact. They all disappear. The room, it is empty."

Miles assessed Joey. "Your job or your sister, Moore. Which one is it?"

Lily struggled against her captors but couldn't escape their iron grips as they dragged her through the woods behind her house. When she tripped over a root, they kept her on her feet. When she twisted her already-sore ankle, they didn't allow her to stop. And when she used teeth and nails to attempt an escape, they awarded her with a gun muzzle jammed into her back and a swath of fabric in her mouth.

Around her pond they marched. Lily pushed back the tears that would suffocate her and clung to the memory of training her dogs with Miles along this very shore. He knew she'd been taken. He found her once. He could do it again. Right?

The five men, dressed in black gear, halted as they came to the other side of the lake. Without a word, one of them wrapped a blindfold over her eyes. She fought back, only to have one of the men swing her over his shoulder like a sack of dog food. Another tied her hands and feet.

All bearings lost, she grasped at any smell or sound. The sweat of the men. The decay of the foliage. The dampness of the marshy lake. Leaves crackled under booted feet. Branches snapped. Then the footfalls became silent. A cold breeze smacked her face. They'd left the woods.

She tried to count steps but couldn't discern where one began and another ended. Then a door squealed and boards creaked. An old building on the other side of the lake? Her mind raced through possibilities until the man who carried her lowered her to the rough dirt floor and reality slammed into her like a bullet.

These men had taken her to a deserted shack, in her nightgown, tied her up … Her mind went wild, and fear pushed her as far into the corner as she could shrink. Maybe being left to die alone in a hole wasn't the worst thing that could happen to a woman.

"What—" Mr. Moore's greeting died as he looked from Miles to Joey, then back to Miles, who inclined his head. "He took her, didn't he?"

"You knew about this?" Joey pushed past his father into the kitchen, the only room with electric light spilling from it.

Miles followed more slowly, weighing Moore's reaction. He'd expected more anger, especially at Miles's failure to protect his daughter.

Miles stumbled to a stop when his eyes landed on Craft, sitting calmly at the kitchen table with a cup of coffee. Fury like he had never experienced shook his hands. He clenched them. He couldn't give in to the urge to grab his boss's lapels and shake the truth out of him. Instead, he forced himself to rest on his sniper training and steadied himself with several slow breaths.

"More guests?" Lily's mother turned from the stove, holding a coffeepot. Her braided hair showed remnants of the same brown as her daughter's. With her chin held high and her eyes questioning, Miles knew from whom Lily had gotten those traits.

"Please sit down, my dear." Mr. Moore spoke gently as he took the pot from his wife's hands.

"This is bad news, isn't it?" Mrs. Moore lowered herself to a chair, color washing from her face. "Is it Lily?"

"Do you know where she is?" Miles watched Craft for any hint of a reaction. He got one.

"Me?" Craft looked as indignant as he sounded. "Your job was to protect her. Now you lost her, just like you lost my men."

The words punched Miles in the gut.

"And who are you?" Joey stopped Craft's indictment.

"Joey, this is my old friend, Karl Craft." Mr. Moore set the coffeepot on the stove and his hands on his wife's shoulders. "He owns a security firm called The Craft Agency. I hired him to find Lily. Miles works for him."

"Not for much longer." Craft glared at Miles. "You're supposed to be my best soldier. Marine sniper. No wonder they let you leave. You can't even keep a civilian safe, let alone have your own team's backs."

Miles clenched his teeth. What Craft said was true. How could he refute it?

"What's worse?" Craft rose like a panther moving in for the kill.

Miles braced.

"You're the one who betrayed them."

"What?" The word was out before he could stop it.

"I have all the evidence, which is what I'm doing here in the middle of the night. You set up your team, Wright. Was it money? Thrill? What?"

"No!"

Joey's hand rested on his gun. Mr. Moore gaped at them. Mrs. Moore silently wept. Miles felt like doing all three but couldn't let his emotion get the best of him.

"I would never do such a thing. Let me see the proof you have against me."

"Not until I see you behind bars."

"Stop!" Mrs. Moore jumped out of her chair. "My daughter is missing. I don't care who did it. I want her found."

"Karl will see to it," Mr. Moore assured her.

No, Miles would.

"Then go see to it!" Mrs. Moore glared at her husband, then Craft.

Miles and Joey exchanged a look that said they both knew better than to draw her attention, and they took a silent step back, Miles edging closer to the door.

"Mrs. Moore—" Craft turned his placating tone onto the distraught mother, and Miles took advantage of the moment to slip outside. He made it to the hood of his car.

"Wright. Stop." Joey had his revolver aimed at Miles's chest. "Is it true?"

"What do you think?" Miles opened the driver's side door. "Get in so we can find her."

Joey hesitated but was in the passenger seat before Miles put the car in gear.

"This is bigger than your father understands." Miles glanced at Joey as he raced back toward Lily's house. "I have evidence that someone from the Craft Agency was in contact with the man I believe shot at Lily and me. Charles Wade. He's a trigger man."

"What does that have to do with Lily being kidnapped? Twice."

"One minute, the incidents point to me being the target—Wade wanted my job—and the next, it seems to be all about Lily. What your father didn't mention is that Booth has been threatening him to stop Saturday's strike."

"I know the senior Mr. Booth is against the strike since it hurts his business … but threats?"

"We think it's why Lily was kidnapped the first time. Why your father called Craft. Now …" Miles let his words trail off. Why couldn't he make sense of it? There had to be a single answer, a reason for everything. One that would lead him straight to Lily.

"I wish Lily would have told me." Joey pressed his head against the back of the seat as Miles maneuvered over Lily's gravel driveway. "I don't know what I think about you or about what your boss accused you of, but Lily chose to trust you over me. It's time I trusted her judgment."

Miles set the brake.

"However …" Joey caught his wrist before he could move. "If you betray her, hurt her, or get her killed, I'll make sure you spend so long in prison, you won't see daylight again."

CHAPTER 34

L ily flinched as someone ripped off the blindfold and removed the cloth over her mouth, catching a piece of her hair. She blinked at the brightness of the lantern.

"Mr. Berkley?" Lily pushed the name past her dry tongue as she pressed into the corner, the two walls on either side giving her a miniscule measure of courage. "What's going on?"

"Hello, doll." Berkeley crouched to her level and trailed a finger down her cheek. "Got a task for you. We need you to draw out Miles Wright."

"We?" Fear trickled down her spine. "Miles?"

"Being a government man don't pay so well, but Miles probably didn't tell you that. He made the switch from the military to my company, but it must not have been enough. Every man has a price, you know, even to betray his friends."

"Miles wouldn't do that."

Berkeley laughed. "Why do you think he's the only one who survived the ambush?"

No. No. No! He wouldn't do that to them or to her. He was different than all the other men who had bullied her, lied to her. Wasn't he? *Please, Father God. Please …*

"We saw an opportunity to use your situation to draw Wright out, but when those plans failed, we had to resort to more drastic measures." He waved a hand around the empty interior of the shed. Wooden slats made up the walls, dirt the floor. Darkness hid the ceiling.

"Why?" The question came out more as a cry, tears slipping down her cheeks.

"Because you're a lonely, pathetic girl who, frankly, won't be missed when this building explodes with you both inside."

Lily turned her chin into her shoulder to keep from throwing up.

"But first ..." Berkley rose and opened the door. "Someone else has business with you."

"Gio?" Miles called out as he and Joey entered Lily's house. "Tell me you've got something."

Smokey barked excitedly when Miles knelt to pet him and Pieter. Both were tied with a rope to the foot of the stove, keeping them in the kitchen where Gio worked.

"I think Charles Wade, he work with the government man, Berkley." Gio replaced the receiver on the phone hook. "The attendant I befriend, he overheard a man with Berkley's description using the hotel telephone to make payment arrangements with a man the operator identified as Wade."

Joey stood beneath the archway that separated the kitchen from the rest of the house. "You trust this information?"

"I do." Gio stuck his pencil behind his ear. "A neighbor of Signore Booth see the car Berkley drive at Booth's house."

"Are you absolutely positive?" Miles gave the dogs one more pat, then stood up. "Craft just accused me of being behind all this."

Gio snorted.

"I take it you believe in Wright's innocence." Joey raised an eyebrow.

"*Del tutto!*" Gio waved his hands, muttering more Italian words. "Of course, he is innocent."

Joey looked about to demand an explanation or cessation of Gio's version of theatrics, but Miles jumped in. "Did you look at Agnes's information?"

"Si, si. Agnes, she suspect sabotage for months but not know who. She learn bomb was a trap. It meant to kill all of you. That is why she leave Eagle."

"Bomb?" Joey stepped forward as if he could physically insert himself into the conversation.

Miles ignored him. "Was Lily also Berkley's target?"

"It did not matter." Gio frowned and shrugged. "Berkley, he want Elite Company dead, but I do not know why."

Pieter whined and lay down facing the back door. A slice went through Miles's heart. The dog wanted his mistress. Miles wanted her back too.

"Explain this bomb to me," Joey was saying, but Miles waved to him to stop as an idea popped into his head.

"The bomb was meant to stop me and my team from rescuing Lily the first time and is not relevant now." Miles knelt beside Pieter. "Pieter is. Look which way he's facing."

"Toward the back." Joey squatted next to him. "Why is that significant?"

"Lily said these dogs can retrieve fowl shot down by a hunter and always return to their master." Miles looked up at him. "Why couldn't those skills let Pieter lead us to Lily?"

"Brilliant, Wright!" Joey clapped Miles on his sore shoulder. "Let's go!"

"Harry. What are you doing here?" Lily swallowed as the young man strolled into the shed, hands in his pockets, a leer in his eye.

She had to keep her wits about her, keep her virtue intact, and keep Miles alive. Whether he was guilty or innocent, she couldn't be responsible for his death. Not just that, she couldn't bear to see him die. She cared about him. Had she trusted the wrong man? Should she have gone to her brother instead?

But Miles had saved her life multiple times. He'd put his own life in harm's way to protect her. And he'd kissed her in a way that showed her the tenderness of his soul.

Lily squeezed her eyes shut, desperately trying to keep the tears inside. *I'm at the end of myself, Father. I can't even trust my own judgment.*

Harry squatted in front of her. "Since your father didn't value your life enough to give in to our demands the first time, we've had to take drastic measures. Mr. Booth sent me to get your signature. You sign these documents, we'll let your family live."

My family live? Her stomach rolled. "What documents?"

"A will. When you die, Mr. Booth receives everything you have. Fair compensation for your father's stubbornness."

Everything she had. Her home, her grandfather's land, her dogs? Her head spun. "You're the one who kidnapped me."

A sneer pulled up one corner of his thin mouth. "Then you had to get rescued."

"You left me in a hole!"

He shrugged. "Didn't want you where your brother could find you."

"And the shootings? My barn?"

Harry glanced at the open door. "Shootings weren't me. But the second one introduced me to the man who works for Mr. Berkley. A partnership was born so that everyone gets what they want from you. And we all see Wright humiliated for ruining a perfectly good plan."

An image of Miles lying on the ground along a cornfield filled her vision. She'd helped saved his life then and again in the barn. If she planned to save it once more, she needed information. Did he deserve saving? She didn't know, but his team hadn't deserved dying to save her. If he was a traitor, she would do this for those men, see their killers brought to justice. And if Miles was being set up again ...

"Is Andy in agreement with what his father is doing?" Lily asked.

"Why do you think I'm here and not him?" Derision filled his tone. "Mr. Booth had high hopes for his son, but your brother-in-law thinks he's bringing integrity to the business. Even postponed his honeymoon trip to try to work things out with the farmers."

"Wouldn't a deal that benefited both sides be better than all this?"

"Don't bother your pretty head about such matters." Harry held out a fountain pen. "Just sign."

If Harry had wanted simple compliance, he'd chosen the wrong words. Then again, she wouldn't risk her family's lives, which left her one choice. She would sign, then find a way to stay alive so Booth couldn't execute this will until she wrote a new one.

Maybe then she'd know whether she should have trusted Miles in the first place.

Trust in the Lord with all thine heart; and lean not unto thine own understanding …

The words from Proverbs 3 filtered through her like a cool breeze, blowing away her emotional fog. She claimed to trust God. Time to prove it by placing her life and her heart in God's hands. Whatever happened, even if she would see Him face-to-face by morning light, He would hold her in the palm of His hand. She knew this. Believed it deep in her soul. Now she would rest in that promise.

She blew out a breath, squared her shoulders, and snatched the pen.

"Good choice." Harry took the signed will. "When I leave, this shack will be wired to explode. When Wright opens the door to save his best gal … Boom! Hope you said goodbye."

Lily bowed her head. She'd done just the opposite. She'd said yes to a future hope that might no longer exist.

Miles double-checked each weapon before strapping them on—his favorite Colt revolver under his left arm, the semiautomatic on his right hip, and a snub-nosed Colt Detective in his right trouser pocket along with his jackknife. He slung his Springfield rifle across his back, scope attached, adrenaline finally silencing the pain.

"Expecting an army?"

Miles glanced at Joey's single holster and handed him the snub-nose. "Never can be too prepared."

"And this is what you do. I know." Joey tucked the extra gun in his belt. "Which means, Wright, if anyone can bring my sister home a second time, it's you."

Miles silently accepted the compliment, then made one last assessment. He hated leaving Smokey locked in the closet again, but he was too young and inexperienced to join the rescue. His heart constricted at the sight of the burnt barn and the windows broken in Lily's house—the home she loved, felt safe in, and retreated to for peace.

"We will find her." Gio clasped Miles's shoulder.

Miles pushed his emotions deep within and took Pieter's lead. The dog whined and looked back at him. The emotions forced their way up. He clamped them down.

"Let's go, old boy. Let's bring our Lily home."

Pieter kept the lead taut, and the three men jogged to keep up. Miles checked their progress against the footprints he tracked as they threaded past the garden plot, past the dog pen, and headed into the trees. The trail followed the edge of the lake where Miles and Lily had trained her dogs and disappeared on the other side. Pieter didn't slow his pursuit.

The hopelessness of this deepest part of the night pressed in on Miles. He tried to keep his mind on figuring out who'd taken Lily and why but couldn't think of anything but her. Her beautiful smile. The way she pinned up her hair. How strength exuded from her soul. Most of all, the feeling of home that drew him to her whenever they were together.

Pieter slowed as they reached a grazing field, eerily lit by the waning moonlight. Lily said the Booths' property was on the other side of her pond. Was this it? He whispered the question to Joey, who confirmed that it was.

Cold air threatened to squeeze Miles's throat. Cold air that would also leave a heavy frost on the ground by the time the sun came out.

Had Booth taken her to his house? He couldn't, not with her sister living there. Had he left her outside? *Please, God, not in this cold.* Visions of his own battle with the freezing temperatures just a few days ago clouded his sight. *I know I keep failing, but, God, You can keep her safe. Please. I don't deserve it, but I can't lose another person I—*

Pieter's tug on the lead brought Miles back. The dog sniffed the air and took off along the edge of the trees, parallel to the fence line and perpendicular to Booth's house. Miles ran after him, followed closely by Joey and Gio.

"Hold up," Miles whispered as a shack came into view. Pieter stopped at his left leg.

"Gio, take Pieter into the trees and stay there." Miles handed him the lead. "Joey, follow me."

Hunched low, Miles crept up to the shack. A wooden bar secured the door from the outside. His heart dropped. There was no telling what he'd find when they opened it.

"You think she's in there?" Joey panted beside him.

Miles didn't answer, just motioned Joey behind him and pulled the semiautomatic from his hip holster.

"I'm a policeman. Let me go first." Joey pulled his own revolver.

"Your sister would kill me if anything happened to you."

"Same here, Wright. Let me do this for her."

Miles raised his gun as he searched the darkness. "On three."

"One ... two ..."

CHAPTER 35

Wednesday, October 18

L ily paced the shack, her nightgown swishing against bare legs, the hem catching on her work boots. She had to think of a way out before Miles found her. Because, when he found her, and she knew he would, Berkley would detonate whatever bomb or dynamite he planned to use to kill them.

Did she dare try the door? What if it exploded? At least she would have saved Miles's life, even at the cost of her own. Was she willing to die for him the way he was willing to die for her? If he could do that, he couldn't be a bad guy, right? She clutched the St. Christopher around her neck.

Father, you said to trust You. I need Your guidance. What do I do?

She ran her fingers over the crack around the door, feeling for anything out of place. Only a cold breeze slipped through. She whispered a prayer and pushed.

Nothing. No explosion. Not even a budge.

A breath *whooshed* from her lungs, and she sank down with her back against the door. Tears clouded her eyes as fear clouded her mind. She didn't want to die. Didn't want to leave her family, her dogs, Miles. She wanted to stop the injustice being forced on her by powerful men. There had to be a way. Had to be a way to live.

Greater love …

The words seemed to whistle through the dilapidated building. She blew on her numbing fingers. Her heart stuttered. Love? She searched her memory for the rest of the verse and gasped as the words came to her. *Greater love hath no man than this, that a man lay down his life ...*

Did that mean she loved Miles?

Did Miles love *her*?

The sound of crackling leaves stopped her questions, and she froze.

Voices. Male voices. Two distinct ones, but she couldn't distinguish their words—until one began to count down. Joey!

"Stop!" she screamed, leaping to her feet and shouting through the door. "It's a trap!"

Trap? Miles yanked Joey away from the door, pulling him to the ground until Miles's body was between him and the door. Joey shoved Miles off, but Miles merely rolled to the side, kneeling with his hand pressing Joey's shoulder to the earth. Still as stone, Miles called on every sharpshooter skill he had to make an assessment. He sensed no danger, but he'd been wrong before.

"Get off me, would you?" Joey swatted Miles's hand out of his way and struggled to his feet. "Lily's in there."

Emotion pierced through Miles's focus, and tears clouded his vision. He'd acted on instinct, not actually comprehending that it was her voice that warned them. That meant she was alive. Despite his choices, his inability to protect her, his failed promises, she still lived.

Joey scrambled for the shed. "Lil, are you all right? Do you need medical attention?"

"I'm fine, Joey." Lily's voice came from inside. "Is Miles with you?"

Miles swallowed back the emotion that clogged his throat. He had to be strong, be the soldier he was trained to be. He approached the shed on shaky knees. "I'm here, Lily. I need to know what you mean by this being a trap."

"Berkley plans to blow up this shack once you find me." Her voice cracked. "Please. You need to get away from here."

Miles exchanged a glance with Joey.

"He understands, Lil," Joey said, giving Miles a pointed look. "But we're going to get you out of there."

"No! I'm the bait, can't you see that? You both need to go. Please." Her plea ended in a sob.

The sound physically brought Miles to his knees. He closed his eyes. Clenched his jaw. Lily sacrificing herself for him wasn't how this was supposed to go. He couldn't live with himself if he got her killed.

He motioned for Joey to squat beside him, not trusting his legs to stand. "I'm going after Berkley. He wants me, so that's what I'm going to give him." *My life for hers.* Just as he promised.

"No." Joey gripped his bicep. "For a reason I don't understand, my sister needs you. Don't you dare break her heart."

Miles snapped into battle mode. Closed off his breaking heart with the hope that his actions would save her in the end. "I need you to get Lily to safety. Tell her—"

The motor of a car interrupted him. Miles waved Joey back, ducking behind the corner of the shack so they could look without being seen. Miles tugged his binoculars out of his bag.

Booth's house stood large on the far side of the field, rising from the frosty ground like a wood-frame monument to wealth. The car he'd heard pulled around back, stopping before the rear door, leaving headlights on and motor running. A Duesenberg. Only one person he knew drove a Duesenberg Model J, or had he purchased the new SJ? Didn't matter. Either model could reach over one hundred miles an hour.

Berkley emerged from the house as the driver stepped from the long convertible, its canvas top down. Miles had only met Charles Wade once, but that was all it took to know the man liked killing. He liked the power he had with a trigger under his finger.

The men shook hands, and a cold pit of certainty took root in Miles's belly. He knew what these men wanted. Knew he was the last obstacle in their way. What had started out as an attempt to stop the strike had developed into something much more sinister.

The anger that had been festering since watching the bomb take the lives of his friends exploded in his chest. Yes, he should have seen the device. Should have been able to warn them. It was his job. His responsibility.

But although he may have failed, God help him, this time would be different. Someone had to stop Berkley and Wade—Booth, too—from continuing their evil plans. Lily's life depended on him doing what he did best—sacrificing himself so another could live.

Assurance and peace gave him strength, and he grabbed Joey's shoulder. Looked him in the eye. "Tell her I love her."

Before Joey could reply, Miles darted into the trees.

Lily shivered, whether from the cold or the expectation that each breath could be her last, she didn't know. She could only hope Miles and Joey stayed away. If they did, would Berkley blow the shack, anyway? Or would she succumb to the freezing temperatures first?

"Giglia?" The voice came from the rear side of the building.

"Gio, you have to stay away!" She tried to stand, but a shiver shook her whole body.

"Do you see wires? On the ceiling or the back wall?"

She stumbled to her feet, her pounding heart deafening her as she ran her hands over the wall. "I-I don't think so."

"*Molto bene.* This is good, Giglia. Stay away from the wall. I rescue you."

"Gio, no!"

A splintering crack shook the shed. She scrambled for the far corner, tucking her head between her knees, the St. Christopher clutched in her hand. *Father God, please don't let me die before I talk to Miles. Before I reconcile with Joey. Please, Father God. I have unfinish—*

With another shuddering crack, the dim light of the predawn poured into the shack, chasing away the heavy fear that filled the place. Hands yanked away a second board, then a third. Gio's curly head, which looked so much like Smokey's black fur, popped through the hole. Nothing exploded. Nothing crumbled around her. Nothing ended her life.

"How?" The shaky word slipped from her numb lips.

"I find trigger wire at bottom of doorway. I think explosives buried underground, but I take no chance trying to defuse it. Better to just break down old wood, and here I am." Gio gave her one of his most flirtatious grins. "Pietro want to see you now, si?"

"Pieter?" Lily scrambled forward as fast as her cold legs could move. Gio helped her through the hole and led her into the shelter of the woods. Pieter sat, tied to a tree, his tail beating a furious rhythm as she came in sight. She fell to her knees in the wet undergrowth, breathed the crisp air that reminded her she was alive, and threw her arms around her dog. Pieter enthusiastically licked her face in return.

"Lily?" Joey stood off the side, tapping the toe of his shoe on the ground.

"Joey!" She staggered to her feet, and he caught her in one of his fiercest bear hugs. "Oh, Joey, I'm so sorry for everything. Can you, could you, ever forgive me?"

"Forgive you?" He held her tighter. "My dearest sister, can you forgive me for being a complete idiot? You're my twin. Nothing has ever separated us before, and I shouldn't have let anything come between us now."

She squeezed his waist again for good measure. "I missed you."

"*Famiglia. Il sangue non è acqua.*" Gio sighed.

Lily tugged out from her brother's crushing embrace, wondering what Gio had said.

"Blood. It is not water." Gio shrugged. "*Andiamo*, we go now."

"Where's Miles?" Lily ran her hand over Pieter again, looking for the man who had become so dear to her.

Joey exchanged a glance with Gio.

Fear turned her stomach. "What did he do?"

"Mi amico, he …" Gio gestured as if it could help him come up with an English explanation.

Joey rumbled out the rest of his sentence. "Went to be a hero."

A mix of relief and terror churned her insides. *Hero* meant she'd trusted rightly. It also meant he'd die to save her when he no longer needed to do so. Panic set in, and she shook her head. "He—he can't do that. He can't die."

"You can't either." Joey tried to grab her arm. "Miles insisted—"

Lily spun away. "You need to arrest Mr. Booth. He's been trying to coerce Dad to stop the strike on Saturday and forced me to will him my land in the event of my death."

Joey stared. "I thought this was about Wright and this Craft Agency business."

"It's both." She didn't have time to explain. "Just take Pieter with you. I need to stop Miles before he does something foolish."

"*Amore.*" Gio clasped his hands to his heart, then raised his hand as if hailing a hansom cab. "Giglia, I go with you."

Heat burned up Lily's face. It wasn't difficult to translate Gio's meaning, and her own heart clung to the word. *Love. Greater love.* She should be ashamed of herself for even the few moments of doubt she had in him. Miles had proved over and over that she could trust him. Now she had to reach him before he fulfilled his promise to show her the greatest love of all. Sacrifice.

Miles sought the cover of the trees as he angled himself toward the house. Berkley carried a satchel to the back seat of the Duesenberg. Usually, Miles would dig into a sniper nest and call on his skills to end the threat, but this wasn't a task to accomplish from a distance. He needed answers. Not an execution.

Using the corner of the rail fence as a shield, he stepped out of the trees and swiveled his Springfield between Berkley and Wade. Fifty yards, no wind. Even in the first light of dawn, it was an easy shot to hit either of them.

"I can't let you get in that car," he called out. Wade's right hand shifted, and Miles sighted it down the barrel of his rifle, moving his finger to the trigger.

Berkley spun, then laughed. "You're outgunned, Wright."

"Did you set us up?" Miles kept Berkley in his peripheral. "Was it your order to kill me and Lily Moore?"

"That was all Craft." But Berkley's grin said just the opposite.

"I have proof otherwise. I just want a confession from you."

The bluff wiped the smile off Berkley's face but had Wade reaching for the revolver on his left hip. As if Miles hadn't already noticed the second gun.

Miles cocked his rifle, stilling Wade's movement. "Turn yourself in, both of you. No one has to die today."

"Are you really willing to bet Wade won't get off a shot before you take him out?" Berkley inclined his head toward the trigger man even as he put the car between himself and Miles. The action had Miles questioning whether there were other shooters he hadn't yet spotted. He took an instant to search his surroundings but didn't lift his finger from the trigger. No movement, but he felt more eyes on him.

He adjusted his grip on his rifle. Refocused on Berkley and Wade. "I'm not going to walk away and let you kill the people I care about."

Berkley's grin returned. "If you'd prefer to die with them, I can arrange that."

A shrill whistle jerked his focus away from Berkley and Wade in time to spot a man aiming a shotgun at him from the back door of the house. He hit the ground as buckshot spit dirt in his face.

"Police! Harry Williams, put your weapon down!" Joey's shout came from the trees behind Miles and bought him the second he needed to turn on his stomach and put a bullet in Wade's right shoulder before the man could fire. Not that Wade wouldn't use his other arm, but it was hard to be steady at a long distance with just one hand.

"Harry! Now!" Joey demanded as he moved behind a large oak twenty feet away and halfway between Miles and the house.

Harry swung his rifle toward the sound of Joey's voice. A crack from Joey's Smith & Wesson and the man doubled over, clutching his side.

"Get us out of here!" Berkley shouted to Wade, climbing into the back seat of the narrow car.

Miles scrambled for the trees, stumbling as his actions woke the fire in his back.

Joey glanced over his shoulder from his position a few feet away. "You hurt?"

"No." Miles covered his head as Wade's shot showered splintered bark around him, then fired at the Duesenberg's front left tire. Missed. "You left Lily?"

Joey jerked his head behind them as he reloaded.

The whistle. Her whistle! Miles lodged a bullet in the tire, then lunged to his feet, needing to keep her away from the gunfire. Dawn filtered through the branches onto Lily darting toward him from tree to tree, her work coat over a dirt-stained nightgown and work boots sticking out from underneath. Never had he seen such a beautiful sight.

"Wade!" Berkley's shout was followed by three shots fired from the direction of the car, and two reports from Joey as Miles pulled Lily behind the cover of his tree trunk.

"Lily, what are you doing here?" Not the first words he wanted to say to her, but they were all he managed around the lump of emotion choking him. "It's not safe."

"I couldn't let you sacrifice yourself before …" Her green eyes glistened like the fading stars in the sky above, and she held out a hand. "Never mind. Give me your binoculars. I'll spot you."

"Wright," Joey called. "The car, disable it. Now."

Miles tore his gaze away from Lily as he handed her the binoculars. Looking down his scope, he saw Wade shift the Duesenberg into gear.

"Clear shot at the back left tire." Lily's voice calmed his heart faster than a lone breath. Miles braced his sore left arm on his knee, sighted the tire, and pulled the trigger.

"Did Gio go for help?" Miles reloaded as the car jolted to a stop, Berkley's frustrated yell reaching the trees.

"Yes, and he took Pieter." Joey tossed down his revolver and grabbed the tiny spare Miles had given him. "I don't have the weapons for this."

"Then go arrest Booth. He's probably in the house."

"Upper left back room," Lily said. "He's peering around the drapery."

Through his scope, Miles watched Berkley push Wade out of the driver's seat and take control of the car, accelerating despite the two flat tires.

"Harry?" Joey holstered the discarded revolver.

Lily shifted as she moved the binoculars. "Hiding behind the bushes near the door."

Miles followed the car through his sight. Before he could line up a shot, a bullet tore through his left arm, just below the shoulder. He glanced down. Wade shot him! Six inches closer to center, and he would be dead.

"Miles!" Lily tossed the binoculars aside.

Pain blinded him, and he fought through the darkness to stay with her. There was a ripping sound, then something pressed to his arm.

"He alive?" Joey demanded from what seemed yards away.

"Yes."

Swallowing back a vicious wave of nausea, Miles raised his hand to cover Lily's. He'd been shot before, and it never got easier.

"Berkley is picking up speed." Frustration amplified Joey's exclamation.

Her mouth firming, Lily tugged the rifle out of Miles's hand.

He tried to grasp her. "Lily, no—"

"We need to stop that car, right?" Concern and determination glowed in her green eyes. "Keep that cloth over your shoulder and stay put."

She moved away, and an all-consuming pain took her place. He had no choice but to trust in everyone but himself. Perhaps here at the end of his abilities, when nothing he could do would change the outcome, prayer was his greatest weapon.

He closed his eyes. *God, make her aim straight and true. And please, bring her back to me.*

CHAPTER 36

In all the years she'd gone fowl hunting, Lily never dreamed it would help her stop a moving car. Shivers spread through her body as she raised the rifle to her shoulder.

Father God, steady my hands.

The car accelerated, bouncing over the uneven ground on its two flat tires, having nearly reached the speed of a grouse. She tracked it easily through the scope.

"This almost isn't fair," she muttered, the powerful lens bringing her close to the fleeing car. She searched it, looking for the next best place to put a bullet. There. The car swerved, giving her an angle on the right rear wheel.

She calculated the distance, the speed of the car, and let out a breath as she pulled the trigger. The car jostled and bucked, but Berkley kept it going. Wade rose out the back seat, and Lily ducked out of view, her heart pounding.

"Get it?" Miles struggled to sit up, blood oozing around the hand that pressed the piece of fabric she'd torn from her nightgown to his upper arm.

"No." Lily reloaded. "But it gave me an idea."

"Lily." The plea seeped from Miles as he slumped to the ground.

"He's losing too much blood." Joey scrambled to Miles's side, a bullet missing him by an inch. He grabbed Miles's revolver and returned fire. "Lily, you stay with him, I'll take the rifle—"

"I'm the better shot." Lily braced against the tree, making herself as small a target as possible as she raised the scope to her eye. Wade gripped the seat back as the car careened toward the road. She had moments left before it either reached the limits of her range or Wade regained his balance. With the rough ground and the flat tires, if she could disorient Berkley … he might flip the car.

She could do this. *Father God, help me do this.*

Lily sighted down the scope and pushed away her fear of Miles bleeding to death. Breathe in. Breathe out. Squeeze the trigger.

The round landed in front of Berkley, causing him to duck and the car to jerk the direction of the two flat tires, tumbling Wade to the floorboard.

Lily reloaded. Aimed beside Berkeley's head. Fired. He wrenched the steering wheel, and this time, the uneven ground and bent tire rims sent the car veering into the air, dumping its passengers as it tipped onto its side.

Lily's breath whooshed out. She did it! She glanced down at Miles, who sat propped against the tree beside her. Conscious.

"Hold this to his arm and stay with him." Joey's command had her laying down the rifle and taking the blood-soaked cloth in trembling hands.

"Nice shooting." Miles's smile didn't clear the pain radiating in his eyes.

She tried to sound teasing. "Are you flirting with me?"

"Trying." He managed a smile. "I'm just glad—"

"You need to stay still." Lily knelt beside him, pressing his hand that covered the wound. Miles winced. "I don't see an exit wound."

"I hate getting shot." He leaned his head against the tree.

"Help, it is coming!" Panting, Gio crashed through the forest and skidded to a stop upon sight of Miles. "Mi amico, you are injured!"

Lily met Gio's stunned stare. "And losing too much blood."

Miles clawed his way through the pain. "I'll be fine. Joey needs help now." He tried to point to where Joey had stepped out of the trees but could only clench his teeth to resist the wave of dizziness that came with trying to move. If only he could manage his rifle, he could be Joey's backup from here.

Gio grumbled something in Italian as he grabbed his knife, tore fabric from Miles's sleeve, and fashioned a tourniquet just above the wound. He sliced through the other sleeve to make a sling, then helped Miles stagger to his feet.

"Lily?" Where had she gone?

Gio pointed. Lily was marching out to help her brother, Miles's Springfield in hand. Jiminy.

Miles leaned into the tree as he shrugged out of Gio's hold and pulled his Colt from under his useless arm. Joey had taken his other revolver. Gun raised, heedless of whether or not Gio followed him, he stumbled from the safety of the trees.

Joey knelt over Wade, angled to keep Berkley—who stood not ten feet away, apparently no worse for wear—in his sights. From here, the assassin's body appeared broken as he lay backward over a fallen log ten feet from the overturned car. Joey's expression lacked the finality of discovering someone had died, which meant that if Wade drew Joey's aim, Berkley wouldn't hesitate to kill him. Or Lily.

Fresh energy surged through Miles, and he quickened his pace.

"What are you doing here?" Joey hissed as first Lily, then Miles, stopped beside him, Miles assuring his body was between Lily and Berkley, even if she gave him her deepest frown.

"Help is coming." Miles adjusted his grip on his Colt. Sweat dripped down his forehead.

A car rumbled into the yard as Andy emerged from the house. "It's over," he called to them after glancing at where Harry must lie. "I've relieved my father of his position in the business. Joey, you can arrest him. He's in his study."

"Well done," said the suited man who emerged from the newly arrived vehicle. He flashed a badge. "Roy Caden. Bureau of Investigation."

BOI?

"The BOI?" Lily echoed his thought in his ear.

"He's with us." Craft exited from the driver's side, Mr. Moore from the back seat.

"Dad," Lily breathed, dropping the rifle to her side.

Joey handcuffed the unconscious Wade as the G-man joined them. Miles blinked through a wave of blackness. It really was over.

"Don't shoot me ... partner." Berkley flashed a grin.

"Partner?" Lily whispered. Miles clung to her voice as to a life preserver. The buzzing grew louder in his head.

"I know you were on the take," Caden said to Berkley as he took his gun and wrestled his hands behind his back. "That's why you joined Craft's agency before Hoover could fire you. You needed your own personal army. Craft refused ... and now I'm bringing you in."

"I am not going to prison." Berkley slammed his head against Caden's nose, pulled another gun from his belt, and pointed it at Lily's chest.

"Drop it, Berkley." Miles's hand shook as he aimed his Colt.

Berkley cocked a grin and pulled back the hammer. Miles fired. The gun fell from his hand as darkness overtook him, his last thoughts a prayer for Lily.

Lily screamed when Miles fell. More cars pulled into the yard, but she dropped to her knees to rest a hand on Miles's scruffy cheek. He didn't respond to her touch. Uniformed policemen rushed over, and strong hands tugged her away as Doc and Gio took her place beside Miles. The government man vanished with Mr. Berkley. Joey's fellow officers and the chief disappeared with Mr. Booth, Harry, and Mr. Wade.

Someone turned her away as Gio and Doc prepared to lift Miles onto a litter. Was he even alive? Arms encircled her, pressing her against a strong chest—a spot she knew and one that had made her feel safe since her earliest memories. Dad.

"I'm so sorry, my daughter." His voice swept over her hair. "It's over now. No one can hurt you. You're safe."

But her heart wasn't safe. She'd given it away to a man she might never see again, might never be able to tell how much he meant to her.

"I never thought Booth would go to such lengths to stop the strike. You understand why I couldn't give in, don't you? I never meant for him to hurt you."

Lily pulled away so her father could see her sincerity. "It's not your fault, Dad. You're standing up for the smaller farms. They need a big voice to fight for them. Especially against a man like Mr. Booth."

Green eyes, the ones she'd inherited, shimmered like emeralds. "I'm so proud of you, Lily. And while I'm at it, I'm sorry I've never understood why you left the farm. I couldn't understand that seeking your own path meant needing room to grow. It was my own stubbornness that made me almost lose—"

Lily tucked herself back in her father's arms, listening to his heartbeat, tears dripping down her cheeks as thankfulness filled her heart.

"There's something else." Her father's words rumbled against her ear. "What Wright did for you, for us, the sacrifices he's made … Lily, if you return any of his feelings for you, don't let him leave town without telling him. Promise your old man that, won't you?"

Lily blinked. Stepped back, unsure she'd heard right. "What are you saying?"

"I have no doubt Doc will get Mr. Wright back on his feet, but you owe it to yourself to be honest with him. That's growth too. Anyway, a woman's love has a way of healing a man better than any medicine. Your mama has taught me that."

Lily pressed her hands to her burning cheeks.

"And if you doubt how he feels about you, don't. His actions have proved plenty. That type of loyalty and love, the kind that is willing to sacrifice as he's done for you, you won't find it often. It's rare and precious, so don't let him get away."

Miles stared out the window into the inky black night. Doc had said the blood loss nearly cost his life, but he'd removed the bullet and sewed up the wound. Now Miles's arm was tightly bound and resting in a sling against his chest.

A strange feeling, how close to death he'd been. He'd spent years in battle, always knew a bullet could be his end. It never bothered him, never made him afraid, as it did so many others. Now, however, the cost of losing his life seemed so high … thanks to a beautiful, green-eyed girl. Death meant not spending a lifetime with her.

A knock at the door tore his gaze from the window. "Come in."

The recovery room on the second floor of Doc Holland's surgery was cold and sterile. Good for a doctor's purposes, perhaps, but bad for convalescing. Even the green walls didn't help. The men who entered, however, made it worse.

"Doctor says you'll be on your feet in no time." Craft's presence filled the room. "The arm could take a few weeks, but we can work with that."

"Glad you came through all right." Caden, the government man, crossed his arms, feet apart, as if he were about to take on an army. Perhaps he was. "The kid—Williams, was it?—will be fine if he can handle jail. It's too soon to tell if Berkley will survive the gunshot to his abdomen or whether Wade will use his hands again. Not too worried about either. Both will be in prison for a long time."

Miles nodded, but knowing he'd caused Berkley's life-threatening wound and Wade's injuries churned his gut.

Craft brought his attention back to the room. "Besides that news, we have a proposition for you."

"Mr. Craft, Mr. Caden, I mean no disrespect, but I'm not ready to hear any propositions. I just lost my team, and—"

Craft held up a hand. "Hear us out."

Miles adjusted his injured arm in the sling, not bothering to hide the grimace it caused. "You have my attention."

"I want you to lead your own company," Craft said.

Miles laughed outright.

His boss's brows drew together. "Listen to the whole proposal before you say no."

Caden stepped closer. "You heard that because of the Lindbergh tragedy, the BOI is now tasked with kidnappings that cross state borders?"

The kidnapping and death of the Lindbergh boy last year had spurred Congress to take immediate action, adding kidnapping to the list of investigations Hoover's government men could conduct.

Miles nodded and Caden continued. "There are still cases where it takes too long to bring in investigators, so I want a privately funded organization that will step in until the BOI can get up to speed."

"So you government men can swoop in and claim credit?" Miles raised an eyebrow.

"We don't want the public to worry." Caden didn't miss a beat. "And you would only be called in when needed. You could even pick your own team. Including Mr. Vella."

"Money would also not be a concern." Craft folded his arms. "I have already agreed to fund the operation."

Miles sighed. Before meeting Lily, he would have lived for a job like this. Now, was it really what he wanted?

"Take a day to think about it." Caden winked as he pointed at Miles. "I am optimistic you'll get on board."

CHAPTER 37

Saturday, October 21

Three days later, Lily paced the kitchen of her parents' home. Her father and older brothers had been gone since they finished milking the cows that morning—hours ago now. Without the need to protest Mr. Booth's dairy processing plant, they'd joined the larger protest aimed at blocking any dairy trucks from leaving the county. They'd taken their own truck filled with five-gallon jugs of milk, which they planned to prominently dump in the middle of the road.

Joey and the other Eagle policemen had been called in to help the state police break up the riots in their county. The fact that her family was split on either side of a potentially violent exchange worried Lily sick, and she had come to keep her mother company until her father and brothers returned.

Pieter whimpered—doubtless, wishing she'd calm herself—and Smokey circled her feet. Her sisters had left her to pace, preferring to join Amy at the Booth residence, where their new brother-in-law was taking over his father's business with plans to make it as fair as possible.

Whether Lily would be able to recover her business, she didn't know. She had to reschedule another week of clients, maybe more if she couldn't come up with a place to board the dogs. Another reason she hadn't been able to stay at her house today.

What she didn't want to admit, however, was how much her agitation had to do with one Miles Wright.

As the afternoon wore on, her mother retreated to the front porch to churn butter. It had been years since Lily had seen someone using the old churn. Since Dad planned to dump the milk he would usually take to the Booths' processing plant, Mom must have cajoled him into leaving a jug or two behind.

"Lily!" Mom's sharp call propelled Lily through the house and out the front door. Katy Wells's truck bumped along the drive with alarming speed. Mom left the churn to grip Lily's hand as they stood atop the porch steps.

"Mrs. Moore!" Quiet, capable Katy tumbled out of her truck, tossing the keys onto the seat before running up the steps to snatch Mom's hands. Tears dripped down Katy's cheeks, her red eyes evidence that she'd been crying for a while.

"What is it, child?" Mom urged. Lily held her breath. Only Joey could cause such a reaction from her friend.

"Joey's been removed as a policeman. Turned traitor, some are sayin'."

Mom closed her eyes and tugged Katy into her arms. Lily's heart hurt for her friend and for her brother. Would Joey continue to court Katy if he couldn't find work? The question pierced Lily's tender heart.

Giving in like the coward she'd been the last three days, Lily left Katy in her mother's comforting arms and retreated to the cornfields on the north side of the house. She was ashamed of herself. She knew Doc had sent Miles to stay under Mrs. St. Thomas's care until he recovered enough to travel, but Lily couldn't bring herself to visit, to risk what Miles would say to her now that the investigation was over.

She couldn't picture him living here, not when he was a world-traveled, skilled sniper. Eagle didn't need someone like that. Nor could she manage seeing the suffering she caused him. He'd put himself in harm's way for her. She didn't deserve it. Or perhaps she just didn't want to hope that maybe God was finally giving her a chance at love.

Miles grunted as he lifted the five-gallon milk jug from the back of a farmer's wagon, letting it rest on his good shoulder as he held it by the handle. They'd been holding up traffic for going on eight hours now as more and more farmers joined the strike. Blocking the road with their cars, carts, and jugs, more and more dairy trucks were refused access to the processing plant behind them.

"If you reinjure that arm, my sister is going to kill you." Joey pushed over a jug, and milk poured onto the side of the road. The sister who Miles still hadn't seen since the morning of the shootout?

Miles swung the jug down from his shoulder, ignoring the pulling skin on his back, and dumped the milk into the ditch. "I can't sit idle for weeks. You sure about the decision you made?"

Joey glanced at his father, who was halting another milk wagon. "I couldn't put down a protest where I had to aim a gun at my own father and brothers. But I'm worried about the threat to bring in the National Guard. They'll do it, you know."

Miles knew it too. He'd seen it before.

"I ain't letting you touch my milk!" The farmer whose horses had been stopped stood between Mr. Moore and his milk, a pistol aimed at Mr. Moore's chest. "Every cent means I can put a slice of bread in my children's bellies. I won't let you take that away from them!"

Mr. Moore raised his hands. "This strike is to help you. We have to stick this out together. Demand we earn more for our milk so our children can eat more than stale bread."

"You can afford to protest. Your children are grown."

"And my sons are all here with me." Mr. Moore swept his hand toward the two older Moore brothers and then around to Joey. The motion included Miles, and when Joey clapped his hand on Miles's good shoulder, he knew Mr. Moore had indeed called him a son.

If Lily was willing, it was something he wanted too.

"I—I can't." The farmer's voice shook, and he cocked the hammer on the pistol.

The sound stirred the protesters into a frantic tangle even as it pushed Miles into action. In a bound, he scaled the wagon, ignoring the pain shooting through his arm and back. Joey grabbed the horses' reins as Miles dropped into the wagon bed on silent feet. As he wove between the milk jugs, the sun reflected off something shiny in the crowd.

"Get down!" Miles lunged for the farmer, his momentum knocking the man from the wagon as two shots fired.

Lily saw her father's truck before it turned into the drive two hours before milking time. Why were they home early? She raced around the house as her mother and Katy left the porch.

Her heart beat an erratic rhythm while they waited for the truck to reach them, but it nearly stopped completely when she saw Miles sitting in the bed of the truck beside Joey. Miles appeared a paler shade than usual, especially without a hat to shield his eyes from the western sun.

Pieter must have sensed her unease because he pressed into her leg. Lily gave Smokey a command to stay and rested her hand on Pieter's head. Why was Miles with her father and Joey? Where were her other brothers?

Her mother and Katy met the truck and threw their arms around the necks of their men. An odd pang pierced Lily's heart, and she rubbed the cuffs of her coat. She wished she'd put on one of her dresses instead of her old work jeans. And maybe bothered with her hair instead of knotting it before stuffing the knit hat on her head.

Miles jumped down from the truck bed with a grunt. The jarring had to hurt his arm, even if it was tightly tied to his chest.

Fear wrapped itself around Lily like a gag. She couldn't face Miles, face his goodbye in front of her family. Before he could see her, she slipped back into the soon-to-be-harvested cornfields, her dogs on her heels.

Lily barely made it five rows before Joey caught her. "Wait up, Lil."

She stopped and wrapped her arms around herself. "You're okay?"

"Don't worry about me. Katy and I will be fine." Joey linked his arm in hers. "Want to tell me why you're running away?"

"I'm just being foolish." Lily shook her head, chagrined at Joey's choice of words.

"You know, I don't need to be a policeman to see how Miles feels about you."

Hope turned in her stomach.

"He's not like any of the men in Eagle, but you knew that from the beginning, and that's why you trusted him."

"I thought you didn't like him." The tease lifted her lips into a smile.

"All it took was seeing how much he cares about you." Joey nudged her shoulder. "And if he hurts you, he'll have to answer to me."

"I'll hold you to that." Miles's voice interrupted them. "Keeps me honest."

Lily's breath hitched.

"I'll leave you two." Joey winked at Lily, then slapped Miles's shoulder.

Miles waited for him to disappear before taking her hand. "It does my heart good to see you."

"You too." Lily forced herself to answer calmly. "How's your arm?"

He cringed. "Doc isn't happy with me and my activity, but he just applied fresh bandages, and the wounds are healing well. No infection, thank God. I've been hurt worse, so I know it will heal. Eventually."

Lily chewed her lip, unsure what to say to this handsome man who'd given so much to keep her safe.

"May I ask you something?" Miles had a strange lilt to his tone.

Lily wanted to wrap her arms around her stomach, as if that could protect her, but Miles kept her hand captive.

"I have a couple decisions to make." He ran his thumb over her knuckles. "Decisions have never been hard for me, but that's because

I've only had myself to worry about. Now I have two paths I could travel. I know which I would prefer, but it's not a decision I want to make on my own. I want to make it with you."

"With me?" Lily blinked, taken aback. "Do we know each other well enough?" Not what she wanted to say.

"That's just it." Miles brought her hand to his chest. "I want us to know each other better. So do I return to my bare old rooms in New York, or do I tell Mrs. St. Thomas to plan for her boarder to stay a while longer?"

⁓⁖⁓

"You mean you want to stay in Eagle?" Lily's voice sounded so small as it drifted up to the cloudless October sky.

Miles didn't know how it was possible, but the woman before him was even more beautiful than before. Her hair was falling out of the knot at her neck, her cap framing her face, causing her eyes to turn the warmest shade of green.

He swallowed. As sure as he was, he needed to give her a way to say no to him. "Unless you don't want me to."

"I do."

The words were whispered, but they set off a cymbal in his soul. She wanted him! His heart soared to the reaches of the setting sunbeams.

"But what about your job? And your life back there?"

"Oh, Lily, I don't have a life outside of my job, and I don't want to live like that anymore. I want to be with you."

"With me?"

"With you."

Tears filled her eyes.

"Which is why I want to give you this." He released her hand to pull a pinecone from his pocket. She held it in the palm of her hand, questions in her eyes. "It's probably a silly gift, but in some species of pine, the cones require heat to free the seeds. The hardships of the past week seem to have brought you out of your protective shell, letting the world see what an amazing woman you are."

Her hand closed on the pinecone, and when she looked up at him, her tears dripped down her cheeks. "Thank you for believing in me."

He cupped her face, wiping her tears with his thumb. "I love you, Lily Moore."

She sucked in a quick breath.

"When I thought I'd lost you, I knew I would search this whole world to find you." He drew her closer.

But she held him back by a hand to his chest. "I don't deserve you, Miles. I—"

"Shh." He succeeded in tucking her under his chin and wrapping his good arm around her.

"What about your work?" Lily tried to pull back, but he kept her close. "You are excellent at rescuing people. I can't let you give that up for me."

How had he stumbled on a woman with such a large heart? "That's the other decision for us to make. The next job I want is to help you rebuild your barn, your business."

"But—"

"Before I became a soldier, I wanted to build things. Work with my hands. Losing my parents changed that. Now I want to put death and destruction behind me. I want to build and rebuild. See hope come from this depression. And I want to do it with you."

He laid out his whole idea while she listened. Talking it out with her, even though she held back a reply, helped shape his own ideas of what he wanted to do. He'd already turned down Caden and Craft, at least until he knew where he stood with Lily. For now, he wanted to settle in Eagle—make it his home, too, if she approved. Help the farmers as best he could with the resources the market crash hadn't taken from him. See the community thrive despite the drought and depression.

"What do you think?" he asked.

"I think it's a tailor-made idea." Her green eyes sparkled. "And I'm proud of you."

"You are?" The observation took him aback.

"Of course I am. You are the most selfless man I know. Helping the residents of Eagle is a perfect plan for you."

"But for us? I want a life besides my work. I want to rebuild that part of my life most of all."

"And you will. With me." She lifted her beautiful face. "Because I love you too."

He fought back his grin so he could kiss her properly.

The End

AUTHOR'S NOTE

The Great Depression began in 1929 and stretched until the United States entered World War II. The year 1933 proved a turning point as Franklin D. Roosevelt began his presidency with a productive first one hundred days. His New Deal included assistance to farming communities, but the help came too late for Wisconsin dairy farmers. Fed up with low milk prices, farmers staged milk strikes across the state. They preferred to dump their milk than sell it to the dairy plants. Three strikes occurred in 1933, each more violent than the last.

Prior to the Depression, innovations in farming, including electricity for milking pumps and horseless tractors, allowed farmers to expand their farms to make up for droughts and dropping crop prices. Though it took until the 1940s for these advancements to make it to most farms, the technology spread through both the prosperity of the Roaring Twenties and the lack of the Great Depression.

The American Water Spaniel is a native Wisconsin dog developed in the 1800s and promoted by Dr. Fred Pfeifer in the early 1900s. The United Kennel Club officially recognized the breed in 1920 and the Field Dog Stud Book in 1938. Helen Whitehouse Walker and Blanche Saunders hosted the first Obedience Dog Trials in October 1933. Helen trained under the Associated Sheep, Police, and Army Dog Society, which used the teachings of Colonel Konrade Most, considered the father of modern dog training.

World War I not only saw the advancement of military dogs but the evolution of the sniper. Called sharpshooters until this point, the development of better scopes, silencers (which President Theodore

Roosevelt indeed used while hunting), and more accurate rifles in the early 1900s increased the sniper's skill and use.

Hunting in Wisconsin changed during the early 1900s as it morphed from necessity to sport, decimating the animal and fish population. Animal refuges were created to protect game populations and hunting tags/licenses carefully distributed. To this day, the Wisconsin Department of Natural Resources uses hunting to manage the animal population with the goal of creating a healthy balance to help nature thrive.

Radio, telegraph, and home security systems developed during the late 1800s to early 1900s, thanks in large part to several scientists and inventors such as Nobel prize winner Guglielmo Marconi, who engineered a wireless wave transmitter used in transatlantic radio communication and Edward Callahan, founder of ADT—or American District Telegraph—who created the first telegraph-based home security network.

Lastly, up until 1933, women who desired to wear jeans had no choice but to wear men's sizes. Levi Strauss & Co. recognized the market for women's jeans, and in the fall of 1934, introduced Lady Levi's, the first jeans made exclusively for women.

I hope you enjoyed Lily and Miles's story. Reviews are one of the best ways to show appreciation for a book, so thank you for leaving your honest opinion on any of the various retail sites, Goodreads, or BookBub. You can also request this book at your local library.

By visiting my website, daniellegrandinetti.com, you can sign up for my Fireside News emails, read my blog where I post book reviews, and find links to my social media pages such as my bookstagram account on Instagram, @danielleswritingspot. I love hearing from readers and look forward to connecting with you there.

**If you enjoyed this book, will you consider sharing
the message with others?**

Let us know your thoughts. You can let the author know by visiting or sharing a
photo of the cover on our social media pages or leaving a review at a retailer's
site. All of it helps us get the message out!

Email: info@ironstreammedia.com

    @ironstreammedia

Brookstone Publishing Group, Harambee Press, Iron Stream, Iron Stream
Fiction, Iron Stream Kids, and Life Bible Study are imprints of Iron Stream
Media, which derives its name from Proverbs 27:17, "As iron sharpens iron,
so one person sharpens another." This sharpening describes the process of
discipleship, one to another. With this in mind, Iron Stream Media provides
a variety of solutions for churches, ministry leaders, and nonprofits ranging
 ̇om in-depth Bible study curriculum and Christian book publishing to custom
publishing and consultative services.

For more information on ISM and its imprints, please visit
IronStreamMedia.com

CPSIA information can be obtained
at www.ICGtesting.com
Printed in the USA
LVHW040301060922
727615LV00003B/305